Death on the Emerald Isle

A *Murder, She Wrote* Mystery

Death on the Emerald Isle

A *Murder, She Wrote* Mystery

A NOVEL BY JESSICA FLETCHER & TERRIE FARLEY MORAN

Based on the Universal television series created by
Peter S. Fischer, Richard Levinson & William Link

BERKLEY PRIME CRIME
New York

BERKLEY PRIME CRIME
Published by Berkley
An imprint of Penguin Random House LLC
penguinrandomhouse.com

Library of Congress Cataloging-in-Publication Data

Names: Fletcher, Jessica, author. | Moran, Terrie Farley, author.
Title: Death on the Emerald Isle : a Murder, She Wrote mystery / a novel by
Jessica Fletcher & Terrie Farley Moran.
Description: Hardcover edition. | New York : Berkley Prime Crime, 2023. |
Series: A Murder, She Wrote mystery
Identifiers: LCCN 2022023108 (print) | LCCN 2022023109 (ebook) |
ISBN 9780593333686 (hardcover) | ISBN 9780593333693 (ebook)
Subjects: LCGFT: Detective and mystery fiction. | Novels.
Classification: LCC PS3552.A376 D434 2023 (print) |
LCC PS3552.A376 (ebook) | DDC 813/.54--dc23/eng/20220516
LC record available at https://lccn.loc.gov/2022023108
LC ebook record available at https://lccn.loc.gov/2022023109

Printed in the United States of America
1st Printing

To Angela Lansbury,
whose talent and grace brought Jessica Fletcher to life

Death on the Emerald Isle

A *Murder, She Wrote* Mystery

Chapter One

Seth Hazlitt, my longtime friend and Cabot Cove's favorite doctor, was sitting at my kitchen table sipping coffee while I was trying to cross as many items off my to-do list as possible.

"Okay, so, now Susan Shevlin checked in with Jed Richardson and has booked all my connecting flights. We're so lucky to have a world-class travel agent as a friend and neighbor. You are going to look after my house. Oh, and I need to ask Maeve O'Bannon if she will keep an eye on my garden, especially those seedlings I planted two weeks ago."

Seth tugged at his eyeglasses, peered across the table at my seemingly unending roster of chores, and said, "Jessica, I don't understand why whenever anyone imposes on your time, you rearrange your entire life to help them out. Doesn't seem fair to me. Would anyone do the same for you? And I sure could use some pastry to go with this coffee."

"Well, then, you should have stopped at Charlene Sassi's bakery before you came by. Since I'm leaving in two days, I need to empty out my refrigerator, not fill it with snacks, although, as you can see, my fruit bowl isn't quite empty."

A thought popped into my head and I jotted, "Temporarily cancel delivery of the *Cabot Cove Gazette*," on my notepaper before I continued. "I don't see why you are making such a big fuss over a little trip. I am simply doing a favor for a friend. Believe me, if the situation were reversed, Lorna Winters would do the same for me."

Seth guffawed. "A little trip? Is that what you're calling it? Let me tell you, driving an hour or two up the coast to Belfast, Maine, might be something I would consider a little trip. Traveling from here to Belfast, Northern Ireland, that is what I call a *looong* trip. Wasn't it only last Tuesday that you claimed to be too busy to go fishing on Moon Lake for a few short hours with me along with Mort and Maureen Metzger? But today, at the drop of a hat . . ."

I counted to ten and then replied, hoping my exasperation didn't show, "Seth, Lorna Winters didn't drop a hat. Since you are a physician, I would think you'd appreciate the consequences of breaking her leg in several places. The leg is now in what Lorna described as a 'torturous cast' from ankle to hip and she is confined to a wheelchair. Her doctor insists that she stay home in Minnesota so that he can look after her. You know how finicky doctors can be, so there is no way she can go to the Belfast Book Festival and accept the American Author Guest of Honor Award without violating her doctor's orders."

"It is only common sense to follow doctor's orders," Seth said.

"But it seems to me some committee member could pack up her award in a tidy box and drop it in the mail, and your friend would have her trophy, or whatever, in no time."

"There is far more to Lorna's participation than accepting a plaque. She is scheduled for interviews and panels specifically geared to American mysteries. So many things would have to be rearranged if there wasn't an American author to take her place."

A firm rat-a-tat-tat on my kitchen door punctuated my last few words and I turned to see my neighbor Maeve O'Bannon through the glass pane on the top half of the door. Her curly gray hair was escaping from a bun fashioned carelessly atop her head, a sure sign she'd been either baking or gardening, which were her two favorite passions.

When I signaled her to come in, she raised both hands, which were holding a dish covered by a white linen cloth. One glance and it took Seth less than a second to push back his chair and pull the door open.

"Maeve O'Bannon to the rescue," he said. "A man could starve in this house."

Maeve sent a meaningful glance to the fruit bowl on my table, which held two apples and an orange. "I guess that would depend on what the man wanted to eat."

"My nose has me hoping that you're holding some freshly baked scones. And that you've come to share," Seth said.

"Half a point to you. Tell me what kind of scones and you'll earn a full point, and a scone besides." Maeve always enjoyed bantering with Seth about her baked goods.

Seth leaned closer to her and inhaled deeply. "Ah, citrus. Orange.

Tell me, Maeve, have you a plateful of your mouthwatering cranberry-orange scones?"

"I have indeed." Maeve took off the cloth and placed on the table a lovely crystal platter piled high with lightly iced scones.

I took some dessert plates from the cabinet, set out napkins, and reached gratefully for a scone. "Maeve, I didn't even know I was hungry, but after one look at your scones . . . Can I offer you tea or coffee?"

"I would welcome a cup of tea if it's not too much trouble," Maeve said as she settled into the chair between mine and Seth's.

I served Maeve a cup of tea and sat down to enjoy my scone, which was as delicious as it was fragrant. I was swallowing my final bite and was about to praise her baking skills to the sky when Maeve interrupted my train of thought.

"Jessica, I ran into Alicia Richardson in the Fruit and Veg first thing this morning and she mentioned that Jed would be flying you off on the first leg of a trip to Belfast."

I automatically reached for my to-do list, hoping to check off "plants and seedlings," but Maeve distracted me by saying, "I was hoping I could impose on you by asking for a slight favor."

Seth interjected, "Maeve, you do know that Jessica isn't merely hopping up the coast to *our* Belfast. She is flying across the ocean to the original Belfast, the one in Northern Ireland."

Maeve nodded. "I do indeed know that and I can tell you that Belfast is so very near my father's ancestral home in the village of Bushmills. That is why I've come to ask a favor."

Although I wasn't at all familiar with the geography of Northern Ireland, I had a momentary fear of traveling hours and hours out of my way so I could snap a picture or two of some ancient ruins of a thatched-roof cottage, the straw and reeds of which had long since given way. Still, Maeve was a good neighbor and I'd always considered her a friend, so I thought it best to hear her out.

"My father was born and raised on a tenant farm just outside Bushmills, but he always had a love of the sea, and with jobs at home being scarce at the time, he left at the age of seventeen to become a seafaring man. Oh, he traveled the world several times over. And many an evening when I was a child, he'd sit with his pipe in his hand and me on his knee and tell about all the places he'd been and the wondrous things he'd seen." Maeve's blue eyes began to glow with the memories.

"How did a sailor from Northern Ireland wind up here in Cabot Cove?" Seth wondered aloud.

"Ah, now, there's my favorite part of the story. It seems he was a deckhand on a ship bound for Nova Scotia. When it arrived in the Bay of Fundy, it had some serious troubles and needed to be dry-docked for repairs for a length of time that was far too long for my da. At this part of the story, he would look me in the eye and say, 'Not being a landlubber, it wasn't my way to sit around and wait,' and we would both shake our heads really fast." Maeve laughed. "So when a nearby ship was looking for a hand for a short journey to Portland, Maine, my da jumped at the chance to fill the days until his ship would be ready to be off again."

I was intrigued, wondering what Maeve's father had seen in Portland that enticed him to stay in Maine. I should have known.

"At this point in the story, my da would look across the room at my mam, who was in her rocker, often knitting, sometimes sewing, and he would smile and say, 'When we docked at Portland, as I was helping to lower the gangplank, I saw the most beautiful girl, with hints of copper flowing through her light brown curls and eyes bluer than the sky, standing in line ready to board for our return trip.' No matter how long they'd been married, my mam always blushed when Da described the scene." Maeve took a sip of tea before she finished her story.

"By the time Mam left the ship at Jonesport to visit her aunt Lottie, my da was totally smitten. As soon as he'd sailed back to Nova Scotia, he said his good-byes to his shipmates and hitched a ride back down to Maine. Six months later he sailed back to Ireland to invite his family to the wedding. By all accounts a number of the relatives came and it was a joyous event. Da worked the lobster boats and over time was able to buy one of his own. Years of hard work led to my parents buying the house next door, where I have lived ever since and where I hope to die."

"And from what I recall of your recent physical examination, that final event won't be coming along anytime soon." As Maeve's doctor, Seth gave his opinion.

Maeve smiled and patted Seth's hand. "Maybe not, but I do know that the years are piling on, one after the other, far faster than they used to. And that brings me to the reason I need a favor from Jessica. I have four watercolors that my grandfather painted for my parents and brought over as a wedding present. They are local scenes surrounding the village. He even included one that was his own interpretation of the Giant's Causeway—beautifully done, I might add."

"The Giant's Causeway? Is that a bridge of some sort?" Seth asked.

Maeve laughed. "If you were Finn McCool, 'bridge' might be the perfect description. I've a book of Irish mythology in the house and it includes a fine explanation of the legend of Finn McCool— or Fionn mac Cumhaill, as it's pronounced in the Irish—and the Giant's Causeway. I'd be glad to pass it along."

Seth nodded but I could see he was disappointed not to get an immediate answer to his question. I decided to bring the conversation back to the reason Maeve had arrived, scones in hand.

"Maeve, you said you needed a favor? What exactly can I do for you?"

"Lately I've been thinking a lot about my grandfather's paintings. I'm not getting any younger and I have neither siblings nor children. But I do have cousins and they have children." Maeve paused.

Although I was quick to see where this was headed, I waited for Maeve to continue.

"Jessica, if it wouldn't be too great an ask, I was wondering if you would be kind enough to escort my grandfather's paintings home. I would arrange for you to stay at a lovely small hotel in Bushmills where I myself have stayed more than once. It's run by the Nolan family, who are gracious hosts, and they will welcome you as my guest. I will ask Dougal Nolan to arrange for a small reception where you can present the paintings to the cousins and their children. From that point on, they can decide among themselves where the paintings should reside, but I think it is important that the family are all together when they see the paintings for the first time. Don't you agree?"

Of course I had no actual view on the matter, but since it was Maeve's family, I accepted her judgment on what was best.

On the other hand, Seth had a number of opinions. "Maeve, don't you think you are asking a lot of Jessica? How is she to carry four paintings? If you've had them all this while, I suppose they are framed."

"Dr. Hazlitt, what do you take me for? A ninny? I have had them removed from their frames and packed in tubes so that they will travel lightly and arrive safely. The cousins can buy their own frames if they've a mind." Maeve huffed.

Seth nodded, satisfied that his concern had been met. "That's the spirit, Maeve. You're giving the paintings. Let the cousins decide how they should be exhibited."

"And suppose they have poor taste? I can't allow that. Jessica, I had planned to write you a brief description of my cousins and their kin. Now I'll be sure to add a letter to them explaining how the paintings should be framed as well as my own suggestions for display."

I sighed as I reached for my to-do list and put a big star next to Susan Shevlin's name. It was becoming obvious that she was going to have to make my return trip open-ended.

Chapter Two

Both Lorna and Susan had warned me that the trip to Belfast would be a long one and require at least one stopover. When my plane landed at London's Heathrow Airport, I was glad to have the longest leg of the trip behind me. Still, I did have a small twinge of disappointment that, while I was on his side of the Atlantic, my friend Chief Inspector George Sutherland of Scotland Yard was in Australia, on assignment with a special international task force. He told me that he would be there for the next several months, which meant I would be gone long before he returned.

I had nearly two hours before my next flight. The first thing I did was take some time to freshen up in the ladies' lounge. After so many hours on a plane, I can't begin to describe how soothing it was to wash my face and hands. Then I dabbed on a bit of lipstick and a spritz of cologne, which helped me feel human again. I walked around the terminal for a bit of a stretch until I found a quiet corner table in one of the dining areas and ordered a pot of Earl Grey tea and a crumpet with butter and honey. Generally I like to watch planes take off and land but there wasn't much activity on the runway that was visible through the floor-to-ceiling window, so after I'd eaten my crumpet, I poured my second cup of tea and decided to read the note that Maeve insisted I take with me so that I would be familiar with her Irish family members.

I have three cousins on my father's side, all living in the vicinity of Bushmills, County Antrim, Northern Ireland. Together they own and run the family cosmetics company, Marine Magic. The business head of the company is Beth Anne O'Bannon Ryan, a sharp cookie if ever there was one. Without Lizzy (don't ever call her that; it's a childhood nickname she hates) at the helm, I am sure the company would still be a small business run from the old carriage house on our granda's farm. Her younger sister, Jane O'Bannon Mullen, is the head chemist and a wiz when it comes to finding beauty-product uses for the seaweed that abounds on the coast. Their cousin and mine Michael O'Bannon is a doctor and it is his professional recommendation that gives authority to the claim that Marine Magic products keep your skin firm and young.

I could almost hear Maeve laughing as she wrote that last line. I knew she was a firm believer that a good night's sleep and vigorous daily activities were the two things that would contribute most to a long and healthy life, the family cosmetics firm notwithstanding. I read a little more of what she'd written about the family, and Maeve ended by thanking me for being her messenger. She promised that when I came home she would make me a full Irish breakfast, complete with extra raisins in the soda bread, which was exactly the way I enjoyed it.

The boarding call for my flight to Belfast came over the loudspeaker sooner than I had anticipated. I put Maeve's note in my purse, gathered up my tote bag, and headed for the gate.

I felt as though I had barely settled in my seat when a flight attendant announced we were preparing to land. I glanced at my watch, which was still on Cabot Cove time. Right on schedule, the flight had taken slightly more than an hour.

I went through the usual deplaning havoc and was relieved to walk through the doorway that led to the airport lobby. I was scouring the overhead signage, looking for directions to the taxi stand, when I was agreeably surprised to see a middle-aged man who was wearing a wool tweed jacket and holding a sign high over his head that read JESSICA FLETCHER.

I stepped directly in front of him and introduced myself. He answered not with the Irish brogue I was expecting but with a clipped British accent.

"Mrs. Fletcher, it is an absolute joy to finally meet an author I have admired for many years." He reached out and shook my hand firmly. "My name is Godfrey Hamilton and I am your festival escort."

"Why, thank you for coming to the airport to greet me. I am delighted not to have to find my way to the Belfast Hilton on my own." I was effusive with my gratitude.

"It is entirely my pleasure, Mrs. Fletcher. Every member of the festival team is elated that you were kind enough to take Lorna

Winters's place at the very last minute. We are indebted to you. Not having an American Author Guest of Honor would have left a terrible hole in our schedule. We all will do everything possible to make your stay comfortable. Tara Brennan, the hotel's festival coordinator, has seen to it that you've a room with a breathtaking view of the River Lagan." Godfrey reached for my suitcase, which I'd set on the floor in order to shake his hand. "Now, if we have all your bits and bobs, come along. I know where there is a nice pot of tea and a platter of sandwiches waiting for us."

He led me out of the airport and straight to a dark gray car parked at the curb.

I was surprised when I saw the easily identifiable script in the emblem on the hood. "Is this a Ford?"

"It certainly is. The Ford Fiesta is a very popular car throughout Ireland." Godfrey popped the trunk and stowed my luggage. "Now, we've a lovely ride of twenty miles or so through County Antrim's enchantingly beautiful countryside until we arrive in Belfast City."

Godfrey was certainly right about the fields and woodlands that dotted our drive. Belfast itself was impressive with an eclectic mix of architecture, some modern and some quite old. He pulled the car up to the curbside and came to a stop in front of an imposing Baroque Revival–style building that took up an entire city block.

"Jessica, this is Belfast City Hall, which was built in celebration of Queen Victoria's designation of Belfast as a city. Not only is this building strikingly beautiful. I want you to know it was strong enough to survive the Belfast Blitz perpetrated by the Luftwaffe in 1941."

I was surprised and said so. "Really? I had no idea. . . ."

"Oh, it's true. Nearly a thousand people were killed and many more were seriously injured in Germany's attempt to dismantle Belfast's contribution to the Allied war effort, but the attacks were for naught. Belfast continued building and repairing ships as well as manufacturing many types of needed goods to hasten the end of the war."

I mentioned to Godfrey that whenever I traveled, I was sure to be fascinated by the history of the places I visited and I was delighted that he'd introduced me to this piece of Belfast's past.

Godfrey gave me a Cheshire cat smile. "Well, if it is history you've a mind for, then you will be delighted with tonight's reception for honored guests and dignitaries, which is being held at *Titanic* Belfast."

I grinned back at him. "Now, that's a piece of history I do know. The RMS *Titanic* was built here in Belfast."

Godfrey started the car and we were on our way again. "It was indeed. And *Titanic* Belfast today occupies the site of the former Harland and Wolff shipyard, where the *Titanic* was built more than a century ago. And now I am sure you'll be happy to know we're minutes away from the hotel and the tea and sandwiches I promised, unless you'd prefer an Ulster fry, which is our favorite breakfast, consisting of eggs, bacon, sausage, baked beans, black pudding, tomatoes, mushrooms, and tea, although as a Yank, you may prefer coffee."

I couldn't help but laugh. "My friend and neighbor Maeve O'Bannon calls that an Irish breakfast."

"Well, whatever it's called, it's a breakfast that will keep you in fine fettle for many hours to come, so if you opt for sandwiches now, be sure and try the Ulster fry in the morning." Godfrey made a swift turn into the parking lot of an elegant modern hotel and parked the car facing a wide expanse of water lapping softly against a seawall.

"Here we are, Jessica. The River Lagan welcomes you to Belfast. We can leave the luggage; I'll send a bellman out for it later. I am quite sure that Moira Callan and Thomas Singh, the festival cochairs, are prowling the lobby like sheepdogs searching for a missing lamb, waiting for your arrival."

The doorman had no sooner opened the door for us than I heard my name.

"Jessica! Jessica Fletcher. At long last. I've been waiting impatiently."

It seemed as though everyone in the hotel lobby turned toward the tall redhead dressed in an olive green silk dress, and then their eyes slewed to the object for which her arms were outstretched. It was all I could do not to shrink from the spotlight, but remembering that I was here not for myself but on behalf of Lorna Winters, the American Author Guest of Honor, I clutched the woman's extended hands.

"Lorna was so disappointed that she could not come herself, but I promise to do my best to represent her. Her accident was so unfortunate, but Lorna asked me to assure everyone that she will be with us all in spirit this year and plans to attend the Belfast Book Festival in person next year."

Godfrey cleared his throat. "Jessica, if I may present Moira Callan, the festival cochair, who is obviously ecstatic to meet you."

Moira flapped her hand in Godfrey's direction. "Don't be explaining for me what I can clearly explain for myself." She turned her head in every direction. "Where has Tom gotten to? Ah, there he is, coming from the dining room."

A tall gentleman wearing a navy blue suit and a light blue turban signaled us to join him. When we got closer, he reached out to shake my hand. "Jessica, I am Tom Singh, Moira's partner in crime for this year's festival. I can't tell you how much we appreciate having an author of your stature stepping in at the last minute. Please join us for lunch."

He turned on his heel and we followed. Moira leaned in close to my ear and said, "Tom's not kidding. Happy as we were when Lorna accepted our invitation, we were all pleasantly surprised when ticket sales jumped as soon as we announced that you would be joining us in her place."

Godfrey must have sensed that her comment caused me some discomfort, because he quickly said, "Now, Moira, you know we always do well with last-minute tickets. Many people wait until they are sure their schedule will allow them to attend before they order tickets."

Tom led us to a corner table covered with a crisp white cloth. Upscale china and sparkling crystal glasses were set out in a service for four. We had barely taken our seats when not one but two servers appeared, each holding two teapots. They offered us a choice of English breakfast, oolong, Irish breakfast, or Ceylon tea. As we made our choices, a third server came and placed a tiered silver tray in the center of the table. Sandwiches cut into dainty triangles were neatly arranged on the top tier while the middle tier was covered with scones and the bottom tier had rich-looking pastries that I decided to forgo the minute I saw them. I took a sip of my Ceylon tea while one of the servers offered us food choices. I opted for a smoked salmon sandwich and a scone with clotted cream.

Once our plates were filled, the servers disappeared as effortlessly as they had appeared. Tom Singh raised his teacup in my direction.

"Here's to Jessica Fletcher, who saved us from certain tragedy."

Godfrey seconded. "Hear! Hear!"

My cheeks burned because I was blushing profusely, so I was grateful that Moira immediately began to explain what was expected of me over the course of the next few days.

"Tonight we are hosting a gala reception at *Titanic* Belfast. Godfrey will be your escort and we expect that you will mingle. Much as we're sure you would like to spend time reconnecting with your fellow authors, we hope that you will focus primarily on the benefactors, whose generosity allows the book festival to be one of Belfast's premier social events." She leaned back in her chair, obviously pleased that she had gotten her message across— play up to the donors.

While I appreciated her directness, if not the message itself, Tom seemed genuinely uncomfortable. He quickly aimed for damage control. "Jessica, if it is not too much of an imposition, we'd appreciate your saying a few words this evening. Perhaps you could give a brief greeting from Lorna. I promise it will take only a few moments and then you are free to enjoy the party as you wish."

He tossed a meaningful glance in Moira's direction. She opened her mouth as if to speak and then must have changed her mind. She took a bite of her sandwich and began chewing resolutely. By the devious look in her eyes, I was sure she was already devising a plan to lure me into meeting with her chosen group of benefactors at this evening's event. And I was likely to go along with her plan. After all, I was there merely to fill in for Lorna, so why not do whatever was required, even if the role was a bit uncomfortable? In a few days I would be off on my own to explore Northern Ireland on my way to Bushmills.

The remainder of our time was social and congenial. Tom told an amusing story about ordering books for last year's festival, and when they arrived, they were printed in French, German, and Chinese, not a word of English in any of them. Then Godfrey surprised me with a heartfelt account of when he'd met my friend and mentor, Marjorie Ainsworth, at a reception in London shortly before her death.

"Mrs. Ainsworth was such a gracious woman. By the time I had the opportunity to speak to her, the evening was drawing to a close, but she patiently listened while I expressed my admiration and appreciation. The she *thanked me* for taking the time to tell her how much I enjoyed her books. Can you imagine?"

"That sounds exactly like Marjorie," I agreed. "She adored her readers and continued to be astonished by how devoted they were to her books and plays."

While the four of us continued to chat, my eyes began to feel heavy. I craved a nap, which I blamed on the time change, so I was grateful when Moira suddenly pushed back her chair and said, "Look at the time. I have a million things to do before the reception. Tom, see they charge the bill to the festival committee. Jessica, it's been lovely. I trust Godfrey will take good care of you for the next few days, but if he doesn't . . ."

"Oh, please," I protested. "Godfrey has been a perfect guide and a perfect gentleman besides. I'm sure we will be fine throughout the festival."

But Moira had ceased listening and was already walking away.

Godfrey was studiously staring at the tabletop but Tom lightened the mood when he said, "While Moira's busy evaluating everyone else's performance, I often wonder if she realizes that people are evaluating that she may well be lacking in the manners department."

That jostled Godfrey out of his funk. "I suppose she can't help it. Moira is an extremely competent organizer and there are times that may require bumping elbows." He laughed and then turned to me. "I suppose you are quite ready to find your room and have a few hours to yourself."

I smiled thankfully. "Godfrey, you are a mind reader."

We took leave of Tom, and when we reentered the lobby, I headed to the reception desk, but Godfrey took my arm and steered me to the elevator. "No need for you to wait at the desk. Your registration has been taken care of."

My suite was quite sumptuous and included a well-stocked refrigerator and a microwave. Next to the usual hotel coffeepot were an electric kettle and an assortment of teas. A charming arrangement of colorful roses, carnations, and lilies sat on a table in front of the wide living room window, which overlooked the lovely River Lagan. From eight stories up, the view was, as Godfrey had promised, spectacular.

I unpacked my things, pleased to see that none of my clothes appeared to need pressing, so I could ignore the iron and the ironing board tucked neatly in the closet. I settled in a lounge chair and rested my feet on the hassock nestled in front of me. Godfrey had pledged he'd place a warning telephone call approximately an hour before he would come to collect me to go to the reception. I sighed peacefully, appreciative of having time and a room to myself. I pulled *An Irish Country Doctor* by Patrick Taylor out of my tote bag. Although the book was fiction, Taylor was a physician who practiced medicine in Ireland and I hoped the book would give me a deeper sense of my surroundings.

Chapter Three

I had already decided against taking a nap, hoping to swing my internal clock to Irish time. After reading for more than an hour, I started feeling groggy again. I stood with determination and opened the window wide. Then I took several deep breaths and fell into the routine of what I called my travel exercises.

I marched in place to get my heart pumping, then started with arm circles, followed by squats and side bends. I ended with a two-minute full-body shake that I had long ago named my loosey-goosey finale.

I followed up with a warm shower, and I was blow-drying my hair when the telephone rang. I expected it to be Godfrey, but when I picked up the phone, I was surprised to hear Maeve O'Bannon's voice.

"And there you be, Jessica, tucked into your hotel room in beautiful Belfast?"

"I certainly am. The countryside is lovely and so is the city, from what I've seen of it. Of course, I haven't been here very long. I am sure there is much more to enjoy."

"Exactly why I called the room and not your cell," Maeve said. "I expect your writer work will keep you hopping for the next few days, and I didn't want to interfere, but I did want to let you know that once your book event is concluded my cousin Jane's son, Owen, has been deputized to pick you up and drive you from Belfast to the River Bush Hotel in Bushmills, where Dougal Nolan has assured me you will be made to feel welcome."

"Oh, that is very kind of Owen, and you, of course, for arranging it. I had thought to hire a car and driver but this is an ideal plan." I was happy to be relieved of the chore.

"A hire car! Jane was all for sending a hire car for you but I know her far too well. She'd direct the driver to take you to the big, fancy house she lives in and you would be trapped as her guest, unable to do the simplest thing or even so much as take a walk without her permission. Owen will follow my instructions to the letter and deliver you to the River Bush Hotel." Maeve sounded very self-satisfied but I was hesitant.

"Surely, Owen wouldn't want to disappoint his mother. . . ."

Maeve laughed heartily. "Did I forget to mention that Owen is engaged to be married to Dougal Nolan's daughter, Maggie? This is not the first push-pull that Owen's had to navigate between his mother and the Nolans. I am sure there will be many more to come."

I joined in the laughter. "Under those circumstances, you are probably right."

After I assured Maeve that her grandfather's paintings were safely in my suitcase, she disconnected the call, but not before reminding me that she would be forever grateful to me for doing her such a brilliant favor.

"And remember, Jessica, that in Ireland the word 'brilliant' doesn't mean 'superintelligent.' It means 'excellent', 'wonderful,' 'amazing'—something of that sort. So again, I thank you for your brilliant favor."

As she spoke, I shrugged her thanks off. After all, I was going to be able to spend a few extra days in the charming Irish countryside, so delivering the paintings was hardly what I would have called an onerous chore.

Little did I know how complicated things were about to get.

The next time the phone rang, it was indeed Godfrey calling, to advise me that he would be knocking on my door in exactly one hour. "I have gotten a look at the schedule that Moira put together. And I am sorry to say that you will be in for an evening that may stretch far into the night. Plus you can expect it to be quite social. Feel free to let me know when you can bear no more chitchat and I will spirit you back to the hotel."

"You are a kindhearted man, Godfrey, but I am well attuned to this sort of gathering filled with writers, publishers, editors, readers, and the press. I assure you I can hold my own," I said.

"Of that, I have no doubt," he answered. "The question is how long you'll be willing to do so. I'll see you in an hour."

True to his word, Godfrey tapped on my door exactly sixty minutes after he'd hung up the phone. He looked quite dashing in his tuxedo, and I was pleased to see him flush ever so slightly when I admired the tiny green shamrock studs on the front of his shirt.

"And you, my dear Jessica, are quite radiant in that gown. I do believe red is definitely your color." Godfrey smiled and crooked his arm. "Shall we go and dazzle them all?"

"Why not?" As I took his arm I noticed that, as a gentleman is wont to do, he had matched his cuff links with his studs.

There were several partygoers in the elevator, and when we arrived on the main floor, the people gathered in the hotel lobby were filled with excitement about the upcoming reception. Guests were greeting one another boisterously and organizing spontaneous carpools, and many were extracting promises as to who would order the first round of drinks when they arrived at *Titanic* Belfast.

"I can see it's going to be quite a night," I observed.

"And now you understand why this is a book festival rather than a conference. The atmosphere is as jolly as a long-overdue family gathering." Godfrey guided me to a side door. "Let's slip out to the car park and make our way so that we can nibble on all the best hors d'oeuvres before that crowd arrives."

As we walked outdoors, I mentioned my surprise that the sun was still high in the sky.

Godfrey nodded. "Most Americans don't realize that Ireland has such long days this time of year. Tourists are disconcerted when they go for an after-dinner walk and nature's light makes them feel as though they have only finished lunch."

Godfrey clicked his key fob and the doors on the Fiesta unlocked. He guided me to the passenger door and opened it. Once we were settled and on our way, Godfrey suddenly became serious.

"I hope you will not think that I am telling tales out of school when I say that my consistent experience has been that Moira becomes more and more agitated as the opening of the festival becomes a reality," he said.

"Oh, I doubt that will be a problem," I answered. "Once the reception is in full swing, even the most anxious hosts tend to relax. It's likely Moira will do the same."

Godfrey guffawed, but said no more.

We drove in silence until, as we were crossing a bridge over the River Lagan, Godfrey said, "The best view of *Titanic* Belfast in all its stateliness is from the car park at the local marina."

He drove alongside the River Lagan for another few minutes until he pulled into a parking lot and stopped the car.

Beyond the sailboats, cabin cruisers, and runabouts that were moored in the marina, and past the smokestacks of a historic ship nestled in an inlet, stood *Titanic* Belfast. I was awed by its sheer size and shape. I'd seen pictures of course but nothing could have prepared me for the huge building, which was shaped like the hulls of several ships all coming together.

I gasped, and when I caught my breath again, I said, "How magnificent!"

"Indeed it is," Godfrey said, and he put the car in park. "We'll just enjoy the view for a minute and then we'll pop over and I'll give you the grand tour. As you can see, the exterior replicates the prows of four seafaring ships and matches the height of the *Titanic*, which in American terms would be more than one hundred feet."

"Quite frankly, pictures do not do it justice," I said. "I didn't expect it to be so massive. And I am definitely curious about the material that covers those prows."

"The facade is made of silver anodized aluminum shards, all pieced together to give it that amazing look. At least three thousand shards, perhaps a few more," Godfrey said as he put the car in gear. "Shall we go see what's inside?"

"I can't wait. My imagination is in overdrive," I answered.

As we drove past the inlet, Godfrey pointed to the historic

ship. "That is the SS *Nomadic*, a former tender ship of the White Star Line. She was built to transfer passengers, baggage, and mail to and from the larger ships RMS *Olympic* and RMS *Titanic* in popular transatlantic ports such as Cherbourg that were too small to accommodate the big ships. The *Nomadic* now serves as a maritime museum since it was built, along with the *Olympic* and the *Titanic*, in the very shipyards that once occupied this land."

As we joined the crowd walking toward the main entrance, Godfrey said, "No matter how busy the night may be, we must be sure to have your picture taken on the replica of the iconic Grand Staircase from the *Titanic*."

"Do you mean the ornate, curved staircase with the cherub holding the lamp at the bottom? I remember it well. It was such a centerpiece in the movie."

"The very one." Godfrey held a door open for me. "Now, there are Moira and Tom greeting their guests. Hopefully we can get through the receiving line quickly and find ourselves some food and drink."

But we had no such luck.

"Jessica Fletcher!" Moira, dressed in a high-necked royal blue evening gown that complemented her red hair and blue eyes, announced my name loudly enough to be heard by everyone in the lobby. And in case someone missed it the first time, Moira raised her voice higher and began clapping her hands. "Ladies and gentleman, we are fortunate to have as our very special guest the famed American mystery writer J. B. Fletcher."

Many of the guests stopped whatever they were doing and joined in the clapping, much to my embarrassment.

Godfrey muttered, "Oh, dear," and latched onto my elbow. I thought he hoped to lead me away, but Moira took a few steps closer and threw her arms around me as if we hadn't seen in each other in decades.

Then she turned to a woman nearby and said, "Ardis, come meet Jessica." And that opened the floodgates. Godfrey and Tom stood helplessly by while a throng of well-wishers surrounded Moira and me. At one point Moira leaned in and whispered, "Isn't this marvelous?"

I thought it was anything but marvelous but was too busy to say so. Dozens of people were reaching to shake my hand and welcome me to Belfast. I saw Tom and Godfrey exchange a look and then they waded into the crowd.

"Mrs. Fletcher will be with us for the entire festival, so there is no reason to snatch a small bit of her attention now when you can have a much larger slice over the next few days." Tom's voice rang with the authoritative tone that I had often used to settle down rowdy classes during my teaching days.

People smiled and nodded. Some waved and most walked toward the entrance to the museum exhibits. I greeted the few stragglers as warmly as I could, and when they were gone I turned to thank Tom for the rescue, but before I could get a word in, Moira snapped, "Now you've done it. Our receiving line is gone and I have no clear count of the important people."

Before Tom could reply, Moira turned her back on us and strode over to a couple who had just entered. "Mr. and Mrs. Quilty, how nice of you to join us."

I raised an eyebrow. "Important people?"

Tom laughed. "Money-wise, definitely. Personality-wise, Dora Quilty, at least, should be avoided at all costs. She talks of nothing but her prized black-faced sheep. I promise you that you can listen for only so long while she blathers about which of her latest crop of lambs will become providers of the finest wool ever shorn in Ireland."

Godfrey laughed. "I once faked a fainting spell to escape Dora Quilty's clutches. Speaking of escape, Tom, do you think Jessica and I have enough time to slip off to the *Titanic* staircase for a few pictures before Moira hunts us down?"

Tom glanced at his ever-present cell phone. "Ceremonies and speeches begin in about twenty-five minutes. As long as you are in the banquet room by then, I see no harm. I'll run interference with Moira if necessary."

Godfrey took my arm and led me to a room he said was named the *Titanic* Suite. He opened the door, and when I stepped inside, I was awed. The replica of the *Titanic*'s Grand Staircase was a perfect duplicate in every way, from the tone of the wood, which appeared to be solid oak, to the graceful curves of the bannisters.

"How magnificent! I feel as though I am on the movie set or perhaps on the ship itself," I said.

Godfrey beamed. "I did not want you to miss this, and knowing how tight the evening's schedule is, I thought it best to get us in here first thing."

I looked around the room. "I'm surprised Moira didn't decide to have the dinner in this room. I would think that the staircase alone provides an opulence that would have a certain appeal to her."

Godfrey shook his head. "As a committee member, I can tell you with the greatest of personal confidence that Moira has repeatedly said she does not want her 'literary stars' to have to compete with a staircase that just might be more famous than they are."

"You're joking," I said.

"Moira's ideas do not generally leave room for humor. Now give me your phone and strike a pose on the staircase. We have time for a number of photos but we will have to be quick about it. Why not start at the top?"

I nodded and walked up the stairs, planning to strike a pose of sorts on the landing, where the side stairs met. That was when I noticed the clock in the rear wall. Its hands were motionless, set at two twenty.

I turned to Godfrey and asked the significance of the time.

"It is widely believed that the *Titanic* fell completely under the North Atlantic at twenty minutes past two in the morning of April 15, 1912. And so it was decided that on this landing the hands of the Honour and Glory Crowning Time clock would remain forever still at that time in memory of the tragedy."

"Honour and Glory? That's a rather fancy title for such an unpretentious-looking clock."

Godfrey grinned. "While I agree that Honour and Glory Crowning Time is quite a designation for such a small clock, I can tell you the name represents the entire neoclassical design surrounding the timepiece. Take a closer look at the elegant carving."

As I stepped closer, I remembered the scene in the movie when handsome young Jack passed a note to Rose asking her to meet him by the clock.

I examined the exquisite carving on the wall while Godfrey

explained that the large angels on either side of the clock represented Honour and Glory.

"The design is taken from a sculpture that Auguste-Marie Taunay designed for the Louis XIV salon in the Palace of the Tuileries in Paris," Godfrey said. "Charles Wilson carved the scene at the top of the Grand Staircase in both the *Titanic* and the *Olympic*. Why don't you stand just there so I can take a few snaps of an authentically iconic author alongside an imitation of iconic art?"

I laughed at his teasing tone and stood where he pointed.

We took several more pictures before Godfrey looked at his watch. "Oh, my, we are cutting it close, Jessica. We'd best move along before Moira has the entire Police Service of Northern Ireland searching for us."

Chapter Four

We'd barely set foot in the main dining room when Moira came charging toward us.

"There you are. I was about to send out a search party. Godfrey, you should know better," Moira scolded. "Jessica is one of our featured speakers and we are due to start momentarily. I've been frantic."

"Moira, dear heart, have I ever disappointed you? Here is Jessica, safe and sound." Godfrey took my hand and held it aloft toward Moira while surreptitiously giving me a wink and a humorous smile.

I couldn't help smiling back.

Moira led me to a platform, took her place behind the podium, and asked—or, rather, ordered—me to stand a few feet to her left. I did so, but apparently not to her satisfaction. She put her hand over the microphone and said through clenched teeth,

"Farther left. How can I invite you into the spotlight if you are already standing inside its perimeter?"

Since there was no spotlight anywhere to be seen, I wasn't sure what I had done wrong, but I obliged Moira by taking a few steps to the left, even as the thought crossed my mind that I hadn't given as much consideration as I might have to Lorna's request that I represent her.

Moira nodded her approval, removed her hand from the microphone, and asked for everyone's attention. At that moment the houselights dimmed and a spotlight encircled the podium area, and I am sure Moira was pleased that I was a few feet outside its rim.

Moira introduced Tom Singh, who I hadn't noticed was standing on the far side of the podium; she thanked everyone for their unending support of the festival and then started outlining the events of the next few days. Just as I sensed a certain restlessness begin to creep through the audience, Moira switched topics and began to describe the long and magnificent career of American Author Guest of Honor Lorna Winters. She segued into the details of Lorna's accident and ended by saying, "Fortunately, Lorna has a dear friend who is also an America author of worldwide repute and who has graciously agreed to join us in Lorna's place. Ladies and gentlemen, may I present Jessica Fletcher, known to many of you as mystery writer J. B. Fletcher?"

A second or two before the spotlight widened to include me, Godfrey reappeared to escort me the few feet to the podium.

The crowd greeted me so warmly that I immediately felt at ease. I recited greetings from Lorna exactly as she had requested and then I added a few words of my own delight at being able to attend the Belfast Book Festival. Within a few minutes, my official task for the evening was completed. Godfrey was once again at my side and took my arm. The audience clapped enthusiastically while we left the podium. As soon as we were out of the limelight, Godfrey slipped a small green bottle from his inside pocket.

"I thought you might do with a sip of sparkling water."

"Godfrey, you think of everything. Between the glaring spotlight and having to read that long speech of Lorna's, plus my own few words, I am quite parched."

As I raised the bottle to my lips, two gentlemen approached us.

The taller of the two reached out to shake my hand. "Welcome to Belfast, Mrs. Fletcher. I understand that you've brought me a handsome gift."

As the confusion spread across my face, he laughed and said, "Sorry. I couldn't help but tease. I am Michael O'Bannon and my entire family is grateful to you for safely bringing family heirlooms to our shores from our cousin Maeve, who I understand has the good fortune to be your neighbor."

I certainly hadn't expected to meet any O'Bannons before I arrived in Bushmills, yet here was one of Maeve's cousins standing before me.

"Ah, the doctor in the family. Maeve told me that you are the medical authority behind Marine Magic Cosmetics," I said.

"Don't let my cousins Jane and Beth Anne hear you say that. They are rather convinced that I am nothing more than an appendage with an education." This time his laugh had a sour edge to it.

That was family business, not mine, and I certainly didn't want him to expound, so I changed the tone and topic by introducing him to Godfrey. Then I continued. "I was certainly fortunate when the festival committee assigned Godfrey as my escort. He took the time to give me a lovely tour of Belfast earlier today, and taught me a bit of your country's history as well."

"If it is history that interests you, Conor, here, is your man. May I present Conor Sweeney, owner of Sweeney Brothers Shipping, a fine company that transports our Marine Magic products throughout Europe? There is nothing about the history of Ireland that Conor can't tell you. Although I warn you, he generally starts the story around the Stone Age, and once he gets warmed up, it can take hours for him to get so far along as the medieval period." Michael clapped Conor on the back. "For brevity's sake, I will jump to a piece of our history your countrymen find interesting. Did you know that your famous seaman John Paul Jones—a native of Scotland, by the way—led a battle right here in Belfast Lough against the British ship HMS *Drake*? Of course Jones won the day—or the story would not be worth telling, eh, Conor? Tell Mrs. Fletcher, when exactly was that battle?"

The blond man with bushy brown eyebrows, who had been standing quietly while Michael rattled on, responded, "It was in April 1778. The American ship that Jones commanded was called the USS *Ranger*. In fact, Mrs. Fletcher, since in your presentation you mentioned that you are a resident of Maine, are you aware that the *Ranger* was built in Kittery, Maine? Is that anywhere near your Cabot Cove?"

"Kittery and Cabot Cove are both on the Atlantic coast but Kittery is far to the south. It is actually quite near the border of our neighboring state, New Hampshire. Your historical information is fascinating. We Americans know of John Paul Jones and his daring exploits against the British navy, which was deemed to be the finest in the world at that time, but I had no idea that he was daring enough to come here to fight a battle on Britain's own turf and actually win. Remarkable." I was astonished and I was sure it showed.

Just then Tom Singh joined us, said a polite hello to Michael and Conor, then smiled apologetically. "I am sorry to interrupt, Jessica, but Moira would like you to join her for a tour of the museum."

"Of course you should go. Enjoy yourself," Michael said, sounding as though I needed his permission, which I found disconcerting. "We'll see you in Bushmills in a few days' time. Conor and I will be glad to talk your ear off about the history of our fine land. And perhaps you'll finally give us a glance at the precious cargo you've brought us from America."

Then he turned and marched away with Conor Sweeney at his heel.

Tom looked at me quizzically. "Did I interrupt something?"

I certainly didn't think so, but Godfrey was quick to respond, "I'm not sure what all this talk is about gifts and heirlooms and precious cargo, but one thing I do know. If Michael O'Bannon shows up at a social event, there need be something in it for him. And he certainly is not known to be a man who participates in a fundraising event such as this evening's unless there is a way to put a pound or two in his own pocket."

Tom Singh nodded. "Sure, I've heard the same thing myself. Now, let's get to Moira before she becomes unbridled."

As he led us to the lobby, I had to wonder what Maeve would have made of Tom and Godfrey's evaluation of her cousin Michael.

Moira was in the midst of a small group of people whom I

supposed to be her top donors. She confirmed it when she said to me, "Jessica, here are the lovely people who give grand support to the festival each and every year."

She introduced them one by one and I responded effusively to each, thanking them for their dedication to the festival and for their love of books and reading. If someone got extremely talkative, creating a queue behind the donors, Godfrey would enter the conversation and manage to guide the person away.

I was speaking to the very last of Moira's supporters, a married couple named Gaffney who were raving about their three-year-old granddaughter and how much she loved books. Her current favorite was *Don't Let the Pigeon Drive the Bus!* by Mo Willems. Godfrey was unable to temper their enthusiasm, and Moira startled us all when she clapped her hands like a teacher trying to quiet a roomful of rowdy children and gave me a stern look. "Jessica, please, we really must begin the tour or you may miss some of the best exhibits."

She snatched at my arm and shooed the Gaffneys away. When she realized Godfrey had remained by my side, she started to object, changed her mind, and muttered mostly to herself, "Oh, what's the harm?"

The exhibit began with a view of Belfast and its residents during the early 1900s. After that we took a ride in a comfortable minicar through an interactive replica of the old Harland and Wolff shipyard to see how the *Titanic* and her sister ships had been built. We moved on to another gallery to see exact replicas of the *Titanic*'s guest cabins from first class to third class, followed by an interactive experience of walking on the ship's deck and sitting on benches as if we were enjoying a normal day at sea. For me, and I am sure for most visitors, it was difficult to stand in the sixth gallery and watch the sinking of the grand ship, while listening to the repeated SOS signals that begged for help. In an additional overlay, we could hear recordings of survivors as they told their stories.

By the time we reached the display of the aftermath of the ship's hitting the iceberg, Moira had clearly lost interest in introducing me to anyone and everyone we came across and was anxious to get back to the main banquet hall, where most guests were eating and drinking. I suspected we'd already encountered all of the most important people on her list.

She clasped my hand between both of hers and said, "Godfrey will see you through these final harrowing exhibits while I check that everything is going smoothly elsewhere. Thank you for your delightful participation this evening."

She vanished as quickly as a magician who had just dropped a smoke pellet.

Godfrey gave me a wink. "Well, that was easier than I thought. I feared Moira was going to be the bell around our neck for the entire evening."

As we stood in front of a reproduction of one of the *Titanic's* lifeboats, he said, "Now let me give you a brief summary of this section of the museum, and then you have the option of joining Moira and her guests in the ballroom or returning to the hotel."

He was not at all surprised when I chose the hotel.

The next morning I participated in a panel discussion about the popularity of cozy mysteries. After a brief lunch break, I was scheduled to be interviewed. I was delighted that my conversation partner was Tom Singh, who I was sure would be more relaxed than Moira. The program clearly stated that we were supposed to discuss the rise and worldwide spread of interest in American mystery authors. However, toward the end of our allotted time, Tom surprised me by asking if I would tell the audience about my personal and professional relationship with the legendary British mystery writer the late Marjorie Ainsworth.

Of course I was more than happy to do so. Time spent with Marjorie over the years had always been fulfilling and rewarding, right up until her untimely death. And even then I was comforted by the fact that I was close at hand and able to help solve her murder. As soon as the book signing that followed the interview had ended, I decided to head to my room for some alone time before I changed for the formal dinner being held later that evening in the hotel ballroom. Writing and research are solitary endeavors, but I have found that once a book is published, I have no choice but to become involved in the social aspects of my profession. As much as I enjoy meeting readers and other authors, I often need to clear a soupçon of time for me to relax and refuel.

Godfrey, who had been shadowing me all morning, told me he would call me later and faded away so swiftly that I was sure he felt the need for some downtime as well.

After I did my travel exercises and took a shower, I began to look through the Belfast Festival tote bag that had been delivered to my room with my luggage. Among the books and magazines, I found a travel guide, and the maps' pictures and the short articles about Belfast and its surroundings kept me quite interested until the room telephone jangled.

As soon as I said hello, a male voice I didn't recognize asked, "Mrs. Fletcher, is it you, then?"

"This is Jessica Fletcher. May I ask who is calling?"

"You may indeed. My name is Owen Mullen and it will be my grand privilege to drive you on the final leg of your journey, to the village of Bushmills to meet the O'Bannon clan, ragtag bunch such as we are." He laughed heartily, and the slight jingle in his laughter reminded me of Maeve.

"Maeve called and told me to expect to hear from you, Mr. Mullen. And I can tell you that the one O'Bannon I've met so far seemed perfectly presentable, so I expect the rest to be the same," I responded to his humor.

"Ah, I agree. Our American cousin, Maeve, is every bit a brilliant person. It is the wild Irish O'Bannons to whom I was referring."

Instantly I realized the confusion I'd caused. "I agree that Maeve is in every way terrific but I was actually referring to Michael O'Bannon. What would the correct term be? Your first cousin once removed?"

"How in the name of all that's holy did Michael manage to show up in your path and no one in the family knew of it?" Owen sounded so concerned that for a moment I thought he feared for my safety.

Then I shook off my foolishness and gave the simple answer. "It was perfectly innocent, I assure you. We both happened to be attending a book festival event at *Titanic* Belfast and Michael was kind enough to introduce himself when he realized I was there."

"Michael O'Bannon never does a thing unless he sees a direct benefit to himself. No, Mrs. Fletcher, I am concerned enough to say that if Michael was at your event, he had a purpose. It may have been meeting you before the rest of the family does or it may have been something more. Never you mind. I will be there tomorrow and we shall have a wonderful drive through the countryside."

I was somewhat surprised that Owen's assessment of Michael O'Bannon was so similar to Godfrey's on the night of the party.

Owen sounded so—well, "suspicious" is the word that comes to mind—that I decided to rapidly change the subject. "I cannot thank you enough for providing my transportation. When I promised Maeve that I would visit the family, I had no idea of the distance from Belfast to Bushmills or if there was a train or bus service. . . ."

"Never mind your trains and buses. I've a fine, peppy Volkswagen Golf that will bring you to Bushmills in grand style." Owen returned to sounding like an amiable host. "And rest assured, no thanks is needed, although I do need your schedule so that I will be waiting in the Hilton lobby when you check out and we can be on our way. I've planned a tea stop on the way home to show you some of the best we have to offer."

We spoke for a few more minutes and arranged to meet in the lobby at two the next afternoon. I was looking forward to wrapping up the business portion of my trip and enjoying a day or so of vacation while I delivered Maeve's paintings and learned more about parts of the island of Ireland I'd never visited. I had no way of knowing that there was tragedy ahead.

Chapter Five

Early the next afternoon, I said my good-byes to Moira and Tom and spent an enjoyable half hour exchanging email and snail-mail addresses with Godfrey, so I was free to start what I liked to think of as "Maeve's adventure."

A rakish young man wearing a brown tweed sports coat was leaning against the far wall when I stepped off the elevator. He smiled and held up a copy of my book *The Corpse Swam by Moonlight*. Even without the book to signal me, I would have known him anywhere. His brown hair had the same glints of red and gold that Maeve's had had in her younger days, and when he smiled his blue eyes crinkled in exactly the same way Maeve's did. I had no doubt the young man was Owen Mullen.

"Mrs. Fletcher, it is my joy of joys to finally meet you. Through the years Maeve has told us so much about the famous mystery writer next door. We even know that you like extra raisins in your soda bread and we will be sure to make some available while you are here. Now, where is your luggage? We're not to be delayed, are we?"

Owen had me by the arm and was heading to the front door but my lack of luggage stymied him. That was another trait he shared with his cousin Maeve: Their personalities required them to be very much on the go when there was something to be done.

I stood still and put out my hand. "Owen, it is a pleasure to meet you, and please call me Jessica. I thought it wisest to have a bellman bring my luggage down and leave it at the front desk while I made the rounds and said my good-byes to all the wonderful people I've met over the past few days."

"Excellent. Then we'll be off in no time at all."

He steered me to the front desk. In a very few minutes, we were in his little silver car speedily leaving Belfast behind us.

"I cannot wait for you to see the lovely countryside. The Glens of Antrim are home to some of the most beautiful scenery on the entire island of Ireland. Be prepared to relax and enjoy it. It will take us a bit longer to get home but it's worth every minute, I assure you. And here to tell you all about the rustic glens is Bridie Gallagher, singing one of my favorite songs, 'The Green Glens of Antrim.'"

Owen tapped a button on his dashboard. A sweet melody and a soft female voice wafted through the speakers.

In short order I had to admit that Owen was right. The countryside was lush, filled with gorgeous plants and a huge variety of trees, including plenty of oak and spruce. Periodically, off to our right, I could see languid waves of a body of water that Owen told me was known as the North Channel, and he assured me it was having an unusually calm day. He described it as the connector of the Irish Sea and the North Atlantic Ocean.

"The North Channel separates Scotland from Ireland, and at its narrowest point, the two are only twelve miles apart, so as you can image, there's been a lot of traveling back and forth—intermarriage and such—gone on for centuries."

"I would hazard a guess that the Scots-Irish, as we call them, who were early settlers in America, came from this region or hereabouts," I said.

"No guessing about it." Owen laughed. "This is exactly where they came from. And in about five more minutes, we are going to stop for tea in Ballycastle. There is a lovely little tea shop that has the best scones you have ever tasted. Right across the road is the most peaceful beach along the edge of Murlough Bay. This time of day, we'll have no problem finding a table overlooking the beach and we'll have a grand view of Fair Head."

I could tell by his tone, Owen thought I should be happily surprised about the stop to see Fair Head, although in truth I had never heard of it.

He parked the car and waved in the direction of the tea shop. "Before we go in, what do you say to a quick stretch of the legs on the promenade?"

I was halfway through answering that I could use a bit of exercise when I saw where he was pointing to now—a pristine cove-shaped beach and, on the far side, a hauntingly beautiful cliff of strange proportions.

"Oh, my. Is that—?"

"Fair Head? Yes, indeed," Owen answered, quite proud that I had been properly impressed.

"The shape is amazing. The entire top of the cliffside looks like columns. Do you know how they were formed?" I asked.

Owen took my arm and we began walking along the promenade for a better view. "It seems there was a volcano some sixty million years ago, and so that we would always know that the volcano had come and gone, it left us Fair Head to gaze upon. One look at those columns, as wide and high as they are, and you can count yourself lucky that you weren't around when the volcano erupted."

"That is certainly true," I said. "Thank you for introducing me to an unforgettable sight."

"'Tis a shame we haven't more time. We could spend an entire day wandering the many paths of Fair Head. Perhaps on your next trip to Ireland, you could arrange a longer visit. Now, I think it's time for tea and scones."

Owen spun around and I followed him back the way we'd come.

The tea shop was empty, save for a woman, clearly on the far side of sixty, wiping down the tables and chairs.

"Saoirse, it's my good fortune to find you all alone. Tell me, have you finally decided to ditch the old man and run away with me?" Owen grabbed the woman's hand and pretended to try to drag her to the door.

"Go on with you, Owen Mullen, or I'll tell your mam and she'll give you a scolding you won't soon forget. Now, who is it you've brought to sample my fine wares?"

Owen introduced us, and from their familiarity with each other, I should not have been surprised to learn that before she married, Saoirse McInerney had been Owen's nanny when he was a boy.

"And he was an outrageous handful. I can assure you of that, Mrs. Fletcher. Now, why don't the two of you settle into this table here with the best view of the beach and Fair Head while I see what I can find in the kitchen?" Saoirse then disappeared through an archway in the far wall.

Owen watched her go and then said, more to himself than to me, "No child was ever better cared for than I was." Then he looked at me and smiled. "We're in for a treat. Whatever comes out of that kitchen will be some of the finest pastries you've ever tasted."

"In that case, we should have taken a longer walk." I laughed as I patted my stomach. "So far I haven't gotten much exercise on this trip and I fear none of my clothes will fit by the time I get home."

"Ah, then I may have a solution. Do you like riding a bicycle?" Owen raised a questioning eyebrow.

"Oh, my, yes. At home in Cabot Cove, I ride nearly every day. Do you happen to know of a bicycle I could rent or borrow?" I was visualizing a quaint little bike shop on the village's main street but Owen offered a better option.

"Well, since you will be a guest at the River Bush Hotel for several days, you will be pleased to learn that they have an old horse barn that now houses a rack of fine bicycles, including one or two Donards handcrafted in County Down. Since I have an in with the landlord, I may be able to ask him to put aside a Donard for you."

From the kitchen Saoirse brought a tray with two teapots and assorted cutlery, and set it on a nearby table. "The freshest teas I have at the moment are this oolong"—she picked up the teapot decorated with tiny pink roses and placed it on our table—"and we have an Earl Grey as well."

She put a silver-trimmed teapot next to the pink one. Saoirse fussed about with teacups, saucers, and spoons and then insisted on pouring. I followed Owen's lead and opted for oolong. She filled our cups, headed back to the kitchen, and returned with a smaller tray.

"It happens that we have apple tarts today, which I know to be Owen's favorite, but I also brought some scones and a dish of soda bread pudding, which might strike your fancy, Mrs. Fletcher." Saoirse set the tray on the table. "Help yourself to whatever pleases, and don't let the boyo eat it all without yourself getting so much as a taste."

She stood over us until I put an apple tart and a small serving of soda bread pudding on my plate.

A couple with two small children came into the shop and Saoirse left to serve them, but not before giving me a nudge. "Now, don't be forgetting the scones."

A few minutes later, the shopkeeper's bell over the front door jangled again and a large man with a bushy dark mustache and a wild tangle of dark hair sprinkled with gray came through the door. He glanced around and his eyes lit up when he saw Owen. His heavy-heeled boots made so much noise as he strode to our table that Owen turned to see the cause of the racket, and he jumped up from his chair.

"James, an unexpected pleasure."

They shared a vigorous handshake and clapped each other heartily on the back.

Owen turned to me. "Jessica Fletcher, here's a man you will get to know when you are staying in Bushmills for any length of time. May I present James Collins, proprietor of my favorite pub, the Dart and the Pint, which you'll find is only a few short steps from the River Bush Hotel?"

"Ah, the neighbor of the Yank cousin. I am happy to meet ye." James shook my hand with far less energy than when he had shaken Owen's, for which I was grateful. "And, missus, I hear you've come bearing gifts."

"But not a one for you," Owen teased. "Jessica, you'll soon find that there are no secrets in a small village like Bushmills. Perfect strangers will greet you and tell you as much about yourself as they've gleaned from village gossip. And they'll hope your response will teach them more about you."

"Then Bushmills is not so different from my hometown. There are no secrets in Cabot Cove."

Saoirse came from the kitchen and said, "James, I could hear your great laugh all the way in the far reaches of the kitchen. Here is a cup. You can fix your own tea and help yourself to something to eat. I'll be back."

And she hurried over to the other table, where one of the children was fussing about something and the young mother appeared close to tears.

James looked at the teapots on our table. "Delicious as Saoirse's tea is, I can guarantee it lacks the kick of a good pint of Guinness. Isn't that right, Owen?"

"As long as we don't say so in front of Saoirse, I agree that no tea can compete with the way you pour a pint. And I promise to bring Jessica to see you do so. But tell me, James, what are you doing this far from home, besides stopping in to see Saoirse?"

James Collins's face darkened. "Well worth the eleven-mile drive, it is, to see a safe and decent doctor." He clamped his lips tightly shut.

I wasn't sure what had just happened but both Owen and James looked exceedingly distressed. James pushed back his chair, stood, and said, "Sorry, Owen." And he left without another word.

Saoirse came to the table and looked at James's teacup and shook her head. "Never knew himself not to finish his tea and a scone or two besides. Says it fortifies him for the ride home. What did you do to chase him off so abruptly?"

Owen shrugged. "I believe he remembered an appointment and didn't want to be late. You've outdone yourself with these apple tarts. What do you think, Jessica?"

I had no trouble saying, "I have never tasted anything so delicious."

Preening at the sound of our compliments, Saoirse dismissed James Collins from her mind.

I, however, did not. Once Owen and I had bade Saoirse farewell and were on our way to Bushmills, I said, "I don't mean to intrude in what may be a private matter, but I am wondering what exactly happened back there between you and James. One minute you two were jovial buddies, the next the tension was so thick, a knife would have had a difficult time cutting it."

In his Father Blackie Ryan series, mystery writer Andrew Greeley often wrote of characters whom he described as having heaved "a west of Ireland sigh." I never quite understood the meaning until this moment, when Owen pitched the deepest, longest sigh I'd ever heard. Greeley might have attributed lengthy sighs to the western part of Ireland, but from the sound of it, the Irish sigh was omnipresent throughout the island.

"I might as well share what is common knowledge in the village. You are bound to hear it one way or another. You know my cousin Michael is a doctor. He keeps a small local dispensary on Main Street. James Collins's wife was one of Michael's patients.

Because she died quite unexpectedly, James continues to believe that my cousin misdiagnosed Audra's tragically serious illness and that Michael's carelessness caused her death. James and I are longtime friends, and it is a topic we've avoided discussing, but today I understood perfectly why he visits medical services in Ballycastle. But I was at a loss to reply and I suspect he was embarrassed to have said it in such a way as to be reminded of old wounds." Owen shook his head as if he hoped to shake off uncomfortable feelings. "Now, I'll be sure to show you some of the natural wonders between here and home."

Chapter Six

When Owen pulled into the River Bush Hotel parking lot, I thought it looked charming, very Irish countryside, with gables and chimneys galore. I hoped it would be as comfortable inside as the outside promised.

Owen said, "I am honor bound to mention that you are more than welcome to stay at my mother's rather grand palace, if for no other reason than my mother will surely ask if I tried to convince you to become her houseguest."

"One thing I have learned in all my years traveling on publicity tours for my books is that no matter how enjoyable an event is, there is a certain serenity in being able to retreat to a nice quiet hotel room. And this"—I pointed to the River Bush Hotel—"seems to be just the place."

"Well, then, let's get you settled in so you can enjoy some of that serenity before we go to dinner," Owen said.

As I stepped out of the car, a pretty young blond woman came around the side of the hotel and began waving her arms in welcome. "Mrs. Fletcher, at last! Did Owen tell you I am your biggest fan? I've a ton of books for you to sign—that is, if you wouldn't mind."

"Maggie, please, let Jessica catch a breath," Owen said, but she kept chattering.

"Oh, Jessica, is it, now? Should a girl be jealous? You two did take a fair amount of time traveling from Belfast to Bushmills. Any stop offs on the way? A little tea shop in Ballycastle, perhaps? Saoirse McInerney—now, there is my real competition. Did you happen to taste her apple tarts, Mrs. Fletcher? Tell me, how is a girl supposed to compete with that?" Maggie stepped back and put her hands on her hips, and her saucy smile showed delightful dimples in each cheek.

"Well, I suppose being bubbly and bouncy as well as pretty as a picture would do for a start. And yes, Maggie, I certainly will sign all of your books, but only if you agree to call me Jessica," I said.

"Done," she said, and stuck out her hand so we could shake to seal the deal.

"Well, I see my Maggie has met her match in you, Jessica. It should be a lively dinner this evening." Owen took us each by the arm and walked us into the hotel.

Maggie looked around the lobby. "Now, where did my father go? Well, you'll have to meet him a bit later, then." She ducked behind the reception desk and took a key off a hook and waved me to follow along behind her. "Jessica, we have reserved the finest room for you, completely en suite, of course. And a writer such as yourself would have to have a window seat that is perfectly cozy for reading. I left a book of Seamus Heaney's poems on the seat in case you've a mind to browse through it while you're relaxing. This is also one of the few guest rooms with a lovely view of the River Bush. There may be a time when you'll see an angler or two if the salmon decide to be kind."

Maggie unlocked the door and handed me the key. Owen had disappeared while we were in the lobby, so I shouldn't have been surprised when she said, "Owen will be bringing your things along directly. Now make yourself comfortable and get some rest before the big do this evening. You never know what will happen in that wicked old house." Maggie deepened her voice, trying to make her words sound gloomy, but couldn't hold back a giggle at the end.

Owen brought my luggage and we agreed to meet in the lobby at seven. He gave Maggie a quick peck on the cheek and was gone. Maggie offered to help me unpack, and while I was insisting I could manage by myself, there was a knock on the door.

I opened it and a slim man with a cleanly shaved head said, "I am sorry I was not here to greet you, Mrs. Fletcher. Maeve O'Bannon gave strict instructions that I was to treat you like visiting royalty and I failed at the first step." He held out his hand. "Dougal Nolan, at your service."

"Mr. Nolan, Maggie has been taking first-rate care of me. In fact, I am trying to convince her that I don't need help in unpacking my things but she has been quite adamant."

"Ah, that's my girl, saving the family reputation." Dougal smiled at Maggie and looked around the room. "I thought I saw Owen's car in the car park. Has he been and gone?"

"He has. He was thoughtful enough to realize Jessica might like some time to herself. He will be back at seven to drive Jessica and me to dinner at Jane's house."

"Good on him, not expecting you to make your way there on your own. Mrs. Fletcher, you'll find Owen is a fine lad who comes from a bad lot—excepting Maeve, of course. Her father was long gone before the O'Bannons went rogue. I'd best be heading to the front desk. I am expecting some salmon fishermen to check in this evening so as to have an early start on the river in the morning for a fishing competition. I need to be sure we are ready for them."

After he closed the door behind him, Maggie said, "Jessica, I am so sorry you had to hear that about the O'Bannons. There are some things that Da just won't let go."

Hoping that she would say more, I nodded. I was increasingly curious about the family that I was here to meet.

"It was about the land," Maggie continued. "You will find in Ireland it is often about the land. When my father was a boy, there was a land dispute among some neighbors and an O'Bannon wrestled parcels of land from some neighboring farmers in what they considered to be an underhanded scheme. My grandfather was one who lost some of his land, and well, Da is not a forgive-and-forget type of man."

"I understand. Believe me, I do. In Cabot Cove, where Maeve and I live, there are any number of families who avoid one another at all costs. In many cases no one can quite recall the incident that started the dispute generations ago," I said.

"I am so glad you understand. I wouldn't want you to think less of my father. I can promise you he is a good man," Maggie said as she reached for the suitcase Owen had placed on the luggage rack.

"What I do understand is that your father is expecting some fishermen to arrive momentarily and I am sure he could use your help downstairs. Now, you scoot and leave the unpacking to me." I used my firm teacher's voice, which generally does the trick with younger people.

Maggie surrendered graciously. "See you at seven." She pointed to the telephone on the night table. "If you need anything at all, just dial zero."

After I unpacked and laid out my clothes for that evening's dinner party, I took off my shoes and stood in front of the window, looking out at the hotel's surroundings. In the distance, the River Bush was coursing through the luxuriant greenery, although at this time of day there was not a fisherman in sight. I toyed with the idea of calling Maeve to let her know I was in her father's hometown, about to dine with the relatives, but then I decided I would have more to tell her in a day or so. I picked up the book of poetry and plumped the pillows on the window seat. A little time to myself was always worth having.

When I walked down the steps to the lobby at ten minutes to seven, Dougal Nolan was on the telephone behind the reception desk. Maggie and Owen were sitting on a settee, heads together in a private conversation. I noticed they were holding hands. Clearly no matter what Dougal thought of the O'Bannon clan, Maggie had no fear of showing her affection for Owen in front of her father.

I didn't notice Dougal had finished his phone call until he said, "And look at the grand lady coming down our staircase. Don't you look lovely this evening, Mrs. Fletcher!"

"Please call me Jessica," I said, and turned to Maggie and Owen. "And my, how lovely Maggie looks this evening."

I had to laugh when both men stumbled over each other to agree with me. I could see that Maggie would guide Dougal and Owen to become sincere friends, regardless of Dougal's feelings about the O'Bannon family in general.

It was sweet of Maggie to invite me to take the front passenger seat on the drive to Jane Mullen's house. "Please, Jessica, you are seeing Bushmills for the very first time. There's no point in your sitting in the back and looking over my shoulder. Every new visitor deserves a first-class view."

Owen drove along Main Street slowly so I had time to absorb the quaintness of the town. When he got to the statue of a soldier in full battle gear thrusting a bayonet, he told me it had been erected in 1921, and added a bit of history about the soldiers from the town who'd been killed in what was then known as the Great War. Decades later the names of those lost in the Second World War had been inscribed alongside those lost in the First.

Owen then changed the topic. "I have to apologize in advance to you two lovely ladies. I'd anticipated that tonight would be a very cozy family welcoming dinner for Maeve's dear friend Jessica."

When he didn't continue, Maggie said, "But . . ."

"Ah, yes," Owen replied. "Jessica, as Maggie has learned, with the O'Bannon family, there is almost always a 'but.' As it turns out, while we are welcoming Jessica, tonight will also be something of a business gathering. For the past few months, my aunt Beth Anne, who is the corporate head of Marine Magic, has been working on a merger with a small company headquartered in France. The company, presently called Belle Visage, is in some financial difficulty. My aunt and her board of directors approached the French proposing a merger, but they are planning to evolve the merger into an absolute takeover that Beth Anne expects will be a great financial boon to Marine Magic."

Maggie said, "Owen, no. Promise me this isn't going to be one of those stuffy business dinners where I don't care to understand a single word while your aunt persists in pushing her viewpoint until your mother and your uncle surrender because they can't stand listening to her relentless hammering."

"I think I can safely promise that." Owen turned off Main Street and seemed to be heading out of the village proper. "For one thing, Jessica will be joining us, so even Aunt Beth Anne can't focus solely on business."

"True," Maggie said. "I hope Jessica and I are sitting near each other at dinner. It would be rude for us to yell up and down the length of the table, talking about books or the best tourist sites in and around town, while everyone else is talking about profit margins, liabilities, and the like."

Owen laughed. "Maggie, I see you have been paying attention to my family conversations after all. And here I thought you were gathering wool at all those boring dinners. Jessica, I should explain—the reason we have this problem is because my parents have the fanciest home, so all business entertaining is done at what I like to call the Castle. Unfortunately, the gentlemen from Belle Visage arrived ahead of schedule, and, well, as my mother likes to say, accommodations must be made."

He drove for a few more minutes and then turned into a driveway opening between two stone walls at least ten feet high. Then he stopped the car and said, "Welcome to the Castle, Jessica."

"Oh, my goodness, I see what you mean."

A long, extra-wide driveway lined by large oak trees opened

into a circular road in front of a brick house of at least four stories with oval turrets rising at the corners. As we got closer, the bronze front door appeared to be nearly twenty feet high.

Owen parked and escorted us to the entryway. I was somewhat surprised that Lurch, the Addams Family's butler, didn't greet us. Instead, Owen simply pushed the door open and in we went.

A young woman wearing a white blouse and black slacks stood in the foyer. Owen addressed her as Nora. She took our wraps and showed us into what I would have called the living room, where cocktails were being served. A well-kept woman in a gauzy pink dress immediately came to introduce herself.

"J. B. Fletcher! For many years Cousin Maeve has been talking about you, your fabulous mystery books, and the gardening interests you and she share. I am Beth Anne O'Bannon Ryan. Welcome to Bushmills."

A shorter woman with a pair of gold pince-nez clipped to her nose came up behind Beth Anne and reached past her to shake my hand. "Welcome to my home. I am Jane O'Bannon Mullen and I also share Maeve's interest in gardening, so we'll have plenty to talk about this evening."

Beth Anne glared at her sister. "Please give Jessica—" She turned to me. "May I call you Jessica? Of course, I can. We are all friends here." Then, eyes still frosty, she looked at Jane again. "While I introduce Jessica to everyone, why don't you check the kitchen to see if the predinner dips and spreads are ready to be served?"

And with that instant dismissal of her sister, Beth Anne whisked me into the living room. I recognized Michael O'Bannon immediately, along with his colleague Conor Sweeney.

A portly man with a fringe of graying red hair greeted me

warmly. "Mrs. Fletcher, welcome to my home. I am Liam Mullen, Jane's husband and, to my credit, father of Owen. I say that knowing full well that he was a proper gentleman. He picked you up on time, did not risk your life by speeding on the roadways, and ensured you had a proper welcome to our neck of the country by detouring up to Ballycastle so that you could be feted by the best baker in County Antrim, Saoirse McInerney. Am I right?"

"It is as though you were riding in the car with us." I laughed. It was easy to see where Owen got his easygoing confidence.

Beth Anne tugged my arm. "Jessica, please, you can talk to Liam anytime. I have important guests who are dying to meet you."

Being sure to emphasize that I was a "world-famous American mystery writer," a phrase that made me cringe, Beth Anne introduced me to Claude Blanchet and Julien Lavigne, who, she explained, were representing the board of directors of Belle Visage. They ignored the description Beth Anne gave of me and greeted me with great charm and in excellent English, which was a relief since my French had become rusty to the point of being nearly nonexistent, although I did manage to say a jaunty *"Bonsoir"* to them both. The evening had begun.

Chapter Seven

Maggie needn't have worried about the dinner conversation being weighed down by boring business talk. Over a delicious meal of rack of lamb and colcannon—a combination of mashed potatoes, cabbage, and onions that Maeve often made by the kettle full and shared with the neighbors—as well as a variety of fresh garden vegetables in a light butter sauce, the conversation was casual and bubbly.

Conor Sweeney told a highly entertaining story about his recent drive along a road near Portstewart and being stopped by a bull that had broken through a fence and was lounging so he completely blocked the road.

"I was forced to make a hasty stop, and as soon as he saw my little Renault Clio, he promptly fell in love. There he was, drooling and nuzzling the bonnet of my car with his great snout. Had the farmer not eventually come along and wrestled him back behind the fence line, I'd be parked there still." Conor let out a mighty laugh and we all joined in.

I noticed, as I am sure the O'Bannon cousins did, the pleased glances that the Frenchmen exchanged at the mention of a car built in their country.

Julien Lavigne turned to me and said, "I suppose, Madame Fletcher, that you drive one of those large American cars, something by Ford or Chrysler, perhaps."

"Actually, I don't drive at all." When I saw the surprise on the faces all around me, I added, "I haven't found it necessary, although I do have a pilot's license for small aircraft."

In short order the conversation turned to flight mishaps, lost luggage, missed planes, and a very funny story Owen told about flying on a business trip to Newcastle and discovering that he'd gotten on the wrong plane only when the pilot announced they would be landing in Glasgow in twenty minutes.

As the table was being cleared, Jane said, "In honor of our pleasure at having guests from both France and America"—she bowed her head toward Claude and Julien and then toward me—"tonight we hope you will enjoy a traditional Irish dessert, cast-iron apple cake, and in honor of our hometown, you may want to drizzle a taste of Irish whiskey caramel sauce on your cake."

Nora and the other server placed cast-iron fry pans lined with parchment paper and brimming with apple cake on filigreed trivets and began to serve us each a good-sized portion. The fragrances of cinnamon and nutmeg filled the room. Then the young ladies moved among the guests with elegant Belleek porcelain creamers that Jane explained held the dessert sauce, which was made with the finest ingredients, including Bushmills Irish Whiskey.

That led to a conversation about the Old Bushmills Distillery, which Maggie said was "just down the road."

Conor Sweeney leaned across the table to Claude and Julien. "Now, there is something you must see. The Irish have been making whiskey at the distillery since 1608. And in my learned opinion, each new bottle is better than the last."

He laughed and the Frenchmen obligingly smiled back at him but no one else said a word. Beth Anne and Jane exchanged a distressed look.

After a small but awkward silence, Jane announced that a few people would be joining us after dinner. "Why don't we settle ourselves in the front parlor?" She stood, walked around the table, and offered her arm to Julien Lavigne. "I've invited our company comptroller, Malachy Gleason, to visit with us for a while this evening. Julien, I thought you two should get acquainted. And his wife, Grainne, has a lovely voice. I am hoping to persuade her to sing us a song or two."

Julien patted her hand as he slipped his arm through hers. "That sounds delightful."

As everyone was following along to the next room, I noticed Conor stood directly behind his chair and was draining the dregs of his wineglass. He looked up, saw that I'd noticed, gave me a sheepish grin, and said, "I heard a wise man say, 'Never let the whiskey go to waste.' I suspect his words would cover wine as well. Shall we join the others?" And he marched out of the room.

I waited for a minute or two until I thought Conor was safely tucked in the parlor with the others; then I walked out into the hall. Earlier in the evening, when we had first arrived, I noticed an open doorway to what appeared to be a sumptuous library and I wanted to take a look. I was sure no one would miss me for a couple of minutes.

Just as I walked into the library, I heard angry voices. At the far end of the room, Michael and Beth Anne were having some sort of dispute. I stepped back into the shadows, hoping they hadn't noticed my coming into the room. Beth Anne was seething, clearly having trouble controlling her anger. Through clenched teeth, she berated Michael. I couldn't make out her exact words but it sounded as though she was accusing him of selling out the company and ruining their chance for the merger with Belle Visage. She raised her voice ever so slightly. "Michael, I promise I will destroy you before I will let you destroy this company."

Just then Nora pushed a door open at their end of the library. "Ah, there you be. Miss Jane says you are wanted in the parlor. The Gleasons are here."

I stayed perfectly still, wanting to be sure that they had passed by the door nearest me before I walked through it. I heard a noise from the middle of the room and was shocked to see Claude Blanchet rise from a brown leather chair. Seated, he had not been visible to me, and I was sure Beth Anne would not have spoken about the merger if she had known either of the Belle Visage representatives was in earshot.

Claude had been sitting quite close to where Beth Anne and Michael had been standing and obviously had been there when they walked into the room. While I had heard snippets of the argument, I was sure that Claude Blanchet had heard every word. I was curious how that was going to affect the business negotiations that everyone expected to transpire over the next few days.

I stood in the doorway of Jane's parlor. It was a large room painted bright yellow and filled with overstuffed couches covered in yellow-and-brown tweed and with wing-backed chairs covered in brown-, yellow-, and green-striped sateen. The furniture seemed to be casually scattered around the room but it was evident that the main focal point was a spinet piano positioned before a wide bay window. A beautiful golden retriever spread out on a plush area rug in front of a fireplace. He ignored the chatter and laughter going on around him, quite happy in what I thought might be his favorite spot, nuzzling a tennis ball that he held comfortably between his front paws. This time of year, the fireplace held a mixed bouquet of flowers rather than blazing logs.

I was so taken with the cozy domestic scene that Jane startled me when she tapped me on the arm. "Jessica, I have been looking for you everywhere. Please come and meet Malachy and Grainne Gleason."

The Gleasons were one of those married couples who looked so remarkably alike that I always wondered if they had searched the world for a mirror mate or if they had grown over time to share each other's look. Both were rotund with sandy hair turning gray, and they each had bright blue eyes and dimpled cheeks. Malachy gave me a shy smile while Grainne, definitely the more outgoing of the two, shook my hand vigorously.

"I was thrilled to pieces when Jane told me that I would have the opportunity to meet J. B. Fletcher and all I need do for the chance is sing a few songs."

"Now, Grainne, dear, Jane didn't say . . ." Malachy tried to interject whatever his opinion might have been but his words were lost on his wife, who prattled on about my books, her singing lessons when she was a child, and her hope that I would enjoy her repertoire this evening.

I did have the thought that this was a moment when I could have used Godfrey to run interference, but alas, that part of my trip had ended. I was now on my own.

I thanked Grainne for her kind words about my books and assured her that I was so anxious to hear her sing that I could barely contain my excitement. That was enough to encourage Jane to shoo me over to join Owen and Maggie on a couch while she moved to the center of the room.

As people began to quiet down, Jane said, "I feel we would be remiss if we didn't offer our guests some traditional Irish entertainment. Fortunately, our very own Grainne Gleason, who has the voice of an angel, has agreed to sing for us tonight."

"Has agreed to? Try to stop her," Owen whispered in my ear.

Grainne sat at the piano and ran her fingers tentatively over the keys. Then she gave her audience a broad smile and began to sing a plaintive melody about a town called Carrickfergus, which had clearly been a haunting place in the songwriter's memory. She followed that with a cheerful and lively song about a girl who was known as the belle of Belfast City before singing two songs that all foreign visitors were bound to know, "Danny Boy" and "Molly Malone."

We clapped with great enthusiasm when Grainne stood and made a graceful curtsy. Malachy rushed to her side and presented her with what he called a "well-earned glass of wine."

The family and guests began to mill around the room, talking and laughing. I noticed Conor Sweeney heading straight for the self-serve bar and refilling his glass while Beth Anne O'Bannon immediately struck up a conversation with the two representatives of Belle Visage. Owen politely offered to get me a glass of wine, and when I declined, he said, "I suspect you are a wee bit tired. You've had a long day. I'm sure you'll be grateful that we'll be leaving shortly."

True to his word, not twenty minutes later he was ushering Maggie and me into his car and we were on our way back to the hotel. The roads, which had been lit by sunshine earlier, were now dark, but the view was just as enchanting. I couldn't wait to explore on my own. As I was leaving her house, Jane had said something about our getting together tomorrow for lunch or tea, but I hadn't committed. Tomorrow would be my first chance since I'd landed at Belfast Airport to spend time alone, and as much as I had appreciated the wonderfully kind hospitality of Godfrey Hamilton in Belfast and of Owen Mullen since, I relished having some time to discover the Irish countryside on my own.

I woke up shortly after six in the morning. I'd heard the patter of rain once or twice during the night, but when I opened the room-darkening curtains, I was happy to see the sun was already high in the sky. I was glad there was no sign of rain clouds, as I'd hoped to find where the guest bicycles were stored so I could take a long ride around the town and through the countryside. I'd be sure to snap some pictures for Maeve. I suspected she'd be anxious to see what had changed and what had stayed the same.

I didn't have to worry about finding the bicycle rack, because when I walked down to the lobby, Dougal Nolan boomed, "Ah, here she comes, the River Bush Hotel's first and only entrant in this year's Tour de France. Good morning to you, Mrs. Fletcher. I trust you slept well. The kitchen is open, if you'd like a cup of tea before you go off."

"Good morning, Mr. Nolan," I answered. "Tea is always welcome, but since I am anxious to explore, I would enjoy having a bottle of water to take along."

"Say no more." He reached down and pulled two bottles of water out from under the counter.

"You do have a knack for anticipating your guests' wishes." I smiled. "That's a sure sign of a successful innkeeper."

Dougal led me outside and I followed him to the rear of the hotel and into the bicycle shed. He pulled a red bicycle from its rack and pointed proudly to the insignia emblazoned on the down tube: DONARD. He spent a few minutes telling me the history of the handcrafted stainless steel bicycle before assuring me that I was about to take the most pleasurable bike ride of my life.

"If we weren't expecting a mountain of deliveries this morning, I wouldn't mind joining you, but duty calls." Dougal gave me a few tips on the must-sees in the area, then cautioned, "But take your time. Enjoying our surroundings is not a race. It's a leisure sport."

The red bicycle was a true pleasure to ride, providing almost effortless speed and not sacrificing a bit of comfort. Dougal had pointed me in the direction of the town center, home to both the long-standing clock tower and the war memorial. I was eager to see both and examine them closely. In a few minutes I rode past the Dart and the Pint and turned onto Main Street; the clock tower, which rose high above the local buildings, came into view, so I had no fear of getting lost.

As magnificent a structure as the round clock tower was, with its nearly one-hundred-fifty-year-old stone exterior design, I was far more intrigued by the war memorial, which stood directly in front of it in the middle of a traffic circle. The heroes of the village and the surrounding area were represented by the statue of a World War One soldier wielding a bayonet at the end of his rifle to ward off the enemy. The inscribed names included ninety-five soldiers who had given their lives between 1914 and 1918. Last night Owen had mentioned the monument had been updated to also honor the thirty-three local lads who had served and died in the Second World War. It was a chilling and awe-inspiring site, standing as it was in the center of the street as we all went about our routine lives. I said a brief prayer. Then I pedaled away to look at the rest of the village before seeking the enjoyment of visiting the nearby fields and meadows.

Once I had traveled most of the village streets, I began to explore the surrounding countryside. There were plenty of dirt roads and picturesque lanes. I'd been looking for a path closer to the River Bush, and when I came across a muddy dirt road filled with puddles but showing signs of both automobile tire tracks and bike tracks aplenty, I hoped I had found one. I pedaled along under the trees while the birds chirped and squawked at the intrusion. I saw a badger eyeing me from under a hedgerow but he scurried away as I got closer.

The road ambled this way and that, bending left or right without warning and always leading me farther away from the village. I was following one of those sudden changes when I nearly crashed into the rear of a dark blue car parked with its hood squashed between the hedgerow and a clump of gigantic trees. I skidded to a stop. The area appeared to be deserted. I looked at the left front window and didn't see anyone, so I pulled my bike away from the car and farther into the roadway, glad I wouldn't have to explain to Dougal Nolan that I had damaged his beautiful Donard bike. As I started to pedal away, I happened to look back at the car and was momentarily shocked to see through the right-side window a man slumped over the steering wheel. I stopped and called out, asking if he was all right, but there was no response. I hopped off my bicycle and ran to the car, talking all the while.

"Sir. Excuse me, sir. Is everything all right? Are you all right?"

He never moved. I reached through the car's open window, and while I thought I tapped his shoulder gently, my light touch was enough to make him fall across the car seat. I winced when I realized the nonresponsive man was Michael O'Bannon and he had a wide gash on the side of his head.

Chapter Eight

I pulled out my cell phone intending to call 911, and then I stopped short when I realized that I had no idea what to dial for a police emergency in Northern Ireland. Fortunately, I had followed through on my usual habit of putting my hotel phone number in my directory. I hit that tag and waited impatiently for someone to answer.

Maggie Nolan answered with a cheery "River Bush Hotel. How may I be of help?"

In that instant I realized that while I had to tell her what had happened, for the moment it would be better for me not to mention who was lying dead in the car.

"Maggie, it's Jessica Fletcher."

Before I could continue, she interrupted. "Ah, Mrs. Fletcher, my da told me you were off on your bike bright and early this morning. Will you be back for breakfast anytime soon?"

"There's been an accident." Even as I heard Maggie's sharp intake of breath, I continued hurriedly. "I wasn't involved. I am perfectly fine, but someone in a car is, er, injured and I don't know how to call for the police or an ambulance."

"Where are you?" Maggie was becoming more fretful by the second. "I'll make the emergency call and then I'll come and get you."

"That's the problem," I said. "I've wandered off the main streets and I am on a dirt road. I imagine it is one of many."

"Well, we've no time to waste if you've an injured party awaiting help. There's nothing to be done but disconnect our call and then you must dial nine-nine-nine. They'll track you by your phone. Once help has arrived, call me back to let us know you are in good, safe hands."

The 999 operator, a soft-spoken young woman who oozed competence, confirmed that my location had popped up on her computer screen and asked me to describe my emergency. Although I was certain Michael had been dead for some time, I reported him as injured and unresponsive in the hope that my diagnosis was wrong. The operator asked me to stay where I was and then she continued to talk.

"Mrs. Fletcher, did you say it was?" she asked calmly, and when I said she was correct, she had another question. "Do you happen to know the identity of the injured party, unresponsive as he is?"

"Yes, I do. His name is Michael O'Bannon. He is a doctor and the cousin of a good friend and neighbor of mine," I said.

"And were you with Mr. O'Bannon when the accident occurred?" She continued to ask questions that I knew I would have to answer all over again as soon as the first officers arrived.

"No. I was out for a bike ride and happened across his car, and, well, there he was, slumped over." I was describing a scene that I was sure would be seared in my brain for days to come.

"You should be seeing a police car arriving at your location momentarily, with an ambulance a minute or two behind."

And when she said that, I realized that our conversation had served two purposes. The first was to keep me unruffled while I was alone at the scene of this tragedy. More important, from the police perspective, the operator was keeping me occupied so I didn't have time to touch or disturb anything.

Still, my own nerves were edgy enough that, while we were talking, I searched the car thoroughly but only with my eyes.

The first thing I noticed was a chip in the blue paint on the driver's-side window frame. It looked clean, as if the damage had happened quite recently. Then I made a mental note of a tiny piece, not much more than a sliver, of frothy pink fabric stuck in the passenger-side door. At that moment a blue-and-yellow police car turned into the lane. Two officers, dressed in very dark green uniforms, got out and walked slowly to where I was standing.

"Mrs. Fletcher, is it? I'm Constable Breen and this is Constable Redding." He pointed to the shorter, younger man. "The ambulance is right behind us. Where is the victim?"

He nodded when I pointed to the car. "Perhaps it's best that you go sit in our car with Constable Redding and allow him to ask you a few questions while I see to the damage that's been done here."

He walked to the car, opened the door, and leaned over Michael's body. Then he stood straight and signaled Constable Redding to move me away from the scene.

Redding held his arm in front of himself, pointing to the car, and said, "Ma'am, this way, please."

I went to pick up my bicycle, which I'd left leaning against a tree, but Constable Breen stopped me. "No need. We'll take care of your bicycle. Staying at Dougal Nolan's, are you?"

Before I could ask how he knew that, he pointed to the insignia of Donard on the down tube of the bike. "Nolan is the only proprietor around here who provides such expensive bicycles to his guests. And of course, the dispatcher told me to look for an American woman named Mrs. Fletcher, so I thought you'd be a visitor of some sort. Now, if you would go with Constable Redding . . ." Breen was beginning to sound frustrated that I hadn't complied immediately, so I thought it best to do as he asked.

A bright yellow ambulance arrived. Constable Redding pointed around the curve in the road, and medical technicians ran past us while the constable ushered me into the rear seat of the police car. I was grateful he left the door open so I didn't feel quite like I was under arrest or, at the very least, under suspicion. He took a few steps away from me and began talking in a low voice on his radio.

Occasionally a breeze carried a few syllables my way, so I heard him say, "Likely deceased," and "American visitor." When he was finished, he came to speak to me. "Given that Michael O'Bannon is well known in the community, Chief Inspector Clive Finley is on his way and he has requested that you wait with us so he could have a word."

"Of course," I replied as if I had another option.

I hadn't been allowed to retrieve my bicycle and I was sitting in the back of a police car with a constable standing over me. It seemed likely I had no choice but to wait. I wished I could see what was going on at Michael's car around the bend but the dense bushes were blocking my view. Several more police cars arrived, and from where I was sitting, I could hear the murmurings of a lot of activity around Michael's car, but I couldn't see a thing. I was getting more and more irritated. Here I was only a few feet away, but due to the geography of the scene, I might as well have been miles away. Since they hadn't removed Michael's body as yet, I was certain that the police had suspicions of foul play. If I could only see and hear some of what was going on . . . I got an idea, so I asked.

"Constable Redding, I am feeling a bit cramped sitting here. And I am extremely parched. Might I stand up for a while and perhaps you could get me a bottle of water from the basket on my bicycle?"

"I don't see that either of your requests would lead to a problem. Please." He offered me his hand and I stepped out of the car. "I'll be back with your water in just a second."

As soon as Redding was out of view, I moved closer to the hedgerow so I could hear more clearly. I gingerly pulled a few branches apart just enough so that I could peek through to the other side.

The only thing I learned was that Michael O'Bannon's body was now on a stretcher, which was not yet being removed from the scene. There were four or five crime scene specialists examining the car and the ground around it. I saw Breen raise a querying eyebrow to Redding. I supposed he was wondering about me. When Redding held up a bottle of water, Breen nodded and then waved him back toward me. Clearly, in Breen's mind, I was not to be trusted.

I took a few steps back from the hedges so that I wouldn't get caught snooping, and I was busily doing calf stretches when Redding brought my water bottle. I thanked him profusely and then I made a show of staring at my wristwatch.

The constable looked slightly uncomfortable and apologized for something completely out of his control. "I'm sure the chief inspector will be here any minute now."

"Redding!" A heavyset man in a navy blue suit was walking our way quite rapidly. He was wearing a gray tweed flat cap but pulled it off his head when he stopped in front of us. A lock of sandy hair fell to his forehead and he briskly pushed it aside. "Is this our American witness? I'm Chief Inspector Clive Finley of the Police Service of Northern Ireland, commonly known as the PSNI."

He held out his hand, brandished his identification card in front of my nose, and then slipped it back into his pocket. "Now, tell me, Mrs. Fletcher—what exactly happened here?"

If the inspector thought that I knew more than he did, well, he was bound to be disappointed. I told him that I was riding a bicycle partially for the exercise but also to get familiar with the area since I would be staying here for a few days.

"While riding on this road, I came across the car parked in an odd spot. When I saw Michael O'Bannon slumped over the steering wheel, I . . . I tried to assist him but he seemed to be beyond my ability to do . . . anything."

Inspector Finley pursed his lips. "In what way did you try to help?"

I explained that I tried to rouse him, and when I couldn't, I called for help.

Finley gave me a long, piercing look. "And just how did you, a newcomer to the village, know Dr. Michael O'Bannon?"

I decided to give him the short version of the story of my trip to his country. "I'm a writer who came to Ireland for the Belfast Book Festival. My close neighbor back in Cabot Cove, Maine, is Michael O'Bannon's cousin and she asked me to stop in Bushmills to bring some gifts to the family."

Apparently, my explanation was so commonplace, it satisfied him.

"Say no more. Everyone here has family all over the globe. The Irish diaspora, they call it." He dismissed me with a wave of his hand in the general direction of Constable Redding's car. "Have a seat if you wish. Stand if you like. I'll be back shortly."

He turned and walked around the bend to where the police activity continued full throttle. I think Constable Redding was slightly embarrassed by the inspector's abruptness, because he struck up a polite conversation as if hoping to make up for his boss's disrespect.

"Now, tell me, Mrs. Fletcher—how are you enjoying your visit so far?" He instantly realized he had stumbled right out of the gate and tried to recover. "Prior to this unfortunate event, I mean."

We talked about Belfast for a few minutes, and he became genuinely enthusiastic when I mentioned stopping by Ballycastle and viewing Fair Head. He relaxed completely and his eyes lit up as he told me about his first time climbing Fair Head, when he was a young boy. At another time, I would have found his stories delightful, but at that time and in that place, I was getting increasingly restless.

Finally, Inspector Finley came back and told me that my presence was no longer required. He actually used the word "required." Then he told Redding to drive me back to my hotel.

The inspector had no way of knowing that I still had a few things to say and was not about to be shuttled off until I said them. I was gratified by the look of surprise on his face when I began speaking.

"Chief Inspector Finley," I began, hoping that his full title would get his undivided attention, "just out of curiosity, did your technical people find any trace evidence on that tiny nick in the window frame of Michael's car?"

He tightened his lips as if deciding how to answer. He opted for brusqueness. "That would be none of your concern. This is strictly a police matter."

But I still had more to say. "Well, then, what did you make of the sliver of pink gauze sticking out of the passenger-side door of Michael's car?"

He shifted his jaw from right to left and back again. "How do you know about that? And why should it interest you?"

"I am certain that the piece of fabric is an exact match to the dress that Michael's cousin Beth Anne was wearing when we had dinner together at her sister, Jane's, house last evening," I said with as much authority as I could muster.

He raised his eyes skyward as if looking for guidance. Then he looked at me and said, "I may have misjudged the usefulness of a longer conversation between us. Redding, never you mind. I will drive Mrs. Fletcher and we can have a wee chat along the way. If you will, Mrs. Fletcher, my car is just over here."

And just like that, his frostiness had turned to sunshine.

"My bicycle . . ."

"Never fear. As soon as the techs are done examining it, Breen and Redding will return it to you unharmed. Now, where are you staying?"

When I told him that I had a room at the River Bush Hotel, he nodded at Redding to make sure the constables would know where to return the bicycle; then he opened his car door for me.

"Ah, a fine establishment. Dougal and Maggie Nolan treat their guests better than some folks treat their family members."

"Well, I cannot dispute you on that. Mr. Nolan and his daughter have been both kind and courteous to me."

Since I had the feeling that I was going to be the subject of a police interview on the ride home, I was subtly letting him know that I thought those two attributes were important.

As he worked his way back to the main road, Inspector Finley asked how long I was planning to stay in Bushmills.

"I have an open-ended ticket home, but now with Maeve's cousin being murdered, well—"

"And with no more than a brief glance at the body, you are sure that Michael O'Bannon was murdered?" His tone of voice switched from social directly back to gruff again.

"Oh, yes, I am positive. I can see no way that wound on the side of his head could have been self-inflicted," I said. "Of course, we can't yet be certain that the nick on the window frame happened last night, but if it did . . ."

Finley smiled as if a long-forgotten joke had just crossed his mind. "Then let me ask: You've ruled out an accidental cause as well, have you?"

"Yes, I have. The driver's-side window was wide open, so we can conclude Michael didn't smash his head on it, break the glass, and cut himself. The window frame itself has nothing sharp about it—my wrist rubbed against it when I reached in to try to shake him awake—so if he bashed his head against that, he might have gotten bruised but he never would have been cut. And last, if he 'accidentally' hit his head on anything else, well, where is it? I didn't see any bloody object in or near the car. Did you?"

Finley laughed. "For a civilian you are extremely observant. Or perhaps you are a police officer back home in the States."

I laughed out loud. "Far from it. As I told you earlier, I am a writer. As it happens I write mysteries, but my crimes are all completely fictional, I assure you."

"So, if you've worked for any length of time in that particular career, I would not be wrong in thinking it is quite possible that you have developed a devious criminal mind."

The chief inspector's laugh was far more forced than mine had been.

Chapter Nine

I decided there was no reason to respond to his insinuation, so I was glad to see the hotel was a few short blocks in front of us. As soon as Finley stopped the car, I opened my door, happy to be free of him, but I knew I could not refuse when he said, "If you wouldn't mind waiting in the lobby, I still have a question or two. Why don't we talk a bit more while sharing a pot of tea?"

Although he framed it as a question, I was definitely being told, not asked. I opened the hotel's main door and immediately noticed a man sitting in one of the lounge chairs, holding a newspaper high in front of his face. No matter that he was pretending to read, he definitely had one eye locked on the front door, and he folded his paper as soon as I stepped into the lobby. When he stood I saw that he was very tall, at least six feet four or five inches, and as he began walking toward me, I noticed he had a pronounced limp on his left side.

The way he kept his eyes focused on me, I assumed that one

of the O'Bannons had sent him to find me. Perhaps they had heard that I was the one who discovered Michael's body. However, when the door opened behind me and Inspector Finley walked in, the man turned on a dime and hurried away.

"Best hope he wasn't looking for you." Finley pointed to the man's retreating back. "You'll come to no harm if you avoid Dermot Kerrigan. Shall we get that tea now?"

I was not the least bit surprised when Finley ordered for both of us without asking me what I would like to have, but since a pot of Irish breakfast tea and a plate of raisin scones suited me, I didn't object.

He took a long sip of tea and then said, "So, Mrs. Fletcher, it seems you spent a long evening with the O'Bannons. What was your impression?"

"First, I'd like you to tell me, who was the gentleman in the lobby? The one you said I would do best to avoid. Mr. Kerrigan?"

"If you insist, although he is not relevant to this conversation. Our Dermot Kerrigan engages in some of what might be called undesirable pursuits. He generally functions as an unlicensed moneylender, and much to the dismay of those he likes to call his 'clientele,' he requires an extremely high rate of return and has some . . . shall I say 'very persuasive' ways of convincing clients that it would be wisest to pay what is due when it's due, regardless of his usurious rate of interest?"

"A loan shark," I said.

"Precisely. We also have suspicions that he traffics merchandise, some stolen and some smuggled from other countries, but we've yet to catch him at it. I wouldn't worry. You're not likely to see him again. Now, tell me—what is your writerly impression of the O'Bannons?"

"I would be happy to, but I am wondering, has the family been notified of Michael's death?"

"You do ask a lot of questions. That is supposed to be my job." The inspector gave a dry chuckle. "We notified the PSNI in Derry City, where his daughter, Deirdre, teaches at university, and asked the Belfast PSNI to contact his son, Niall, who lives there and works as a solicitor. I suppose you are really interested in his two cousins. I sent word to my superiors as soon as I saw the body. The deputy chief constable is going to break the sad tidings if he hasn't, in fact, already done so."

He brought his teacup to his lips, but before he actually drank, he asked politely, "Might I have your impressions of the family now?"

"Well, the three O'Bannon cousins who own Marine Magic share a grandfather with my friend Maeve O'Bannon. When she discovered I was going to be in the neighborhood, so to speak, she asked me to deliver to her cousins some landscapes that were painted by their mutual grandfather."

I took a small bite of my scone and swallowed before I continued. "Owen Mullen was kind enough to come to Belfast and drive me here, to the River Bush Hotel." I could see he was getting impatient, so I cut to the chase. "Last evening we were all together at Jane Mullen's house for dinner, along with two Frenchmen who represent a cosmetics company called Belle Visage. After dinner a couple named Gleason joined us. It was quite a normal social evening except . . ."

I hesitated to be sure I would be able to describe the scene without pointing a pejorative finger at Beth Anne.

"Yes? Go on," Finley prompted. I suppose he wanted me either to hand him a murderer on a platter or to stop talking.

"I happened to walk into the library at Jane's house just as

Beth Anne and Michael were having a disagreement. I caught only a few words, but they were arguing about the business. Beth Anne seemed to think something Michael had done was going to jeopardize the upcoming merger with Belle Visage. She was furious, while Michael was unpleasantly defensive," I said.

Finley caught the waitress's eye and held up the teapot. She brought over a full teapot and freshened our cups.

After she withdrew with the empty pot in hand, Finley said, "If people routinely killed their business partners over disagreements about the correct methods to proceed, there would be no one left to run the world's companies and corporations. I understand arguments, even vicious ones, but murder . . . I don't think so."

He went quiet for a few seconds, then said, "You have the same look on your face that one of my sergeants gets when he has more to say but is politely waiting for me to finish telling him he is wrong, so he can explain why he is right."

"Actually, I can't say that you are wrong, but I can tell you that I was not the only person who overheard the conversation. After Beth Anne and Michael left the room, I saw one of the representatives of Belle Visage rise from a chair where he'd been sitting unnoticed by any of us. I am sure that he heard far more of the conversation than I did. He surely had to be more interested than I was. After all, mergers generally have great financial interest for all the concerned parties," I said.

"You've a right sharp point there," Finley conceded. "And was there anything else about this grand party that you think I should know before I speak with the family?"

I thought for a moment. "I can say only that taken on their own, each member of the O'Bannon family seems nice enough, but when you see them all together, well, there is an undeniable tension, although I am not sure of the cause. It may be business related. It may be something else entirely."

Inspector Finley raised his eyebrows. "Now, that is something I will certainly keep in mind as the day progresses."

He swiftly drained his teacup, pushed his chair back, and stood. "Thank you, Mrs. Fletcher. I appreciate your time and our conversation. Never fear. I will see to it that your bicycle is returned shortly."

Left to my own devices, I sipped my tea slowly, quite lost in thought until the waitress asked if I required anything else. I looked at the grandfather clock in the corner of the room and realized that much of the morning had slipped by. I needed to shower and change out of my sweat suit and into something more presentable for whatever the rest of the day might bring. I went upstairs and was unlocking the door to my room when Maggie Nolan came along the hallway. I could see she had been crying. She repeatedly dabbed her eyes with a wad of tissues.

"Mrs. Fletcher, I am so very glad you are all right. I've been bothered ever since you called. Then I heard from Owen a few minutes ago. The family's been told about Michael. What a tragedy for them all. And how terrible it must have been for you to be out in the countryside for a peaceful bicycle ride and come across a horrible accident, such as it was, only to find the victim is someone you know."

I found it interesting that the family had been told Michael died in an accident. Or had they simply assumed he had? I unlocked the door. "Maggie, please come inside for a few minutes. We needn't talk in the hallway."

I steered her to the sun-filled window seat and poured her a glass of water from the bedside carafe. Then I sat in the nearby club chair.

After a few moments' silence, which I hoped gave her a chance to compose herself, I said, "I know this is upsetting because you have grown so close to the O'Bannon family, but I suspect that you are also worried about how Michael's death could possibly affect your future with Owen."

"I sound so selfish when you put it that way," Maggie said. "But I cannot deny that I fear Michael's untimely death could have a detrimental effect on Owen's plans. And as you rightly perceive, our futures are entwined."

"Exactly what are Owen's plans, if you don't mind telling me?"

Maggie was able to show a glimmer of a smile. "Sure, his plans are no secret. Owen studied architecture and his head is filled with ideas for designing grand buildings all over Europe."

"And what makes you think Owen's future as an architect would suddenly be in jeopardy?"

For the life of me, I couldn't see a connection, but Maggie's next sentence gave me insight into the cause of her dread.

"Marine Magic is an O'Bannon company," she said, "and Owen is an O'Bannon."

"I must have misunderstood. I thought Michael's role was primarily that of a figurehead, the medical consultant who could assure clients and customers that the products would work wonders for their skin. How could Owen, a trained architect, fill that role?"

"It is all about personality. You met Beth Anne and Jane. You are far too observant not to have noticed that Beth Anne is abrasive and extremely bossy, while Jane, preeminent botanist though she may be, is best left dealing with her flora and fauna. She is rather awkward around people and coarsely transparent when she pushes for what she wants. Michael, on the other hand, though he may be a bit of a chancer, is—or, rather, was—always charming and extremely sociable. People tend to like him and remember him." Maggie held out her hands palms up as if she had completely explained the family dynamic.

To my mind she had, except . . . "Tell me, Maggie—what is a 'chancer'?"

She laughed. "Ah, then, a chancer is a bit of a dodgy fellow. Let's call him one not quite to be trusted. He's a person that the auld ones—that is, folks like my grandparents—would call a gombeen man."

"And what about Owen's father, Liam Mullen? What is his role in the workings of the company?" I asked.

"Liam has no interest in Marine Magic, other than the fact that it provides a nice living for his family so he can dabble in his passion. He owns a small antiques shop down along Castlecat Road, where he sees patrons by appointment only. Liam is a personable sort but only if you want to have a lengthy conversation about a glass plate that was handblown in someone's barn in 1827. More to the point, he is not an O'Bannon."

"And Owen is both affable and an O'Bannon, at least by blood. He checks all the boxes, you might say." I appreciated that Maggie had given me a very clear picture.

Maggie glanced at the wall clock and jumped from the window seat. "I apologize for having taken up so much of your time. My father will be wondering where in the world I've gone."

I told her that I was happy to spend time with her and that I hoped she would feel free to stop by whenever she needed to talk. I neglected to mention that I was grateful she had given me more information about Maeve's family.

I also realized that notifying Maeve of Michael's death was going to fall on my shoulders. My watch, still set to Cabot Cove time, told me that Maeve would be up and about. I gave it some serious thought and decided to call her a bit later in the day, when I hoped to have some additional information about whatever had happened to her cousin.

There was a knock on my door. I assumed it was someone from housekeeping who wanted to straighten my room. I decided to ask them to come back in an hour. I pulled the door open and was shocked to see that the man from the lobby, the one Inspector Finley had warned me to avoid, was now standing in my doorway.

I started to close the door over. My goal was to leave as little space between us as possible until I could find out what he wanted. He put his foot between the door and the frame to block me from closing it any farther.

"I mean you no harm, Mrs. Fletcher. My name is Dermot Kerrigan and I've come to ask a favor," he said curtly.

"I know who you are, Mr. Kerrigan, and I see no reason to let you into my room." I increased my pressure on the door, hoping he would release his foot.

Kerrigan gave me a shrewd smile. "Press all you like; it will do you no good. I lost that foot, and much of the leg I was born with, in what I now refer to as an accident, some years ago. My hard plastic-and-wooden replacement doesn't feel a thing, no matter how hard you push. I need only a minute of your time. It would be simpler for us both if you allowed me to come inside."

I decided to open the door wide enough for him to enter, and while he did so, I made sure the door was unlatched before I closed it.

By way of apology Kerrigan said, "I would have approached

you in the lobby but I can't say I have much liking for the company you keep. Having the copper around, I thought it best to wait my turn."

"Chief Inspector Finley was kind enough to drive me back to the hotel and offer me a cup of tea after an incident on the road this morning. Now, tell me what business you think you have with me." I made a show of looking at the clock as if I were on a tight schedule.

"Ah, 'business.' The very word. Business is exactly what I have come about. I've recently heard the disastrous news about Michael O'Bannon. I can tell you that he and I have been business associates of a sort for many a year. His unfortunate and sudden death has left our most recent professional arrangement in limbo, you might say." He stopped and looked at me expectantly, but if he was waiting for a response, at that point, I had none to give.

He tipped his head to one side. "I see I need to give you a fuller explanation. Michael and I have had a commercial relationship for all these many years. Now his sudden death has left me with what you might call the short end of the stick."

I'd had quite enough of his dancing around. "Mr. Kerrigan, I know that you are a loan shark, and from what you are saying, I presume Michael O'Bannon died owing you money. I assure you that has nothing whatsoever to do with me."

"As it turns out, last evening while I was having a wee drop at the Dart and the Pint, I heard talk of an American visitor bringing family treasures from a wealthy relative in the States to be delivered to the O'Bannon clan." Once again he raised his eyebrows with that expectant look he seemed to have perfected.

When I did not reply, he drew in a deep breath. "Michael owes me plenty and it would seem you have the treasure that could easily settle his debt. I'm sure he would want you to do so."

"Now, see here, Mr. Kerrigan. Whatever rumor you may have heard about my visit to the O'Bannon family has nothing to do with Michael's debt to you. Now I'd like you to leave my room." I pointed to the door.

"You listen to me, missus. I am not some chancer you can dismiss with a wave of your hand. I am entitled to what I am owed and I intend to have it."

"Then I suggest you take your case to whichever solicitor will be handling Michael O'Bannon's estate. I am not going to tell you again, I'd like you to leave." Even to my own ears, I sounded loud and firm.

At that exact moment, a strong knock on the door startled us both.

"Who's there?" I asked, hopeful that Kerrigan hadn't left a couple of thugs downstairs who had gotten impatient waiting and were here looking for him.

"It's Constable Breen, ma'am."

"Come in, Constable. The door is unlocked. I have company but he is just leaving."

I couldn't help chuckling when I saw the look on Kerrigan's face.

Chapter Ten

Constable Breen stepped inside and began to speak but clamped his jaw shut when he saw Dermot Kerrigan. The constable took two giant steps to stand in between us and shield me with his back while he faced Kerrigan. In a commanding voice, he asked, "Is everything all right here, Mrs. Fletcher?"

Before I could answer, Dermot Kerrigan said, "Of course it is, Constable. Why wouldn't it be? At any rate, I was just leaving. Mrs. Fletcher, it has been a pleasure. I'll be sure to see you again before you leave."

He tipped two fingers against his forehead in a mock salute and slid out the door.

Constable Breen studied me carefully, and then, as if he couldn't contain himself another second, the words burst forth. "What in the name of all that's right and holy was that man doing in your room? Have you any idea—"

I held up my hand to stop his flood of outrage. "I do. Inspector Finley gave me a rundown of Mr. Kerrigan's activities both proven and suspected."

"And yet you allowed him into your room? Woman, are you completely mad?" Breen's eyes popped wide, as if he was as shocked by his own words as he was by my carelessness. Then he heaved one of those deep Irish sighs I was getting used to, and said, "I apologize. I've no cause to blame you. He should have known better than to make the approach to you, a respected guest in our country. Now, as I'm sure the chief inspector will be asking me to provide a reasonable explanation, do you have any idea what Dermot Kerrigan wanted so badly that he would chance coming to your hotel room even knowing you were in our sights due to your proximity to Michael O'Bannon's body?"

"Mr. Kerrigan is under the mistaken impression that I have brought 'family treasures' to the O'Bannons from my neighbor, their cousin Maeve O'Bannon, who Mr. Kerrigan presumes is a wealthy woman, and therefore whatever she sent must be quite valuable," I said.

"And is he correct? Are these gifts of great value?" Breen asked.

"As far as I know, the gifts are four Irish landscapes painted by the mutual grandfather of the O'Bannon cousins. I presume their value is primarily sentimental," I said.

"That is probably so. Still, I will give the chief inspector a full report and I am sure he will wish to speak to you about your encounter with Mr. Kerrigan. In the meantime, I am here to report that your bicycle is in fine fettle. I brought it with me. Mr. Nolan examined it and put it in the shed. He asked me to tell you that the bike wasn't damaged in any way, so you can take it out again whenever you've a mind to." Breen's eyes clouded over. "Not that I would suggest you go riding alone. Mr. Nolan also mentioned that, should you prefer a different bicycle for future rides, he has more than one Donard bicycle ready and at your service."

I thanked Constable Breen for bringing my bicycle back safely and assured him I looked forward to several more rides around Bushmills before I departed for home. "But I promise to stay on the main roads."

"And while you are riding, as soon as you have a free minute, be sure and stop by the Old Bushmills Distillery. You can see how the finest whiskey in all the world is made, and you might be lucky and get a free taste as well." Breen smiled. "I sincerely hope the rest of your trip is happier than this morning has been. Be sure, now, to lock this door. Yer man isn't likely to come back but he is a bold one, so we can't be sure. Now, I'd better leg it before my sergeant comes searching for me. My day will be all the better if I avoid a run-in with the likes of him."

As soon as Constable Breen had left, I turned the lock and got on with my original plan to shower, change, and get ready for the rest of the day, one I hoped would hold no more surprises.

While I was drying my hair, my mind wandered to the O'Bannon family. According to Maggie, they'd been told of Michael's death. I was thinking about what their individual reactions might have been. Knowing that would help me decide how to break the news to Maeve.

The gentle tap on my door caused me to raise my eyes skyward in the universal "What now?" expression. Then a soft voice followed.

"Mrs. Fletcher, have you a minute to spare?" Maggie said.

I opened the door. She was no longer crying but her eyes were red and her face was still blotchy.

"Come in, please, and for heaven's sake, sit down. You look exhausted."

Maggie said, "I wish I could, but I'm here on an errand. Owen called. His mother has asked if I would drive you to the house. Jane and Beth Anne would like you to join the family for a while."

"Oh, that can't be right. They've had a family death. Why would they want a total stranger in their midst?"

"Owen didn't say. I'm not sure he knows. He sounded as though he was under a tremendous amount of pressure, trying to hold the family together. Oh, that might be it. Jane probably wants to talk to you about the American cousin. Has she been told or who should tell her, something like that? So will you come?" Maggie looked so worried that I might refuse, I instantly patted her cheek.

"Of course I will. I'll meet you in the lobby in, say, ten minutes. Will that work?"

We'd barely parked when Owen, who must have been watching for Maggie's car, came barreling out the front door and ran to us. After giving Maggie a quick hug, he said, "Jessica, thank you for coming. My mother and my aunt are completely at sixes and sevens. One minute they are talking about funeral arrangements. The next they are reminiscing about the time Michael broke his arm falling from a spruce tree behind their grandparents' house when they were all still at school. Then a few tense words about the business, followed by funeral arrangements once again. I just don't know what to do with them. When mother asked me to invite you, I saw my opportunity to call in support."

"I am glad to be here and I'm more than willing to help in any way I can, but before we go inside, do you happen to know if anyone notified Maeve about Michael's death?" I asked.

"No one has mentioned Cousin Maeve but I am guessing that as of yet they have not. They know that notifications must be made and when they, for the briefest time, talked about letting people know, Mam pulled out her personal address book of friends and family, while Aunt Beth Anne opened a manila folder filled with pages of business contacts."

"Oh, dear." I could see the potential for conflicts brewing. Notifications were small things compared to how to replace Michael within the company, and I had already begun to wonder what his children would want to do with his share of the business. Hopefully none of that would come up today. "Well, let's go inside, and perhaps we can find a way to be of help."

Owen led us to the yellow parlor, where we found Jane sitting on one couch while Beth Anne occupied a lounge chair. Liam was pacing back and forth. With his hands clasped behind his back, he looked for all the world like a father waiting for an errant child who had missed curfew. A young woman I'd not met before was sitting on the piano bench, plunking odd keys while matching no rhythm I'd ever heard.

"Caro, please stop that incessant noise. How do you expect anyone to think clearly?" Beth Anne snapped.

Caro answered, "Sorry, Mother." She stood and walked away

from the piano. I noticed she didn't move nearer her mother, but instead sat by herself in a chair at the far end of the room.

Jane and Beth Anne both rose from their seats and came to greet us. I offered them my deepest condolences. Jane gave Maggie what looked to me like a warm and sincere hug. It seemed that she, like Dougal Nolan, had no objection to the match between Owen and Maggie, regardless of whatever difficulties the history between the families might have presented.

Liam stopped his pacing long enough to give us a wholehearted welcome ending with "Please, please, sit down. Nora was kind enough to come in today to do for us in the kitchen. Can we get you a cup of tea and a scone or two?"

I would have declined rather than inconvenience anyone but Maggie replied, "That would be lovely."

I was beginning to realize that for fear of giving offense, one simply did not turn down the offer of tea anywhere in Ireland. We sat looking out the bay window and made small talk about how lovely Jane's garden was this time of year, until Beth Anne said, "Maggie, do you know if Messieurs Blanchet and Lavigne are still at the hotel? They haven't heard the news about Michael and scurried back to France, have they?"

Beth Anne's question shocked Maggie, along with everyone else in the room. Beth Anne's daughter Caro, who'd ignored us all thus far, said, "Mother . . ."

But the rest of her remark was drowned out by Maggie, who answered loudly and firmly, "Beth Anne, I am sorry but I have no idea. I haven't seen them all day, nor have I checked the register. Let me call my father and verify their guest status."

She pulled her cell phone from her purse, instantly realized that she'd best not dial while standing in the midst of us all, and left the room.

Jane pushed herself off the couch as if it were suddenly on fire. Hands resolutely on her hips, she stood in front of her sister. "How can you . . . How dare you think about business at a time like this? Michael is dead. Our cousin is dead and we are not even sure how that happened, but all you can think about is your ridiculous merger. Can you, just this once, give it a rest?"

By the time she stopped talking, Jane was flushed and gasping for air. Liam hurried to her side while Owen picked up her teacup and brought it to her, quietly urging her to take a sip.

Beth Anne did not appear the least bit concerned that she had upset her sister. She sat up a little straighter and waved her arms, indicating her surroundings. "Take a good look around you, Jane. Marine Magic allows you to live in this ostentatious house. Marine Magic affords you those trips to Paris twice a year to buy the latest fashions. How far do you think you'd get on what Liam earns by dabbling in that hobby he calls an antiques shop?"

Beth Anne noticed Maggie frozen in the doorway and demanded, "Well?"

Maggie cleared her throat and said, "The Frenchmen have not checked out, although my father said they are not on the premises at the moment. He is not sure where they have gone."

Beth Anne clapped her hands. "Well, that is some good news, at least. I may be able to keep you all living in the style to which you have become accustomed."

We were all mesmerized by Beth Anne's outlandish behavior, so none of us noticed Nora entering the room. "Sorry to be interrupting, but Chief Inspector Finley of the PSNI is here. I showed him to the library. He would like a word with Mrs. Ryan."

Beth Anne raised a hand to her throat. "Me? What could he want with me? Oh, I suppose he wants to report their findings about the cause of Michael's accident. I'll be back shortly."

As soon as she left, I looked around. Beth Anne's daughter Caro was thumbing through a magazine, ignoring everything that had gone on during the past few minutes. Maggie and the Mullen men were huddled around Jane, offering comfort.

Jane sniffed. "It's not as though we haven't had sisterly spats before. She'll calm down."

Liam was outraged. "*She'll* calm down! She *wasn't* upset. She was rude. Your sister was absolutely insolent to you. To all of us. If I were you, I would demand a full apology."

"But you are not me. And Beth Anne is not your sister. I will handle this in my own good time. But for now . . ." Jane walked over to me, and as if the blowup with her sister never happened, she said, "If you all will excuse us, I am going to treat our guest to a tour of the house. Jessica, I have collected many fine heirlooms. I insist that you take pictures so we can share them with dear Cousin Maeve. Why don't we start in the sewing room?"

As we walked up the stairs to the second floor, Jane said, "You mustn't mind my sister. She is all business all the time. I think she uses it as a shield to hide her loneliness. She lost her husband long ago to cancer and her girls are grown and on their own. Caro is a teacher at a primary school over in Limavady. She lives quite nearby, although she doesn't visit often. As soon as Owen called to let her know we lost Michael, she came right home. Beth Anne's other daughter, Sheila, lives in London, so we won't see her for a while yet."

Jane opened a door to what she called the sewing room. I

would have been inclined to call it a display room. One wall was lined with bed-sized quilts, each with a different intricate pattern. A few quilts had faded streaks, making it obvious they had dressed beds for many years and the sunshine coming through the bedroom windows had left its mark. And yet some of the quilts were so pristine, they looked brand-new. A small table was covered with a pleasing arrangement of candlesticks along with a copper kettle and cast-iron fry pans similar to those used to make the apple cake at our recent dinner. Next to the table stood a glass-topped case that held embroidered linens of varying styles and sizes.

"You have such a lovely assortment of household items. Are all these things O'Bannon memorabilia or have some items come from Liam's family?" I asked.

"Oh, except for my grandmother O'Bannon's kettle and old Mrs. Mullen's candlesticks, all the things you see are recent acquisitions that I picked up here and there around the county at church sales, charity shops, and the like. When I die, I intend for Owen as well as Michael's and Beth Anne's children to all have their pick. These may not have come directly from their ancestors but each piece spent its useful time somewhere in the area of Bushmills where generations of O'Bannons have lived and died. That's close enough for me," Jane said.

I was admiring one of the embroidered pillowcases trimmed with an exquisite lace edging when Jane said, with what I felt was a deliberately casual air, "As you can see, Jessica, this room will be the perfect place to display the heirlooms Maeve has sent over. I'm sure things will have settled down enough by tomorrow that I'll be able to come to Nolan's hotel and take that responsibility off your shoulders."

"Oh, Jane, I am sorry but I thought you understood. Maeve made it quite clear that she prefers that her cousins and as many of their children as possible all be together when they see your grandfather's paintings for the first time."

Jane didn't respond, so I continued. "You do realize that I am honor bound to carry out her wishes, don't you?"

"I won't say I'm not disappointed, but I suppose if that is how Maeve wants things done . . . Let's say no more about it for the time being." Jane slapped her hands together a couple of times as if shaking off bread crumbs. "We'd better get ourselves back to the parlor before that police inspector puts us on his missing-persons list."

Beth Anne had not yet returned from her interview with Inspector Finley. It did seem to me that she'd been gone an awfully long time. And now Nora was standing near the serving table with a bottle of whiskey in her hand. The label read "Bushmills."

"Can I offer you ladies a wee drop?"

Jane said, "Ah, now, tea with just a taste of Black Bush might do the trick on an afternoon such as this. Will you try some, Jessica?"

Normally whiskey would not have been my first choice, but to be polite I asked, "What is Black Bush?"

"Only the softest whiskey on God's green earth," Liam said.

"In that case how can I refuse?" I said but was immediately distracted when Beth Anne came back into the room escorted by Constable Breen.

She was pale and drawn and looked totally exhausted. Could it be that in being interviewed by Chief Inspector Clive Finley she had at last met her match?

It appeared I was the only person in the room who was not

surprised when Breen said, "The chief inspector would like to speak to Mrs. Mullen now."

Jane blanched and turned to her husband. "Why? Why me? Liam, will you come with me?"

Breen was firmer than I'd known him to be. "'Tis only you the inspector requested." And he escorted her out of the room.

Chapter Eleven

Beth Anne stood just inside the doorway and said, "What a horrible experience," as her eyes wandered the room, looking for sympathy.

Liam immediately picked up a crystal glass from the serving table and signaled Nora, who poured an inch of Bushmills whiskey. Liam twirled the glass twice and then drained its contents. I'd foolishly thought he was going to offer it to Beth Anne.

Caro dropped her magazine on an end table, walked over, and gave her mother a hug. "Come and sit. Do you want a cup of tea or would whiskey serve you better?"

"Tea would be grand. But first I have an announcement." Beth Anne took her daughter's hand and said, "I hate to be the bearer of such distressing news, but according to the inspector, Michael's death was not an accident."

The room went silent. Liam recovered first. "So what was it, then? Heart attack? Stroke?"

"Inspector Finley believes"—Beth Anne paused; I thought it likely she was hoping for dramatic effect—"that Michael was murdered."

Everyone started talking at once. Caro guided her mother to the nearest seat and Nora quickly handed her a cup of tea.

Liam was the loudest by far. "Impossible. If the inspector thought Michael was murdered, why would he ever want to talk to Jane? She couldn't possibly be a suspect. Jane is the least violent person in the world."

I was sure he would have continued in that vein for a good while longer but Owen stopped him. "Da, don't you suppose this inspector will want to speak to every one of us? We are Michael's family, and more important, since all of us, except for Caro, were with him for dinner yesterday, we may be the last people to have seen him before— Well, you know, before it happened."

"I am sure Owen is correct. My guess would be that the inspector is at the fact-gathering stage rather than at the 'suss out the culprit' stage of the investigation," I said.

Liam seemed to settle down. "Of course. That's it. Fact gathering. I'm not sure how Jane can help him. Beth Anne, what did he ask you? What kind of facts is he looking for?"

Beth Anne shocked us all by bursting into tears. Nora hurried over to the couch and handed her a fistful of napkins while Caro wrapped her arms around her mother and began murmuring words of comfort I couldn't quite catch.

After a while Beth Anne's sobs lessened; she moved away from Caro and sat straighter. Nora took Beth Anne's damp napkins and offered replacements. Beth Anne thanked her and asked for a fresh cup of tea. Owen moved a small table so that Nora could set the tea directly in front of Beth Anne, who picked up the cup, took a slow, deliberate sip of tea, and replaced her cup in its saucer. Once she was sure she had everyone's attention she spoke.

"Liam, I'm certain the inspector has no reason to suspect Jane of anything. I rather believe he has his eye on me." She looked around, perhaps expecting outrage, but there was none. We were all waiting to hear more, and in her own good time, Beth Anne continued.

"You may recall that Michael drove me to the dinner party last evening, so naturally he drove me home. When I got out of his car, somehow the hem of that flowy dress I was wearing got caught on the door panel and I never noticed that a small piece ripped off and became trapped in the door."

Owen said, "That explains what Michael was doing on the old cow path. As he often did, he was taking it as a shortcut from your house to his."

Caro brightened. "Yes, always. Even when we were children and the path was still used by some local drovers, Michael would drive along the path to avoid driving through the village. I still remember the few times a flock of sheep or a herd of cattle got in his way. He'd be furious at the delay, but sure as it rains in Ireland, the next time he was driving us kids from one house to the other, he'd take the cow path."

My first thought was that everything Beth Anne told us put a different spin on Michael's death. When I saw the gauzy pink fabric trapped between the passenger-side door and its frame, it appeared to me that it was likely to fall out once the door was opened. I'd have to check with Inspector Finley, but if that was what had happened when his techs opened the door, then no one else entered the passenger-side door after Michael dropped Beth Anne off at her home.

If Beth Anne was telling the truth and the techs could establish that no one was in the car with Michael, the question became, whom had he met on that dirt road in the middle of the night? Had it been a chance encounter or had someone who knew his habits been waiting for Michael O'Bannon?

Beth Anne seemed somewhat cheered by the family support she must have been feeling, so I was surprised when she blurted, "I certainly hope that after today the inspector will busy himself with finding the actual killer. The publicity of Michael being murdered is bad enough. How will it look to our business partners and clients if one of us is arrested for the crime?"

"Never fear, Aunt Beth Anne. If it comes to that, I'm sure the inspector will have the good grace to wait until after the funeral."

Owen laughed, expecting us all to join in, but the only reaction he got was from Maggie, who slapped his knee and said, "Behave," as if talking to a puppy she was trying to train to stay off the furniture.

When Constable Breen escorted Jane back to the parlor, she wasn't nearly as ruffled as her sister had been. Then Breen asked Liam to meet with the inspector. As soon as they left the parlor, Owen asked his mother about her interview.

She looked at her sister. "I suppose Beth Anne told you the really shocking part. Michael was murdered. Once I heard that, I didn't pay much attention to the rest of what the inspector asked. I still don't understand why he bothered questioning me about money and business entanglements. I told him Beth Anne handles all those boring details. I'm a chemist and a botanist. I can explain the complexities of seaweed or hyaluronic acid in skin care products, but when it comes to profits and losses, that's my sister's department." Jane looked around, clearly seeking agreement.

"He did ask me some questions about the company finances, but frankly I was in no condition to give concrete answers," Beth Anne said. "Did he give you any idea when we could begin to plan Michael's funeral arrangements? Deirdre and Niall will be here soon. I'd like to be able to tell them something besides 'A maniac killed your father' and 'No, we don't have any idea who or why.'"

Some sort of gong reverberated through the house and I was the only one who jumped at the sound of it. Nora left the room and came back with Conor Sweeney, who was carrying a large bouquet of white lilies.

Conor expressed warm condolences to Beth Anne, Jane, and all the other family members present and then he seemed to become confused. I don't think he could decide to whom he should give the flowers. Maggie saved the day by asking Nora to take them to the kitchen and arrange them in a suitable vase.

Owen offered Conor a glass of whiskey.

"Ah, there's yer man," Conor said. He emptied the glass in one swallow and offered it back to Owen. "I wouldn't refuse more of the same."

With his refill in his hand, Conor took a seat next to me. "Tell me, Mrs. Fletcher, how are you getting on? I stopped by the Dart and the Pint this morning and the proprietor told me the news. Bad luck to you, finding Michael like that. I suppose the PSNI have been full of questions, you being a foreigner and all."

"Inspector Finley and his colleagues have been considerate while proceeding with their investigation. You may have noticed a police car outside. The inspector is here, speaking to the family. Liam is in the library with him right now. Jane and Beth Anne have already been questioned."

Conor looked toward the bay window for a few seconds. "Really? It being such a grand, sunny day—one of the days my mother always called 'a good day for drying'—I rode over on my bicycle. As I racked it by the far side of the house, I never so much as glanced at the cars in the driveway."

"Since I don't have a driver's license, I really enjoy riding a bicycle. It's my main form of transportation at home in Cabot Cove," I said. "I was delighted that Mr. Nolan has bikes available for his hotel guests."

"We must see if we can find the time to go for a good long ride together before you leave us," Conor said as Constable Breen and Liam came through the doorway.

Liam greeted Conor but passed right by us in order to give Jane what I would have called a bear hug. "The inspector assured me they will be done with us fairly soon."

Breen stopped in front of Conor and me. "Might I ask your name, sir?"

Conor replied, "Conor Sweeney, president of Sweeney Brothers Shipping, close friend and business associate of the family. I've come to support them during this terrible time."

The constable nodded. "I see. You were on the dinner party guest list as well, were you not? If you wouldn't mind waiting a wee bit, I am sure the inspector would like a word."

Before Conor could answer, Breen signaled Owen to follow him out of the room.

Conor looked puzzled. "Interviewing dinner party guests? Isn't that a bridge too far when tidying up loose ends after an accident?"

I lowered my voice, not wanting to get Jane and Beth Anne in a renewed tizzy. "I can tell you that Mr. Collins at the pub did not have the most accurate information. Michael O'Bannon's death was not an accident. A short while ago Inspector Finley informed the family that Michael was murdered."

Conor's mouth dropped open. When he recovered, he said, "That can't be right. Why, Michael was a man without an enemy in the world. He was . . . he was a prince among men."

In my experience everyone has enemies. Michael had at least one that I knew of: the loan shark Dermot Kerrigan. And with the squabble I'd witnessed between Beth Anne and Michael, although they might have been cousins, they could have been enemies as well. I know Inspector Finley disagreed with me but arguing over business decisions could cause an irreparable schism between even the closest of friends or family members. Still, I said nothing in response to Conor, surrounded as I was by Michael's family and business associates.

Inspector Finley's interviews seemed to drag on and on. Nora brought in a tray of sandwiches—ham and cheese on bread, chicken fillet on rolls, and plain bread and butter. Snacking on them did help fill the time. At long last Constable Breen invited Conor Sweeney to meet with the inspector. I assumed that would be the end of it. It seemed as though everyone in the parlor had long since run out of small talk. We were all hanging on, waiting to be dismissed. For my part, the time had long past for me to call Maeve and give her the dreadful news.

Since the inspector had interviewed me already, I didn't quite understand why, when Breen and Conor Sweeney came back to the parlor, the constable said, "Mrs. Fletcher, the inspector would like a word, if you please."

There was no point in saying it didn't please me at all. I followed Breen to the library.

When I came into the room Finley rose in a gentlemanly manner and directed me to a chair that looked quite comfortable. But he threw me off with his first question, which was a doozy. "So, tell me, Mrs. Fletcher, what were your impressions of everyone in the house as they absorbed the information that Michael O'Bannon was deliberately killed?"

"My impressions? Didn't we just discuss my impressions over tea earlier today? And I wasn't sure you found them at all interesting," I said.

"Well, upon reflection, it seems to me you are a perceptive woman, which leads me to hope that you are willing to share your impressions of how everyone in the parlor reacted to the news that Michael O'Bannon had been murdered."

"Well, honestly, Michael's cousins Beth Anne and Jane, while they may be sisters, work hard to exhibit the differences rather than the similarities in their personalities. Beth Anne constantly reminds us that she is all business. I would imagine that she sees profit ledgers, advertising plans, and future expansions in her every dream. In truth, each sister is quite determined to be a huge success at whatever she does. Jane, as the chief botanist and chemist of the company, actually considers herself to be completely responsible for all the leaps and bounds of progress that Marine Magic has made, especially in recent years," I said as if that explained everything. It certainly did to me.

Finley leaned forward, clasped his hands, and rested his elbows on his knees. "And Michael O'Bannon? Where did he fit within the family push-pull as they scramble to take credit as the person most responsible for the company's success?"

"Now, that is an interesting question," I said. "If you ask either of his cousins, Michael was nothing more than a figurehead, the face in the company advertisements merely because he had a medical degree. Both ladies seemed to think the company could easily move on without him—until now."

"You mean, now that he is actually gone, they realize he served a purpose." Finley's statement sounded like conjecture.

"No, I mean that your declaration that Michael was murdered means the company is in for a slew of unwelcome publicity, and since Michael's only role in their eyes was to increase the firm's public credibility, the sisters both fear they are in for a rough ride. Beth Anne said it out loud, and although Jane seems to fight her every step of the way, she did not disagree." I couldn't have said it any more plainly.

"And the rest of the family? The men? What is your opinion of Liam and Owen Mullen?"

"As far as I can tell, neither of them has any interest whatsoever in the day-to-day operations of the business. As an aside, I can tell you that Owen's fiancée, Maggie Nolan, is worried that Jane will use Michael's death as a way to entice Owen to come into the business."

Finley raised his eyebrows.

I raised mine right back at him. "Oh, come now. I doubt any woman would kill her cousin as a means of guilting her son into joining the family business."

"As a motive it is a wee bit thin. I'll grant you that," Finley agreed. "And what can you tell me about Conor Sweeney? How did he respond to the word 'murder'?"

"He was shocked, quite wide-eyed, as I recall, but you can't judge by that. Everyone you interviewed today had a similar reaction. Any killer, even the fictional ones I invent for my books, knows that the concept of murder is too horrific for people to contemplate, so in order to look innocent once the crime is discovered, the murderer is prepared to be appalled.

"What I can tell you is that Conor Sweeney and Michael O'Bannon seemed to have a close business and personal relationship, but I had a sense there was tension, something that I can't identify. They both seemed to work a little too hard at projecting the image that they were besties." I wished I could have been clearer, but to tell the truth, I wasn't quite sure myself.

"One final note." Finley shook his finger in my general direction. "Let me remind you that allowing Dermot Kerrigan into your room was not the wisest thing you've ever done. How much longer will you be in possession of the 'treasure' that interests him?"

"Given the family circumstances, I can't honestly say." I neglected to tell him that Jane too was quite anxious to take charge of the paintings.

We spoke for a few more minutes and then Inspector Finley walked with me to the parlor. He thanked us all for our time and said he would probably be in touch soon. After he and Breen left, Jane Mullen was kind enough to invite us to stay for an early supper, but I was delighted when Owen said that he and Maggie had plans to meet friends, so we'd be leaving.

Once in the car, Maggie said, "Owen was rude not to ask if you wanted to stay here for supper, Mrs. Fletcher. If you would like to do so, we'd be happy to return to drive you back to the hotel."

"Goodness, no. As much as I appreciate your kind offer, I think it is time for me to telephone Maeve O'Bannon and tell her about Michael's death."

Chapter Twelve

I kicked off my shoes and sat on the window seat. Even though over the past few days, I'd thought I had adjusted to the time difference, the very sight of my bed had me longing for a nap.

Short of knowing that I wasn't going to open with *Hello. Michael O'Bannon has been murdered*, I was still unsure exactly how I was going to tell Maeve about her cousin's death. I decided to call Seth Hazlitt first so that he would know what had happened and be set to check in on Maeve as necessary.

He answered on the second ring.

"Hi, Seth. It's Jessica."

"Well, I am disappointed. Here you've been in Ireland all this time and there's not a hint of a brogue in your voice. Still a New England gal, by the sound of you." Seth laughed. "My final patient of the day just left, so I have plenty of time for you to tell me how your trip has been so far. You can start by reassuring me that Maeve's relatives aren't all as crusty as she is."

"Now, Seth, Maeve is not crusty. She's just busy with her own interests and doesn't like to have her time interrupted by anything she considers unimportant."

"I'll stick to what I said. Jessica. There is no denying Maeve's a crusty one. Oh, and did you unload those old paintings yet? I hope you followed her exact instructions. If not, you'll come to see her crusty side right quick. Count on it."

"I am in her family's home village of Bushmills, and from what I've seen so far, it is a lovely place, and the people I've met have been very open and friendly," I said.

"Why do I sense a major 'but' coming?" Seth asked.

"Probably because there is one. My next phone call will be to Maeve. I have to explain that her plan for me to call the family together and show them her grandfather's paintings will have to remain on the back burner for a while."

"That doesn't sound good. Are you having a hard time arranging for a 'gathering of the clan,' as the Irish or the Scots might say?"

"No, it's far worse. At the present time it is impossible. One of Maeve's cousins has died unexpectedly."

"Jess, when you say 'unexpectedly,' that could cover anything from a heart attack to an accident." Seth had moved quickly into doctor mode.

There was no point in holding back the truth from Seth when I knew I was going to have to tell Maeve everything in a few minutes.

"Michael O'Bannon, who was a doctor and functioned as the medical authority behind the family skin-care company called Marine Magic, was found in his car on the side of a deserted road. He'd been bludgeoned to death."

"Poor Maeve," Seth began, but I stopped him.

"Maeve doesn't know yet."

"What do you mean? Didn't her cousins think to tell her? Here, Maeve sent you across the Atlantic Ocean to deliver gifts and they can't be bothered—"

"Seth, calm down. That is not what happened. First of all, I discovered the body only this morning." I regretted saying it as soon as the words were out of my mouth but it was too late.

"Naturally, you're the one who found the body," Seth thundered. "How many people live in this quaint little town? Hundreds? Thousands? Couldn't one of them manage to come across a dead body in a car on a roadside in their own town? Oh, no. Jessica Fletcher, girl detective, found the body and is, no doubt, actively on the case."

"Seth, will you stop making a mountain out of a molehill? All I did was go for a bike ride." I hoped to settle him down so I could get to my request.

"Sorry, Jess. I just don't like to think of you in danger. And who knows where the murderer was while you were poking around the murder scene?"

"Seth, I know better than to poke."

"I hope you do. Now, if you are telling me before you are going to tell Maeve, you must want my help. What can I do?"

I smiled to myself. No matter how grumpy Seth might act, when he feared I was getting myself into danger, he was always willing to render any possible assistance.

"We both know how fiercely independent Maeve is, so I'm going to suggest that when you stop by to check on my house a few hours from now you knock on her door and ask her how she thinks my seedlings are doing. Use your doctorly eye to judge how she looks."

"Jessica, you know full well I've done this same silly routine hundreds of times with my patients. As soon as I get a look at her, I'll be quick to determine if this news has caused Maeve any potential health difficulty."

"I knew I could count on you. I'd better hang up so I can call her now."

"Before you do, remember we have a date for breakfast at Mara's the first morning you are home," Seth said.

"You can count on it," I said, and disconnected the call.

To make myself a cup of tea I heated the electric kettle that stood on the dressing table. Then, while it was steeping, I dialed Maeve's number.

As soon as I said hello, she was filled with questions.

"Jessica, now that you've gotten out of big-city Belfast and seen the Irish countryside, I'm sure you will agree it is amazing, especially Bushmills Village. I hope you are bringing lots of pictures home to me. Now, tell me, how is the family? Did Owen pick you up on time? He's a fine, trustworthy lad," Maeve said.

"Not only was he on time, but he went out of his way to drive me to Ballycastle so I could see Fair Head, which, I admit, was truly remarkable. I'd love to go back sometime to climb its pathways."

"Ah, and I suppose he managed to stop at Saoirse McInerney's tea shop in the hope of an apple tart or two." Maeve laughed. "The boy hasn't changed since he was a toddler. Speaking of climbing around, I'm sure that before you left I mentioned the Giant's Causeway to you. It is only a couple of miles up the road from the village. See that Dougal Nolan arranges for someone to take you there. Once you stand on the basalt columns, look out over the North Atlantic, and see the glory of the spume as the waves swell, your spirit will feel renewed."

Listening to Maeve so joyfully reliving her memories of her father's homeland, I hated to get to the purpose of my call.

"Maeve, I have some news. It may be difficult for you to hear. Perhaps if you are not sitting down, you should find a chair," I began.

"As it happens, I was in the kitchen having a cuppa when the phone rang, so here I am at the table. Now, don't keep me in suspense. You didn't lose my granda's paintings, did you?" Alarm was palpable in Maeve's voice.

"No. No. The paintings are fine. But I do have some dreadful news. Your cousin Michael O'Bannon died last night quite unexpectedly," I said.

Maeve's reply was not what I anticipated, although I should have realized that she'd be as stoic about that as she had been about every troublesome problem for all the years I'd known her.

"Ah, that Michael. He was always one for the sweets and the whiskey. I suppose that's what did him in in the end." Maeve sounded resigned.

Although she didn't mean it as a question, I replied, "Unfortunately, no. Michael was attacked and died as a result of his injuries."

"Where did this happen? Surely not in Bushmills . . ." Maeve trailed off as if she needed time to process what I had told her.

I explained what I knew, leaving out the fact that I had discovered Michael's body. It was nearly half an hour before I felt that

Maeve accepted Michael's death and the fact that it would delay my delivering the paintings in the manner she'd requested.

"Under the circumstances, if you want me to present the paintings to Jane, I'll be happy to do so. Then she can follow your instructions at a later date." I made what I thought was a reasonable suggestion but Maeve was having none of it.

"Jessica, blood she may well be, but I don't trust Jane Mullen to honor my wishes if they don't coincide with her own." Maeve went silent for a few seconds. "I see now I should have made the trip myself. More's your misfortune that I did not. If I'm not asking too much, can you manage to stay in Bushmills until things quiet down a bit, and then you can follow the original plan, gather the family, and finish the task?"

Naturally I agreed, and Maeve was much comforted when I reminded her that Susan Shevlin had kept my return trip open-ended, so I needed only to make a phone call when I was ready to head back to Cabot Cove and Susan would put everything neatly in place.

I hung up the phone. I looked through the window and was calmed by the sight of the fields and the River Bush totally at peace with one another. It was easy to understand why Maeve, or anyone for that matter, would find it hard to believe a violent murder could have happened in that peaceful, bucolic place.

A loud knock on the door interrupted my revery. *Now what?* I thought.

I opened the door and Chief Inspector Clive Finley said, "Well, now, you've gone and failed the test. You were supposed to ask who was knocking, and if I answered, 'It's Dermot Kerrigan,' you were supposed to tell me to go away. But here you are opening the door to all and sundry."

"Come in, Inspector. I hardly think Mr. Kerrigan will waste time coming back to see me. He's more likely to shake down the family for whatever he thinks he's owed. That's where the real money is."

"'Shake down,' is it? Now that's a corking good American phrase. I know you are a mystery writer, Mrs. Fletcher, but can it be that you are a fan of pulp fiction as well? The likes of Lawrence Block or James M. Cain. They are masters of such language."

"I've read them both. My favorite is Cain's *The Postman Always Rings Twice*. But that is enough about literature. Tell me what I can do for you, Inspector. It has been a long day."

"That it has, ma'am, for us both. I was wondering if I might take a look at the family gifts you brought from America. I'd like to see for myself what might attract the likes of Dermot Kerrigan."

"Inspector, I thought you understood. Mr. Kerrigan has not seen any of the gifts I brought. He has no idea what I brought or its value," I said.

"I understand quite well, Mrs. Fletcher, but in order to prevent any type of calamity, I would like to see these treasures for myself and decide whether to allow you to keep them here or if I should store them at the police station for safekeeping until you are ready to turn them over to the family."

He must have noticed me bristle as soon as he said the word "allow," because he quickly amended himself. "It would be up to you. I've brought up the idea only because your safety is my primary concern. Dermot Kerrigan has been known to play rough to get what he's after."

I decided that showing the paintings to the inspector was the easiest way to get him to leave me in peace. My brown tweed suitcase was on the luggage rack in the small alcove next to the closet door. I unzipped it and took out the large plastic bag that held the four heavy cardboard tubes Maeve had packed so carefully, and I handed it to him.

"Here you go. The O'Bannon family fortune." I am sure he detected the sarcasm in my voice.

Inspector Finley opened the bag and pulled out a tube, which Maeve had sealed with caps at both ends. "Do you know what is in these tubes?"

"Maeve O'Bannon's paternal grandfather, who lived hereabouts his entire life, painted four local landscapes and presented them to Maeve's parents as a wedding present. Since she is the last of her O'Bannon line, Maeve decided that she wanted to gift the paintings to family members still living in Ireland so that they wouldn't wind up at a rummage sale or, worse, in the trash after she is . . . gone." I wanted the inspector to understand that this was a sentimental bequest, not a monetary one.

"Would you mind if I opened this tube?" he asked.

"Feel free. Open them all if you like. But be careful not to damage the paintings in any way or Maeve will have my head." I was only half jesting.

He was extremely cautious as he removed the painting, unrolled it, and laid it flat on the dressing tabletop and said, "Well, would you look at that? I can tell you for sure it was painted by a local. I know the exact location."

Now, there is a surprise, I thought, although I said nothing.

"It's a grand fishing spot, for sure, just north of where the River Bush crosses under the A2 roadway, and then the river curves, curves, and curves again, heading back toward Ballaghmore Road. I won't be giving away the secret if I tell you that one of those curves is a place where the salmon practically jump into your net. And the artist knew it, for sure. Look how he's painted a tackle box, a rod, and a long-handled net at the base of that tree."

"But this painting is not something that would have value to a man like Dermot Kerrigan, is it, Inspector?"

Finley laughed. "Being a local, sure, even Kerrigan has his secret fishing sites, so I doubt he'd find great interest in old Mr. O'Bannon's favorite spot."

He rolled the painting up, replaced it carefully in its tube, and handed it to me.

"So I needn't worry about Mr. Kerrigan?" I asked.

"He's a worrisome fellow and that you can bank on, but as far as these paintings, I will put out the word first thing that there is no financial interest to be had in the package you've brought over from the American relative. Mind, that is no guarantee that Kerrigan won't find some other reason to come sniffing around, but he won't be looking to grab away your pictures."

"And what about his relationship with Michael O'Bannon? Kerrigan told me that Michael was deeply in his debt. Is that true or was he merely trying to get me to part with the gifts I brought from Maeve?"

Finley took a moment before he answered. I could almost see the wheels turning as he decided how much he was willing to tell me. "According to the people who know about this sort of thing, O'Bannon owed Kerrigan a nice sum of money, but"—he raised his hand, fingers spread wide—"Dermot is a man who would be far more likely to order O'Bannon to be kneecapped rather than killed. Dead men can't honor their debts, now, can they?"

"That's certainly true," I said, although I wasn't ready to give up on Dermot Kerrigan as my number one suspect. "Perhaps, besides the moneylending, there was another connection between the two."

"Nice try, Mrs. Fletcher, but from what I hear, Kerrigan is otherwise occupied. He has taken a strong interest in a small import-export company situated on Bayhead Road. So I suspect his attention has turned more to developing his fledgling smuggling operation. He'd have no interest in killing a doctor. It would be no help to his own prosperity, and one thing I know for certain is Dermot Kerrigan is quite fond of his own prosperity."

The inspector left me in a funk. I had hoped for a quick resolution to Michael's murder so I could present Maeve's paintings to the family and be on my way home. I decided to go for a walk; maybe a little window-shopping would cheer me up.

Chapter Thirteen

Dougal Nolan was alone in the lobby when I came downstairs.

"Aye, Mrs. Fletcher, I do apologize for the unfortunate beginning to your stay here in Bushmills, and if I can do anything to make up for it, you've only to let me know."

"You are very kind. I think all I need is a short walk and perhaps some window-shopping to clear my head," I said.

"In that case, make a right turn and walk a couple of blocks. Just past the Dart and the Pint, you will come to Aunt Aggie's Attic. Agatha Mason stocks every kind of this and that you could imagine. Some of it old, some if it new, all of it worth a browse."

"Thank you. That sounds perfect," I said, and headed out the door.

I strolled along Main Street, and when I reached the Dart and the Pint, I did wonder if James Collins might be available for a chat and decided I would stop by on my way back to the hotel. For the next little while, I would be a tourist out to do some shopping.

As soon as I looked in the window of Aunt Aggie's Attic, I knew it was everything Dougal Nolan had promised and more. When I opened the door, the shopkeeper's bell tinkled gently and caught the ear of a woman who immediately came out from the back room.

"'Tis yourself, the American visiting the O'Bannons and all. I have been hoping you'd stop by. We have some fine merchandise you'll be wanting to take home to your friends and family. I'm Agatha Mason. Happy to help you. Sorry about Michael O'Bannon, though. You must have taken that as quite a shock."

Her brown hair was woven in two untidy braids and she tugged on the left one as she spoke.

I was at a loss. I couldn't decide which part of her speech to answer first, so I said, "Good afternoon. I am Jessica Fletcher. I'd like to look around if I may."

"Sure, give it a go. Take your time, enjoy what you see, and if you need some help or a bit of explaining, I will be waiting right here."

The shop was small, but with floor-to-ceiling shelves there was more space than I would have imagined from the outside. The center of the room was filled with racks—some holding books, some holding clothes—along with two display cases of jewelry.

In short order I found handsome tweed flat caps for my nephew Grady and his son, Frank; a pair of Celtic knot earrings for Grady's wife, Donna; and an Irish cookbook for Maureen

Metzger. Maureen's husband, Cabot Cove's sheriff, Mort, would be the happy beneficiary of all her trials. It took a while longer for me to decide on a tan cable-knit sweater vest for Seth. However, try as I might, I couldn't find anything that I thought would be the perfect gift for Maeve.

Agatha sorted through the gifts I'd placed on the counter. "And won't the family and friends find themselves to be lucky to receive such lovely keepsakes of your trip here to Bushmills? I hope you will take the time to visit the distillery for the tour and a sip or two."

"Well, I'll certainly try," I said vaguely.

"And your American O'Bannon, she's a nice one, as I recall, although I could be thinking of someone else entirely, seeing as her last visit here was donkey's years ago," Agatha said as she began totaling the cost of my purchases.

I handed her my credit card while she continued to talk about Maeve.

"The American is breaking up the estate, I hear. I hope it's by choice and not because she's ill or having difficulties."

Obviously, every resident of the village was curious about whatever the rumor mill had conjured up about the gift I was delivering to Maeve's relatives. I thought it best to clarify.

"Actually, my friend asked me to deliver some family memen-tos to relatives because I happened to be traveling nearby."

Agatha shrugged. "If you say so. Now, will you be taking your purchases or do you want me to send them around to the hotel when the boy comes back from rugby practice?"

The packages were not cumbersome, so I carried them easily as I walked back toward the Dart and the Pint. I had two hopes: the first that James Collins would be behind the bar and the second that the pub wouldn't be busy this time of day, so that he might be inclined to chat with me.

I admired the inside of the pub. The wooden walls were intricately carved and they surrounded decorative stained glass above the door and the window frames, which gave the pub an old-time look, but the chairs and tables appeared sturdy and modern. Three old men were having a lively conversation at one table while a lone man nursed his glass at another. James Collins was behind the bar polishing glasses.

"Mrs. Fletcher, how nice you've come to visit." He looked at the packages I was carrying. "Been to Aunt Aggie's, have you? Good pickings there."

"Oh, yes, I did quite well. I bought some lovely gifts to bring home to my family and friends."

"And where is it you would like to sit? We do have a snug. That stained glass window is the pass-through. That's if you'd be wanting some privacy." He pointed to a corner behind the bar. "The snug has been here since my grandfather opened the pub nearly a hundred years ago. It even has its own door from the outside. If I leave that alley door unlocked you could enter the snug, and unless you open the stained glass window a wee bit to order a drink, the publican or his barman would have no way of knowing you are in there."

"I know snugs became popular during a time when it wasn't seemly for a woman to be in a pub but I think today I can chance staying in the main room." I chuckled as I hoisted myself onto a barstool.

James joined in. "Ah, you know your history. Fair play to you. You have earned a drink on the house. What will it be?"

"Perhaps I could manage a half-pint of Guinness."

"Done," he said, and moved to the taps.

James set my glass down and toasted with a matching one. "*Sláinte!*"

"Good health," I replied.

"Must have been quite a scare you got, finding Michael O'Bannon on the ole cow path as you did."

James gave me an opening I was only too glad to take in the hopes of leading him into a conversation.

"I imagine finding a dead body is always upsetting, but it was devastating because I actually knew the man." I shivered slightly as if the experience was still with me.

"I suppose you'll be having nightmares for a night or two. Be sure to ask Dougal to give you a nightcap to help you drift off."

I nodded. "That is a fine idea. And you, Mr. Collins—how will you sleep, knowing that the doctor you hold responsible for your late wife's death is now dead himself?"

He leaned both elbows on the bar and lowered his voice to a whisper. "I'll tell you this. I only wish he'd died before he killed my Audra. Would have saved me a lifetime of grief. Now, if you'll excuse me, I have to tend to the storeroom."

He turned away and disappeared through a doorway off to the side.

I had mixed feelings about James Collins. While it was logical that murdering Michael wouldn't have given James any tangible benefit, vengeance is a powerful motive for some. Still, I had no concrete reason to suspect him of murdering Michael.

I was so deep in thought that I started when someone said, "Aye, Mrs. Fletcher, all alone, are you? Do you mind if I sit?"

I almost didn't recognize Constable Redding without his dark green uniform, which had been replaced by jeans, a plaid shirt, and a denim jacket.

James Collins must have heard the new voice at the bar, because he came out from the back room and immediately asked, "The usual, is it, Tim?"

When Redding nodded, Collins went right to the tap and filled a pint glass with Guinness. As he set the glass in front of the constable, Collins spoke to me.

"Ah, Mrs. Fletcher, have you met Tim Redding, only one of the finest constables the Police Service of Northern Ireland has to offer?"

"Yes, we have met. Constable Redding was quite kind to me earlier this morning."

I was pleased to see my words made Redding blush.

He looked at me and said, "Surely we can put this morning behind us, and while we are sharing a Guinness, you can call me Tim."

"That would be my pleasure, Tim, but only if you'll call me Jessica."

"Jessica it is. So, tell me, Jessica, have you fully recovered from coming across Mr. O'Bannon as you did?" Tim studied my face as he waited for an answer.

"That is difficult to say. I was out for a peaceful bike ride in a lovely village. The disruption of that tranquility was so abrupt, so disturbing, that I am sure it will stay with me for a long while to come."

Tim took a sip of Guinness, then said, "I can tell you that I have been in the PSNI for nearly three years but I have never gotten used to dead bodies. They sadden my heart. I find myself saying a prayer for their souls even as I am checking for a pulse."

"Tim, that is a lovely sentiment. You are able to see the person, not just the corpse of what once was a living, breathing human being. I think that sort of spirit makes you a stronger, more empathetic police officer." I patted his hand, causing him to blush again.

"Thank you kindly. I suppose there is no harm in telling you that I went with Inspector Finley to meet with the medical officer who examined Michael O'Bannon postmortem—that is the after-death exam."

I nodded to indicate that I understood and he went on.

"One thing that surprised me—and I'm sure Inspector Finley, although he didn't question it—was that O'Bannon's body showed signs of being beaten a week or two before his death. According to the medical officer, the body still had fading contusions—that'd be bruises—about the arms, legs, and back. There was also a small, nearly healed cut on his neck, behind his left ear. They said it looked as though someone had held a sharp, pointed object, probably a knife of some sort, to the victim's throat as if threatening to slit it. His skin was punctured a few times to make sure the message had been received."

"Enough of that serious talk. Here, nibble on these crisps and talk about happy times. I have a grand story a fisherman told me just yesterday about a friend who fell in the River Bush."

James Collins placed a bowl of what I'd call potato chips on the bar and began to regale us with comical stories of local fishermen. More than a few stories involved "the one that got away."

The pub started to get crowded, and I was feeling sluggish as the afternoon was turning into evening. Tim Redding offered to walk me back to the hotel and was kind enough to carry my packages.

I described some of the presents I'd bought and he told me I couldn't go wrong at Aunt Aggie's Attic. When we got to the hotel's front door, I reached for the packages but Redding insisted on walking me inside. As we entered the lobby, he took a long look around before surrendering my parcels.

At that moment I realized that while I remained in the country, the PSNI would be keeping a sharp eye on me until they were satisfied I was neither the killer nor the killer's next victim.

Tim bade me good evening and said he'd enjoyed our time at the pub. "We must do it again, ya hear now?"

I agreed, wondering to myself if the next time he'd bring Breen and Finley along for good measure.

Dougal Nolan was at the registration desk. "Ah, there you are, Mrs. Fletcher, and I see that you were able to find a bauble or two at Aunt Aggie's. You've two messages. Now, where did I put them? Here you go." He handed me two pieces of paper, but before I could look at them, he said, "One is from Belfast and the other is local."

"Thank you, Mr. Nolan."

As I turned toward the lobby stairs, he said, "It's been a long day for ye. I'd not be averse to sending a pot of tea, some slices of bread, and a bit of cheese and ham up to your room. Save you coming down to dinner."

Until that very moment I had not realized how exhausted I was. "Mr. Nolan, you are a mind reader. Your kindness is much appreciated."

As I walked up the stairs, I was quite happy that I wouldn't be walking down them again until morning.

I stowed my packages on the top shelf of the closet and then washed up so I'd be ready for the tray Dougal was sending up from the kitchen.

My local telephone message was from Jane Mullen. I set it aside when I saw that the Belfast message was from Godfrey Hamilton.

I was cheered when I heard his voice. "Shall I rev up my shiny Ford Fiesta and rescue you from the murderous den that Bushmills has apparently become?"

"Godfrey, how nice of you, but I am not in need of a rescue, at least not yet," I said. "However, I will keep your offer in mind."

"As soon as I heard about Michael O'Bannon, I remembered his conversation with you at the fundraiser, so I knew it was his family you were visiting. How awkward for you to be their guest when the tragedy occurred."

"Fortunately, I am staying at the River Bush Hotel rather than with the family, so I have some degree of separation. The position I am in is exactly as you describe it—awkward. You may not have heard that I was the one who came across Michael's body, while I was exploring the town on a bicycle ride. I was alone and didn't even know what telephone number to dial for help. I called my hotel and they told me to dial nine-nine-nine."

"My dear lady, that does surpass 'awkward,' and I suppose this all interferes with you accomplishing your mission of delivering the gifts from the American cousin," Godfrey said.

"Yes, it does. At this moment everything is on hold while Michael's death is being investigated, so here I stay," I said. "I think it is wisest for me to remain here until things are resolved. Godfrey, I don't know if word has reached Belfast but Michael didn't die accidentally. He was murdered."

Godfrey immediately reiterated his offer to come and drive me back to Belfast but I again refused, reminding him that since I found the body, I might easily still be considered a likely suspect.

He scoffed and told me that was preposterous but he was willing to accede to my wishes. The last thing he said before we hung up was "Remember, I am at the ready. If things get the least bit difficult, give me a jingle, and I can be there in a little over an hour—or under an hour if I push the Fiesta!"

I was deciding whether to call Jane or wait until after I'd had my tea when a knock at the door made the decision for me.

Before I turned the lock, I asked who was there, not wanting to fall into Inspector Finley's trap again. I was pleased when a soft voice said, "It's Breeda from the kitchen, ma'am. I was asked to bring you a light supper."

I opened the door and Breeda set the tray she was carrying on the dressing table. "Now, there's your pot of tea. It's strong brewed. Mr. Nolan ordered ham and cheese sandwiches with the tea but we in the kitchen thought you might like a bit of fresh broccoli, and a biscuit or two as a sweet treat."

"You've outdone yourself, Breeda. This is perfect."

After she poured my first cup of tea, Breeda left, but not before reminding me that if I found anything wanting, I needed only to ask.

As I sat sipping my tea and munching on the tastiest broccoli stalks I'd ever eaten, I realized that this was the first time I'd relaxed since discovering Michael's body. I thought about where I had found him and how his injury had looked, and I couldn't help but think that the murder had been an impulsive act. I wondered if Inspector Finley thought the same.

Chapter Fourteen

Much as I enjoyed having a light supper in my room, the next morning I was glad to have breakfast in the dining room. Menus were set out on the tables in anticipation of hearty morning appetites. As soon as I spied oatmeal with a side of fresh fruit, I knew I had a winner.

"Good morning, Mrs. Fletcher. Can I pour you a coffee? And I hope you enjoyed your light supper last evening." Breeda was at my side with a coffeepot in her hand.

"My supper was delicious and now I expect my breakfast to be the same. May I have the oatmeal with the side of fruit?"

"For the fruit, would you prefer chopped apple, chopped pear, or a mix of the two with some cranberries tossed in for good measure?"

"The fruit mix sounds perfect," I said.

"I'll have your breakfast out in two shakes. And before I forget, Maggie said that if you were to come in for breakfast, I was to ask you to kindly stop by to talk with her sometime this morning. When you've finished your breakfast, you'll probably find her in the office."

I left the dining room with two chores on my mind. I knew I should return Jane Mullen's telephone message from last night, and I wanted to find Maggie to learn why she wanted to speak to me.

As soon as I walked into the lobby and saw Claude Blanchet and Julien Lavigne deep in conversation with Dougal Nolan, I was completely distracted from my own plans and much more interested in their conversation.

I was curious if the two Frenchmen were checking out of the hotel and heading home, so I walked over and said, "Good morning, gentlemen."

All three greeted me cordially and then Claude turned back to Dougal. "I have been telling Julien that it would be *bête*—silly for us to be so close to a World Heritage Site without spending some time admiring its beauty."

"You are right about that," Dougal said. "Those basalt columns are sixty million years old, give or take a day, and they will last another sixty million unless a volcano such as the one that formed them comes along and wipes them out. I tell everyone that comes to Bushmills to travel up the road to the Giant's Causeway, take a hike and a gander, because you'll not see the likes of it again. And the birds that spend their time splashing in the water and nesting in the grass are wondrous to see."

I was waiting for an opening to become part of the conversation and there it was. I asked, "Could you tell us something about the birds? What kind are they? Where do they nest?"

Julien kindly took a step to one side, allowing me to move in between Claude and him and making me fully part of the group.

"Those science fellas who follow these things are a bit worried about the curlews. After breeding in the fields, they spend their time at the coast, and the causeway has always been a favored place for them to live for at least part of the winter season. Sadly, we are seeing their numbers decline, although I have not heard of any specific reason. Still, there are plenty of oystercatchers and redshanks that wade all around the basalt columns, not to mention ducks and razorbills that nest. For sure you'll see plenty of birds. Butterflies as well."

"That sounds spectacular." I looked at Claude Blanchet with just a hint of entreaty in my eyes. "Might I be so bold—"

He interrupted instantly. "But of course, Madame Fletcher. Julien and I insist on your charming company. Mr. Nolan, we will now need transportation for three to the Giant's Causeway. We will meet back here in, say, half an hour? You can have our ride secured by then?"

"Without a doubt," Dougal replied.

The Frenchmen thanked him and went into the dining room. I asked Dougal where I might find Maggie and he directed me down a hallway behind the reception desk.

The door was open and Maggie was sitting behind an oversized oak desk, with her nose only inches away from her computer screen.

"Good morning, Maggie. Are you busy? I hope I am not interrupting."

"Not at all. I wanted to talk to you about . . . Well, it's about

Jane. And I do hope you'll keep this conversation between the two of us. Not even Owen needs to know." Maggie was far from her usual cheery, confident self.

I nodded. "I've learned that sometimes an outsider is the best person to talk to about family problems, especially when you are not a member of the family just yet."

"I can see you do understand my position. Last night Beth Anne spoke to Michael's daughter, Deirdre, about assuming Michael's role as spokesperson for the company. Deirdre teaches nursing at the university and she's a highly regarded nurse herself."

"Ah, I see. Beth Anne is trying to keep the medical side of Marine Magic front and center by having a nurse from the family replace the doctor for interviews and such," I said, and then waited for the rest.

"Well, Jane got wind of Beth Anne's conversation with Deirdre, and not to put too fine a point on it, Jane is insisting she will have none of it. She is determined that Owen should become the new spokesperson in spite of the fact that he has no interest whatsoever." Maggie threw up her hands in frustration.

"And you fear Owen may accede to his mother's wishes," I said.

"Exactly. Honestly, I wouldn't care if Owen took the position and we stayed here in Bushmills for the rest of our lives. But that's not what Owen wants. I know it isn't. He has worked too hard to get his architecture career off the ground. And now his opportunities are right in front of him. How do I prevent his mother from ruining Owen's life?"

I selected my words carefully. "Owen is a grown man and has to make his own choices. Besides, Beth Anne is still the head of the company and has a lot to say. Everyone is at such a high emotional level right now. Any major decisions about the company are probably best left to a future date when cooler heads can prevail."

I couldn't think of anything else to suggest, so when Maggie thanked me for my input, I hurried off to grab a jacket and change into sturdy walking shoes for my trip to the Giant's Causeway. As much as I was looking forward to seeing the legendary landscape, I was far more excited at the possibility of having with Messieurs Blanchet and Lavigne a conversation that could give me better insight into Marine Magic and the future merger, if it was still in the offing, with Belle Visage.

When I came downstairs, there was a group waiting for me in the lobby. Julien Lavigne was carrying a black camera bag and he had two cameras hanging around his neck, while Claude Blanchet had added a white straw fedora to his dapper tan suit.

Dougal waved me over to meet a man wearing a blue tweed flat cap and a shiny blue rain jacket. "Hugh Tierney, here is your final passenger, Jessica Fletcher. She's an American over for a short visit."

Hugh's green eyes sparkled when he said, "And she's a smart lass if she'll not go home without spending some time at the Giant's Causeway. It is a scene you'll not soon forget. And now we are on the move."

We followed him outside and he opened the rear door of a white Citroën. I noticed my companions exchanging a look of approval at the sight of a car made in their country. I was delighted when Julien Lavigne insisted that I sit in the front.

As he pulled out of the driveway, Hugh said, "It is a short drive to the causeway but I will give you a bit of the history."

"Monsieur Nolan told us about the volcano," one of the men said.

"But not about the giant, I'm supposing. So let me tell you what many believe to be the true story. This area of Ireland was once home to an enormous giant named Fionn mac Cumhaill, known in English as Finn McCool. "

I had to smile, remembering that Maeve O'Bannon had made the same distinction when she told Seth and me about the Giant's Causeway.

Hugh continued. "It has long been believed that Finn built the causeway by flinging columns into the sea. He wanted a road to Scotland, where he would find his rival, a giant named Benandonner, and fight him to the death. Unfortunately for Finn, he found that Benandonner was much larger and probably much stronger, so Finn scooted back to Ireland and devised a plan. He wrapped himself in a diaper and cuddled in a hastily made over-sized cradle. When Benandonner crossed the causeway and came searching for Finn, he came across Finn's wife, who admitted she was married to Finn McCool and introduced the huge baby in the massive cradle as her son.

"Benandonner was no fool. If the baby was that big, he didn't want to meet the father, so he turned on his heel and hustled back to Scotland, tearing up the columns behind him, and he was never seen in Ireland again," Hugh finished and, with a flourish of his hand, said, "And in the time it takes to tell the story, here we are."

We got out of the car and Hugh gave us each a business card. "Now, I'm going to walk along with you for a bit and then I have agreed to drive a granny to babysit her daughter's bairns for a few hours. Should you need assistance or want to leave earlier than I think you will, it is best for us all that we keep in touch. Send me a quick text right now, and that way I'll have your numbers as well. Now, I suggest you hike down to the causeway itself and afterward stop by the visitors' center, which, as you'll see, has interesting exhibits, including interactive ones, plus refreshments and rest facilities."

We walked for a few minutes, and when the causeway came into view, I was stunned by the vastness.

Hugh clapped Claude on the back, tipped his cap to the three of us, and said, "I'm sure you'll be fine on your own. Have a grand time. I'll see you soonest."

After he took his leave, we three continued on. I'd expected the causeway to be a visual place, which it certainly was. I hadn't realized that we'd be able to climb and walk on thousands of hexagonal basalt columns, some appearing to be nearly forty feet tall. Those formed high walls in clifflike formations while the shorter ones went right into the sea. People were scattered here and there, some climbing, some resting. I'm sure that they all were as enthralled as I was.

Julien was in his glory snapping pictures, sometimes with both cameras simultaneously.

As we walked along, Claude Blanchet said, "It is truly amazing, is it not, Madame Fletcher?"

"Yes, it is. I had no idea this area would be so captivating, completely open to one and all. But, please, call me Jessica."

"We are honored to be invited to do so. *S'il te plaît*, you must call us Claude and Julien," he replied.

We climbed to the grassy top of the highest columns, often using the hexagonal tops of various pillars as stepping-stones. I offered to take pictures of Julien with a variety of views of the causeway as his backdrop.

He returned the favor by insisting on taking some pictures of me. "These will be wonderful. Keepsakes, and you can give some to the O'Bannon who lives in America. I am sure she would love to have them, *non?*"

"She would indeed. Thank you for thinking of her."

And for reminding me I would be remiss if I didn't take more pictures in Bushmills before I returned home, I thought.

We walked to the farthest edge of the cliff, which jutted deep into the North Atlantic Ocean.

"Amazing, is it not? According to Monsieur Nolan, fierce waves have been lapping against these pillars for sixty million years and still they stand straight and firm." Claude pointed to the waves, which were consistently reaching, receding, and reaching the columns, again and again. "We see it right here."

"This place is absolutely one of nature's finer miracles. Or perhaps it was the hard work of Finn McCool that gave us this glorious vision." I laughed.

"I confess that I prefer to believe in nature rather than mythical creatures," Claude said.

I was about to agree when Julien said something in French and sprinted away. I looked at Claude askance.

"The *photographe* has become inspired. He is going down there." Claude pointed below us to where several teenagers were jumping from column to column at the very edge of the ocean. "Julien has decided to stand on the spot where those young ones are cavorting, turn his back on the ocean, and take pictures of the entire landscape. This trip has been far more stressful than we could have imagined. I am glad to see him happy."

"It sounds as though you two are good friends," I said.

"We have worked closely together for more than thirty-five

years. In that amount of time two colleagues either become friends or they struggle to hide that they loathe each other." Claude laughed. "Julien and I managed to avoid loathing. Our wives are also good friends, which makes our relationship nicer, more *amical*."

We stood for a while saying nothing, taking in the natural beauty that surrounded us. I decided to take the opportunity to have a "just between us" conversation and chose to start it rather bluntly.

"I guess it is time I confess that I also overheard bits and pieces of the argument Beth Anne and Michael had in the library on the night of the dinner party."

Claude gave me a pointedly measured look but did not reply, so I continued. "I'm sure you didn't notice me, but after they left, I saw you rise from your chair. I realized instantly that you not only were closer to them but must have been there for the entire quarrel and heard much more than I did."

When I stopped speaking, it took him a while to answer. "Truthfully, Jessica, I was astounded. Their conversation made so little sense. Beth Anne and Michael were disagreeing over shipping, of all things."

I had to concur. "Now, that is surprising. Product distribution is the heart of any business. Without distribution nothing can be sold."

"Very true. In all of our discussions about the upcoming merger, it has been agreed by all concerned that we would continue on our usual distribution path because it worked for our products, mainly because our factories are located near our suppliers. Marine Magic would continue with their supply chain for the same reasons."

I could see the sense in that. "There is no advantage in changing what works. I still don't see the cause of the argument."

"Privately, I can tell you that as the negotiating team, Julien and I wanted the shipping to stay the way it has always been because Julien's brother-in-law owns the company that we have always used and Belle Visage *is* his foremost customer. Michael wanted to bring in a new company, one completely unknown to those of us who do business on the Continent."

On one level, that made sense in terms of billing and trustworthiness, but with Sweeney Brothers here in Ireland and Belle Visage manufacturing their products somewhere in France, I had to wonder what the overall cost would be. I thought I was catching on.

"You mean, he wanted Conor Sweeney and Sweeney Brothers Shipping to integrate your product distribution with Marine Magic's shipping."

Claude stared out over the sea for a few moments before he said, "You would think that would be the issue, but *non*. What had Beth Anne so upset was that Michael had in mind a shipper who would be completely new to both companies. She thought it was the worst possible time to make additional changes and I must say I believe she was correct. In business it is often best to make a modification and evaluate its effect on the company before implementing another change. I am sure she would want to complete the merger and iron out any problems that may cause before considering additional alterations to the business plan."

I was dumbfounded. "By any chance did Michael mention the name of the shipping company he was proposing?"

"I am not likely to forget. He called it Worldwide and I think that was the point. That shipper has a name that fit with the image Michael wanted for the new, international company that would develop from our merger."

I had more questions but Claude ended the conversation by suggesting that we climb back down, and signal Julien to move inland before an ocean wave knocked him off the low basalt columns he was jumping between and floated him clear to Scotland.

About an hour later, after Julien had taken pictures of the Giant's Causeway from every possible angle, Claude suggested we go into the visitors' center in search of a cup of tea. Once there we immediately got caught up in the interactive exhibits, and I wandered through the gift shop, but among all the excellent choices, I could not find quite the right present for Maeve. Probably because my mind kept drifting back to Claude's account of Beth Anne and Michael's conversation. I couldn't help but wonder how far Beth Anne would have gone to prevent Michael from making changes if she thought they would hurt the company.

The three of us were having tea and biscuits when Hugh Tierney texted to say that he was on his way back to the causeway and ask our whereabouts. Claude replied that we were in the visitors' center, and Hugh answered that he would join us in two shakes.

When Hugh arrived, he greeted us like long-lost friends he hadn't seen in a decade or more. Then he settled into his tea and biscuits and asked what we thought of the Giant's Causeway. Claude and I praised it but Julien ran away with the conversation, vividly describing every bird and plant that he'd photographed. He also surprised at least me when he mentioned that he had seen basalt columns that had four or eight sides rather than the usual six.

"'Tis observant you are and that will do you well. I've decided we'll take the long way back to the hotel, let you see a bit of the countryside," Hugh said.

None of us objected, but I, for one, was anxious to get back to familiar territory in the hopes I would be able to gather some information on a shipping company named Worldwide.

Chapter Fifteen

Hugh regaled us with jokes and stories as he drove along country lanes and roads, showing us this church or that two-hundred-year-old thatched-roof farmhouse. He did stop in front of the Old Bushmills Distillery to spend a few minutes telling us the history of the buildings and the whiskey. He reminded us not to go home without taking the distillery tour.

It had been a wonderful afternoon but I was relieved when we finally pulled into the hotel driveway. After we'd all gotten out of the cab, Hugh started to pull away and then stopped, rolled down his window, and said, "I hope to see you all at the trad session tonight." He waved and was gone.

Julien was puzzled. "Trad?"

Claude laughed. "I am sure we will learn of it from the Nolans."

However, when we walked into the lobby, there was not a Nolan to be seen. I said good-bye to Claude and Julien and was about to hurry to my room when the young porter who was manning the reception desk called my name. According to the message he handed me, Seth Hazlitt had called shortly after I'd left for the Giant's Causeway. I called back immediately, hoping to catch Seth outside of office hours.

"Jessica, good to hear from you." Seth sounded more cheerful than I'd expected.

"Is everything all right? It's not like you to make an international phone call. I assumed you would call my cell if it was an emergency."

"Calm down, woman." Seth raised his voice a tiny bit. "There is no emergency here, which is exactly why I called your hotel rather than your cell. I certainly couldn't be sure what is going on in your part of the world. I have no reason to interrupt whatever you might be doing."

"I spent a lovely afternoon playing the role of tourist, and I can tell you, it relaxed me a thousand percent. Everything else is not going well. The police are investigating, although I don't see much progress. Maeve's family members are completely topsy-turvy. They were in the middle of a business merger and everything has come to a standstill. One minute they are in mourning. The next minute they are arguing about the business. Until they settle down, I can't find a way to fulfill my promise to deliver Maeve's grandfather's paintings in the way she has asked me to do. Speaking of Maeve—"

"That's one of the reasons I called," Seth said. "I want to reassure you that I stopped by to spend some time with Maeve this morning. From a medical standpoint, she seems fine. Even let me take her blood pressure, which was one hundred percent normal. I'll keep my eye on her at least until you get back, but I think she's going to weather this storm pretty well."

"Oh, Seth, I hope you are right. There is one cousin, named Beth Anne, who is wound so tight that if Maeve knows her as well as I suspect she does, Maeve might think Beth Anne had a motive to get Michael out of her way in the business. Another cousin, Beth Anne's sister, Jane, doesn't seem likely to kill a spider, much less a relative, but I've seen tiny glimpses underneath her 'sugar wouldn't melt in my mouth' facade, and there is a woman with a will of steel when she is determined to get what she wants."

"And what exactly is it that you've decided she wanted badly enough to kill for?" Seth sounded as though he was humoring me rather than being actually curious.

"That is the problem. I can't find any compelling issues between Jane and her cousin Michael. I don't know enough about any of these people to figure out how their relationships are going." I was feeling more dejected by the moment.

"Jess, I know that when something like this happens, your curiosity gets the best of you and you cannot rest until the murderer is brought to justice. But as it happens, you are in a foreign country. The only person you really know who has been involved with the victim for a lifetime is back here in Cabot Cove tending to your seedlings—which, by the way, Maeve mentioned are doing quite well. So please let the police do their job, and as soon as you can comfortably do so, hand over those paintings, call Susan Shevlin, and come on home." Seth sounded firm yet caring.

"You are right, of course." I sighed. "It's just that—"

"You hate to leave a puzzle unsolved." Seth laughed and I joined in.

"Okay. I surrender. I will continue enjoying Ireland as a tourist if you will cross your fingers in the hope that Michael's body is released and properly buried. Once that happens I can fulfill Maeve's wishes and skedaddle."

We hung up but not before I again charged Seth with keeping an eye on Maeve, and in turn, he again encouraged me to come home as soon as was practical.

I took off my dampish clothes and shoes, freshened up, and changed into a pleated navy blue skirt and a beige sweater set. In case I had to walk a distance, I took a couple of minutes to choose a pair of shoes. As I slid into a comfortable pair of pumps, I got an idea.

I went downstairs and asked the young man at the reception desk where I might find Dougal or Maggie. He hesitated about Dougal but was quick to tell me that Maggie was in the back office. I thanked him and moved away before he could tell me that she did not want to be disturbed.

Maggie's door was open; still I tapped gently rather than barge in. When she looked up from her work, she gave me a broad smile.

"Jessica, I heard you went exploring the Giant's Causeway. And what did you think of the sixty-million-year-old attraction that brings visitors to our quiet corner of Ireland every day of the year?"

"Before I left home, Maeve told me that a visit there would

renew my spirits and I believe that was totally accurate. I feel completely energized," I said before I moved on to the real reason I'd sought her out. "I have a chore to do and thought perhaps you could help me. Can you tell me where I might find a shipping company named Worldwide?"

"Hmm, I've actually never heard of them but I can refer you to a few places in town that handle transport of all kinds of goods all over the world," Maggie said.

I decided to be as close to honest as I could. "I can't tell you how I know but I think Michael had some business dealing with them, er, recently."

Maggie looked alarmed. "Even if we knew where it was, do you think it is wise for you to look for this Worldwide company all alone?"

Discouraged, I said, "Suppose Michael's only connection to the place was that he mailed a package? I really didn't want to bother Inspector Finley."

Maggie opened her desk drawer and pulled out her purse. "Who said anything about the PSNI? Come along. I'll introduce you to the very man who'll know the exact spot if this place exists anywhere in County Antrim."

She marched off at such a stride that I had to pick up my pace to keep up with her. We moved quickly through the lobby and the dining room. When we got to the swinging doors to the kitchen, Maggie pointed to the right-hand door and said, "This way."

There were at least eight people bustling around in the kitchen. Breeda looked up from a corner where she was emptying a dishwasher and gave me a shy wave while everyone else ignored us and continued with their food prep.

Maggie stood in the center of the room, hands on her hips. "Can anybody tell me where Old Joe Fogarty is hiding now?"

A pert young woman laughed. "He isn't hiding, ma'am. He's out the back seeing to the potatoes."

"Thank you, Eileen." Maggie signaled me to follow her.

We went through a door to what looked like a food storage room piled high with crates of boxed goods, canned goods, and some hardier produce items such as turnips and apples.

Maggie kept walking until she opened a door to the outside and called, "Mr. Fogarty, sir, are you out here?"

"I am indeed, Miss Maggie. How can I serve ye this fine day?"

We stepped outside and a man I could describe only as ancient was standing over a table. A bulky pile of potatoes was to his right. He pointed to a huge stockpot filled with water and potatoes that had been peeled and quartered.

"Ye can check the billycan yourself, miss. I've not been slacking."

Maggie laughed. "As if you'd ever be on the slacker rolls. No, I'm here because I want you to meet my friend and our honored guest, Jessica Fletcher. Jessica, this is Joe Fogarty. The only reason we tolerate him is that he's the best kitchen hand in all of Ireland."

He smiled at the compliment, not at all self-conscious about his few missing teeth. "Happy to meet ye, missus." He raised his wet hands, the right one holding a potato peeler, and said, "Best we don't shake on it."

I smiled and said I was pleased to meet him.

Fogarty looked at Maggie. "And I suppose there's a reason for it?"

"Ah, there's no fooling you, is there? Jessica is looking for a place I never heard of and I knew there was only one man who knows every nook and cranny of County Antrim, and that would be you, Joe Fogarty."

He grinned, held out his left hand, and fluttered his fingers. "Bring it on, then."

Maggie looked at me and gave a nearly imperceptible nod.

"I hope you can help me. I am trying to find a shipping company called Worldwide. Do you know of it?" I asked.

"Worldwide, is it, then? What are you ladies planning to do, ship stolen diamonds at half price, or maybe restock Ireland with the wild boars that have been gone these many centuries?"

The incredulous look on Mr. Fogarty's face told me that I had hit on something. I just wasn't sure what. I was trying to think of an answer when Maggie said simply, "So you know it, then?"

"'Course I do. It's only that I'm gobsmacked, seeing a fine lady such as herself would know about the likes of Worldwide, but there's nothing to be said for these modern women." Fogarty shook his head.

I was searching for a snappy answer but there was no need. He continued speaking. "Prepare yourselves to be in the car for a while. You need to be taking Main Street until it becomes Castle-cat Road. Go along there for a good while, and once you've passed Derrykeighan but before you get to Dervock, you'll come across Worldwide."

Fogarty looked quite satisfied with himself but Maggie was not so sure.

"That's all farmland between the two. Wouldn't I have noticed ages ago if there was a big shipping company along the road?" she said.

"And who said anything about the size of it? You've only to look out your driver's-side window. There'll come a time when, among the farms, you'll see a farmlike group of buildings, including a barn, homes for the livestock, even a bothy or two. Keep an eye out, for there'll be a small sign next to the drive telling all who pass that it's the location of Worldwide Shipping."

"Well, that's new to me but I'm sure we'll find it. Thank you for your time." Maggie turned to go back the way we came.

As I was beginning to add my thanks, Mr. Fogarty signaled me to silence and pointed to Maggie's retreating back. "She's a bright young thing, innit? That Owen Mullen could do far worse. And ye can do me the favor of telling the O'Bannon clan I said so."

With that, he pulled a potato off the bulky pile and began to peel it.

Maggie left a note for Dougal at the front desk and off we went in a minuscule white two-door car.

When I said I'd never seen one quite like it, Maggie said, "It's an Abarth. Made in Italy. Sporty and good on mileage. I love driving it. Now, you should have a bit of a tourist look-see, because we'll be on the road awhile before we need to examine every turnoff and driveway in our search for Worldwide."

As soon as we were out of the village of Bushmills, we rambled through farmland with well-tended fields on both sides of the road. Twice I saw a flock of black-faced sheep herded by long-haired black-and-white border collies.

Maggie slowed down as we entered a village square. "This is Derrykeighan and you can catch one or two buses just there." She pointed out the window. "According to Joe Fogarty, somewhere once we pass here is the sign that should introduce us to Worldwide Shipping."

We continued on and the road remained the same, mile after mile of tidy fields, many planted and a few lying fallow. I was so entranced by a dozen or so cows resting comfortably in a field, I nearly missed the sign, but Maggie was sharper eyed.

"Look, Jessica, right there. There are two cars behind me; I'll have to turn in the next drive and come back."

Sure enough, nearly hidden in the hedges on the far side of an extra-wide driveway was a small white sign about six inches high. It read WORLDWIDE SHIPPING in faded blue letters.

Maggie circled in the next driveway and went back, and we drove onto a rutted driveway that led downhill to some terribly broken-down barnlike buildings. She stopped the car and said, "I suppose we should look around for an employee who can tell us about the company."

I agreed. "We've come this far. It looks as though either they have gone completely out of business or perhaps they moved and neglected to put up a sign with the new address."

"Well, that is certainly possible if they transact most of their business by telephone or over the Internet. We rarely get any walk-ins looking for rooms at the hotel. I daresay far more than ninety percent of our business is by phone or email. But I think it's more likely you are right about this place. They seem to have gone out of business entirely."

Chapter Sixteen

Before we got out of the car, Maggie tooted the horn several times. "You never know when there is a watchman asleep on the job. But not likely he could sleep through that. Shall we have a look, then?"

We walked toward the closest building. It was nearly two stories tall and I was amazed it was still standing. One of the extra-wide doors was closed while the other was missing entirely. As soon as we entered, we could see the sky through holes scattered about the roof. Pieces of wood were hanging from what was once a hayloft.

"Mind your head." Maggie pointed to a cracked plank forming a vee a foot or two in front of us. "We're in serious danger of any of this lumber landing on us like a guided missile. What a disappointment there is nothing here. I expected at least to find a broken-down lorry kept for parts that might have a name written on the side. Should we bother taking a look at the shanty next door?"

The small wooden building with broken windows and no door at all that Maggie called a shanty turned out to have once been the office of whatever company had occupied the site. Inside, we found two desks and four file cabinets. If they had been made of wood, exposure to the weather would have destroyed them, but they were all made of metal. Most of the drawers were missing, and the few that remained seemed to be empty until Maggie discovered a file folder in the bottom drawer of the smaller desk.

Her yelp of joy turned to disappointment when she opened it only to find—nothing. It was absolutely empty.

"Lot of good this will do us," she said.

But I noticed something that might be helpful. "Let me see. Look here."

I pointed to the file's tab, where a small piece of label remained. There were only two typed letters still visible, RT, followed by a symbol, ☼, that I thought looked like a circle with prongs.

"We have no idea what the folder was named but I'm going to hang on to this in case something comes to mind. The symbol may give us a clue."

Maggie nodded but I could see she was still dejected, so I tried to cheer her. "I have been writing mysteries for quite a while now, and the one thing I am certain of is that anything, even something as seemingly insignificant as an empty file folder, can lead to an answer. Now let's go have some tea and biscuits."

We pulled out of the driveway and headed back the way we had come, and we hadn't gotten far when a large black car zoomed past us in the other direction. I was sure I recognized the driver.

"Maggie, slow down." I craned my neck and watched the black car turn down the driveway we'd left only moments ago.

"Jessica, what is it?" Maggie braked while she looked in the rearview mirror to make sure there wasn't a car right behind us. "Did you forget something?"

"Dermot Kerrigan! I am sure that Dermot Kerrigan was driving the car that passed us, and I saw it turn in to the Worldwide driveway."

Without any warning, Maggie sped to the next driveway and made a U-turn. Then she said, "I will pass by very slowly while you look down the drive and see what he's about."

"I must say, Maggie, you have a knack for sleuthing."

As soon as we reached the driveway, I spotted Dermot Kerrigan coming out of the barn and walking toward his car.

"I am not sure what he could have done in such a brief span of time but it looks as though he is getting ready to leave. Keep going so he doesn't see us."

"Don't you want to confront him?"

I could see Maggie had some tiger in her even as she did as I asked.

"I very much do but not at this time. Trial lawyers have a saying that goes something like 'Never ask a witness in court any question if you don't already know the answer.' And our problem is, we have no idea what Kerrigan is doing on the site. He could be the landowner, for all we know."

"Hmm, true." Maggie slipped into the next driveway and turned the car around again. "If I speed up, perhaps we can follow him."

"We may not need to. Are you familiar with Bayhead Road?"

Maggie hooted. "There aren't so many roads around Bushmills that I wouldn't have driven on any one of them a thousand times."

"Well, I did hear in passing that Kerrigan may have an interest in an import-export firm on Bayhead Road." I decided there was no real reason to mention that Chief Inspector Finley was my source.

Maggie didn't press the issue. She merely said, "Haven't you done well for yourself? Barely here a minute and you have your own pipeline to local gossip. Old Joe Fogarty would be extremely jealous, should he ever find out."

"Then we'd best not tell him," I said, causing us both to laugh.

We headed back north, passed through the village of Bushmills, and then stayed left until the road ended.

"Here we are," Maggie said. "Now, do you want me to make a right or a left turn? As you can see, going straight will put us right in the North Atlantic."

"Since we don't know exactly what we are looking for, turn as you like. I must say, this is a lovely road, houses on one side of the street and dunes and ocean on the other," I said.

"A far cry from the mess we saw at the Worldwide site. Not a dilapidated or abandoned building in sight."

"That's it, Maggie. That's the missing puzzle piece," I said. "Suppose you wanted to move goods of any kind, from something as small as handkerchiefs to something as large as a tractor, from one country to another. In the United States, I know I would have to follow rules and get permits. I assume it is the same way here."

"It is. I can't imagine any country in the world that doesn't have rules for transport." She stopped. "So are you saying this is about running a business but going to ground, as it were? Keeping it hidden, so to speak?"

"I suspect it is. Suppose a business like Worldwide was heavily in debt or failing for some other reason. Someone could come along and buy it. Not for the location or the equipment or even the customer base but for the transport permits," I said.

"Brilliant! And if anyone was to question a shipment, well, all the paperwork would be in order," Maggie said. Then she said, "But I don't get the why of it. Why would anyone go to all that trouble? Why not start a company of their own? Get permits of their own?"

"Probably because you don't want anyone to know the business is yours, or—"

"Or"—Maggie was growing more excited by the moment—"if you are the likes of Dermot Kerrigan, you can't afford to have the permit office look too closely at your background. You'd stand a good chance of being turned down. Let's go home. I think we've earned our tea and biscuits."

We walked into the hotel lobby, laughing like two longtime friends who'd shared their hundredth adventure together. Dougal was standing at the reception desk. He gave us a stern look, which didn't bother Maggie a bit.

"What have you two been about? Owen Mullen is looking for you." He handed a message slip to Maggie. "And so you don't feel unwanted, Jane Mullen has called you twice." He handed me two small memos.

Jane. I'd completely forgotten that she'd called me last night.

I looked at Maggie and Dougal. "Now I've done it. This is her second and third call. I'm sure I am in trouble."

"Not at all. I took her last call a wee bit ago and I told her that you were enjoying this fine day at the Giant's Causeway. Not one bit of untruth there, since she never asked about the time you left or the time you'd return."

Dougal's grin reminded me of some of my students who hadn't done their homework but were hoping to be forgiven.

"And don't either of you accept any invitations for this evening. There's a trad session at the Dart tonight and it's promised to be a right hooley. Danny Donovan and the boys are driving over from Rosnashane. No one blows the whistle quite like Danny."

I looked at Maggie, who said, "The tin whistle—it's like a flute of sorts."

"Oh, yes, I know. I've heard it played many times. My mind was still elsewhere for the moment," I said.

"No wonder after the day you've had," she answered.

"I don't like the sound of that," Dougal said. "Have you two been causing trouble while you were out and about?"

"Don't be silly, Da. We wouldn't think of it." Maggie turned to me. "Early dinner, then, Jessica, because we have a grand evening ahead: a traditional Irish music session with lots of singing and perhaps even a dance or two."

As soon as I entered my room, I kicked off my shoes, plugged in the kettle, and dialed Jane's number. She didn't seem the least bit upset that I'd taken a while to return her calls but that might have been because she was in full hostess mode.

"Jessica, I do hope you enjoyed your trip to the Giant's Causeway. Such an unforgettable place." Without waiting for my reply, she continued. "Michael's children, Deirdre and Niall, are here. I've persuaded them to stay with me rather than rattle around in their father's house. I can only imagine how uncomfortable that would be for them both. Just think of how sad it would be. At any rate they are anxious to meet you, so I was hoping that you would come to tea tomorrow. That way we could all spend some quiet time reminiscing about Michael."

I thought "reminiscing" was an odd choice of words and said so. "Jane, I am certainly willing to join you and your family for tea but please don't expect me to contribute much in the way of memories. I met Michael only twice, once in Belfast and then here at your house."

"Ah, but, Jessica, I'm sure you'd have plenty to contribute. We've been told that you discovered the body and that is an experience none of us can imagine. See you at four, then." And she hung up.

I stared at the phone in my hand. Had Jane actually invited me to tea tomorrow so that I could tell Michael's children any gruesome details that the police might have omitted when notifying them of their father's death?

I was determined to figure out a work-around for that, but in the meantime I was going to have my dinner, and then I'd be off to the Dart and the Pint to enjoy some music and fun. I put my phone on its charger to be sure I'd have enough power to record a song or two and send it off to Maeve.

Inspector Finley was standing in the lobby and talking on his cell phone when I came down the stairs. He waved me over as he slid the phone into his pocket. "I am just after signing out for the evening. I am now officially off duty, so I can assure you that when I say, 'How are you?' it's a social question, not an interrogation." He laughed at his somewhat awkward jest.

"I am quite well. Thank you. I have had a lovely day. I was fortunate enough to spend much of it at the Giant's Causeway with Messieurs Blanchet and Lavigne."

The inspector's face became guarded. "And how did that go? Did you enjoy the gentlemen's company?"

"I did but I am surprised that is what you asked me rather than whether I enjoyed visiting what Hugh Tierney told me is often called the Eighth Wonder of the World."

"Hugh Tierney, was it? And did he happen to drive the three of you to the causeway? Or did you meet up with the Frenchmen later on, by accident, like?" Finley asked.

"Inspector, in spite of your earlier declaration, this is beginning to sound far more like an interrogation than a social conversation. Why don't you tell me what really is on your mind?"

"You've seen right through me, Mrs. Fletcher. Let's step outside."

He took my arm, and as we headed for the door, Dougal Nolan called from the reception desk, "Is everything all right there, Mrs. Fletcher?"

Finley answered for me. "Only after a breath of fresh air. She'll be back momentarily."

I raised my eyebrows. "Well, that's a comfort to know."

"Don't get testy on me. It's only a bit of privacy I'm after," Finley said as he led me to the middle of the parking lot. He looked around to be sure there was no one in earshot.

"As we've discussed, I have a high regard for your powers of observation of what I suppose could be called the human condition, so since you spent so much of the day with Claude Blanchet and Julien Lavigne, I am curious as to your impressions of the two. I'm only after finishing my second interview with each of them and I continue to get the feeling that they are holding something back. Why do you think that is?"

"Inspector, I'd be hard-pressed to determine anything about what prompts your feelings." I smiled as though we were discussing the weather, or a sale at Aunt Aggie's Attic.

Finley's return smile had an annoying aura of "gotcha" even though I was sure I hadn't dropped any hint of my thoughts about the Frenchmen. "No need for you to play watching and waiting with me. If you know something, anything at all, about the men, their company, or their relations with the O'Bannons, this would be a good time to tell me."

I decided that for the moment, mentioning Claude's eavesdropping in the library would not add anything of significance to the inspector's case. After all, I had already told him that I had overheard part of the disagreement between Michael and Beth Anne. Wasn't it up to Beth Anne to tell Finley the subject matter? And for all I knew, if the Frenchmen had raised the hackles on the back of Finley's neck, the cause might well have nothing at all to do with the argument, although even I wondered what else would have caused the Frenchmen to be evasive.

"Inspector, I wish I could help you, I really do, but between Hugh Tierney's fascinating jokes and stories and the breathtaking splendor of the Giant's Causeway, I am afraid I paid very little attention to my companions. I can tell you only that they were complete gentlemen."

"Well, that's a disappointment." As soon as Finley realized

how it sounded, he tried to correct himself. "Not their being gentlemen—that's as it should be—but I was hoping they'd dropped a crumb or two of guilt and that you'd picked it up."

"I'm sorry that I couldn't be more help. Have a good evening, Inspector," I said.

"I intend to. The wife's making my favorite supper: sausage, potato, and onion all cooked together in beef broth with a touch of bacon. You might know it as Dublin coddle. Enjoy your night as well." And he strode across the parking lot to his car.

I walked back into the hotel in search of a light dinner and hoping I'd done the right thing. Perhaps the shipping issue was more important than I realized, but if so, I would still have bet on Kerrigan being the troublemaker rather than the Frenchmen.

Chapter Seventeen

I needn't have worried about dinner, as there was plenty to eat along with the drinks that were being served when Dougal, Maggie, and I arrived at the Dart and the Pint. The atmosphere was lively in anticipation of the evening's entertainment. James Collins passed our table, carrying an extra chair to a group gathered in a far corner. On his way back to the bar, he stopped.

"I'm glad you've come to join us for this grand evening, Mrs. Fletcher. You won't regret it." Before I could reply, he looked at Maggie. "And what have you done with Owen Mullen this fine night? Tossed him aside for Danny Donovan when the entire town knows Ellen Clancy has her sights set on him good and proper?"

Maggie shook her head. "The cousins are all in town and having a quiet evening together, catching up and that. Better for Owen to join them."

"Aye, that's the truth of it," James said. "I'd little respect for the man who's now gone but his children deserve to grieve. Is there no date set for the funeral service?"

Dougal said, "The family arranged with the McAvoy brothers to take care of everything but Michael hasn't yet been turned over to them. There is nothing to be done until such time. . . ."

James smiled at Maggie. "Well, you tell Owen he was missed, and when he has a spare minute or two, his first pint is on me. Speaking of, shall I send over pints?"

Dougal and Maggie agreed and James was not at all put out when I asked for tea.

The band was organizing their instruments and getting ready to play. An older man was tuning a violin that there in the pub would surely have been called a fiddle while the accordion player was wiping his keyboard with a soft cloth. A third man opened a long case and took out a flute. I assumed that he was Danny Donovan and that the short case that rested on his knee held his tin whistle. Next to him, a stout man wearing a typical Irish cable-knit wool sweater was examining a round framed drum about a foot and a half in diameter.

"I've seen that type of hand drum before but I can't remember what it's called," I said.

"You mean the *bodhrán*," Dougal said. "My own da used to play one. Made them himself from goatskin and the odd piece of wood."

"Goatskin—I had no idea," I said.

"Probably not that one." Dougal nodded his head toward the band. "Today most *bodhráns* are made of synthetics. Ah, and look who is here."

For a second I thought he was appreciative of the drinks the waitress began setting on the table, but just over her shoulder, I saw Conor Sweeney moving past.

Dougal called out to him, "Conor, boyo, there's an empty seat right here."

"Thank you kindly, Dougal, but I've arranged to meet with some of the lads." He pointed to a group of men on the other side of the pub. "Mrs. Fletcher, it's good to see you out for a bit of fun after all the stress you've been under. Enjoy your evening, now."

He moved to his table, where there was a general roar of greeting.

Dougal furrowed his brow. "Now, that's an odd matchup for a night in the pub. Conor Sweeney usually fancies himself socially above those in his employ and yet here he is having a pint with some truckers and movers. I wonder what's the occasion."

Maggie laughed. "Don't be so nosy, Da. Maybe it's a birthday or someone is getting married."

Danny Donovan stood, which silenced the pub crowd almost instantly. After he introduced the other band members, they went right into a stirring mix of what he promised would be reels, jigs, and flings. In short order nearly everyone, including me, was clapping their hands or stamping their feet.

At one point a young couple in the back of the room came forward and did a traditional dance, which Maggie told me was called the Stack of Barley. Having one couple on the dance floor wasn't enough for the band, so they began to play a waltz, which brought three more couples along. I was pleased to see that Tim Redding, dancing with a petite blond girl, was among them. He gave me a wave and a smile as they danced by.

At the end of the waltz, Danny Donovan announced that the

band would take a short break. "But no one's to leave, ya hear? We've a special treat tonight. Aileen and Orla Byrne are here. . . ."

Apparently, he needed to say no more. Everyone cheered and clapped. I looked at Maggie, who said, "Only the best Irish step dancers in the county. You couldn't have picked a better moment to visit. We're in for a fine time tonight." Then she squeezed my hand. "I do hope that seeing how the town and its people really appreciate life will help erase the memory of your coming across Michael such as you did."

"Maggie, you are very sweet to be concerned. But I learned a long time ago that the only person responsible for a crime is the person who committed it. No matter how often we hear on the news that the murderer claimed that the victim or some other person or a confluence of events caused his actions, we know and he knows that he has only himself to blame."

Maggie's smile was filled with relief. "I've been so worried that you'd gained a bad feeling about the town and we'd never see you again. What a loss to Bushmills that would be."

A loud bang startled us and we turned to see Conor Sweeney bending to try to lift the chair he'd apparently knocked over when he stood. He looked around and gave his tablemates a crooked grin. "I need to use the facilities."

And he loped away toward a long hallway even as James Collins was coming around from the back bar. Conor's shoulder bounced off the wall at least once that I saw.

Dougal said, "This is happening far too often of late. Conor has always had a reputation for not knowing when to slow down his drink, but this sloppiness . . . He's lucky James hasn't refused him service, although that may yet happen. I'd hate to see it. Conor is a fine man with a wee problem."

Most of the patrons resumed their conversation but we three watched as one of Conor's tablemates righted the chair. James thanked him and then followed Conor down the hallway.

Dougal grimaced. "Well, that's the end of it. We won't be seeing Conor again this evening. James isn't going to take a chance of having so fine a night ruined by—I have to call it as it is—by a sloppy drunk."

"How do you know?" I didn't doubt Dougal's assessment, but I did wonder how he'd reached it.

Dougal smiled. "As a landlord, who in my turn has had to turn out a person who's drunk one too many, I can tell you that while we each have our own style, the goal is to remove the person from the premises with as little fuss as possible. You can just ignore those movie scenes where the owner comes from behind the bar carrying a bat and loudly orders the drunk to leave. That is bad for business.

"We all have our tricks of the trade. I can tell you exactly how James will handle it. He will wait outside the gents', and when Conor comes out, James will politely escort him to the rear door, which is a few feet farther down the hall. And that will be the end of it."

"Oh, but if Conor couldn't stand up without knocking over a chair, surely he is in no condition to drive home," I said.

"You're right about that and even Conor agrees with you. He gave up his car-driving license a year or so back. He'll probably walk home. It's not that far. Or he'll ride his fancy new bicycle—nice one that, but not nearly in a class with our Donards. Speaking of pints, I think I will have another." Dougal stood, ending a conversation that I suspected might have been making him uncomfortable. "Can I get you ladies anything? Perhaps some crisps?"

The Byrne sisters were young, talented, energetic dancers. They held their torsos ramrod straight while their feet went flying. The entire room stood cheering when they took their final bows. Danny Donovan made a glowing speech, thanking Aileen and Orla, and everyone clapped and stomped.

Then the band began to play a set of softer tunes and the audience settled down. My seat was facing the front door, so I was the first one to notice the door open and Owen Mullen walk in with another young man.

Maggie saw them as well, and while I thought she would be happy to see Owen, she whispered half to herself, "Oh, dear Lord, what is he thinking?" Then she leaned over and said to me, "I hope that won't make the rest of the evening too thorny for you. Owen's gone and brought Niall O'Bannon with him."

When Owen and Niall arrived at our table, Dougal stood and shook Niall's hand. "I am sorry for your trouble. Your father was a fine man. Here, use my seat. I'll be after finding us some more chairs." And he moved away.

After Maggie expressed her condolences, she introduced me to Niall. I was saying how sorry I was about the loss of his father when Dougal came back with two chairs and offered to get Owen and Niall drinks. Owen opted for sparkling water while Niall said a straight whiskey would do him no harm.

The band picked up in both volume and tempo just as we all settled around the table. Niall and Owen accepted my offer to share the crisps that Dougal bought earlier and we listened along until the band took their next break.

Owen's glass was half empty but Niall had yet to sip his whiskey, although I had noticed him turning the glass in his hand a few times.

When the music stopped, both Dougal and Maggie tried for small talk. Dougal asked about Niall's trip from Belfast and Maggie inquired about his sister, Deirdre. Niall obliged with minimal answers. Then he tossed back his whiskey so decisively that he garnered all our attention.

"When I asked Owen to bring me here tonight, I am sure he thought it was so that I could see my lifelong friends and neighbors, the Nolans, or possibly to meet Mrs. Fletcher, who, I've been told, discovered my father's body. Neither is correct. I came here to confront the man who some people believe murdered my father." His eyes filled with tears. "Everyone knows James Collins held my father responsible for Audra's death. There was even talk about a lawsuit, which I for one would have relished, but that came to naught. I've been told that James's anguish continued to grow and his hatred of my father more so. But I can see this is not the time for me to face him man-to-man. I am sorry to have disturbed your evening. Mrs. Fletcher, I will see you at tea tomorrow. Good night, all."

He got up and headed for the door. Owen looked at us helplessly until Maggie said, "Go, would you?"

Then he too went out the door.

Dougal drained his pint. "Aye, that put a damper on the evening, didn't it? Sad enough to lose a loved one for any cause but when it was a deliberate killing and there is no known reason . . . I understand the lad's sadness, but for his sake and James's, I am truly happy he decided not to cause a scene. One awful scene a night is enough in any pub and we had Conor for tonight."

While I agreed with Dougal that Conor Sweeney's falling down drunk was more than enough, I couldn't help but wonder who it was who had pushed Niall O'Bannon in the direction of James

Collins when there was so little evidence pointing at him, or at anyone else, for that matter. Just then Tim Redding stopped to wish us a good evening on his way out the door. As I watched him go, I remembered that he had told me about old bruises—contusions, he called them—that had shown up on Michael's body. Perhaps it was time to ask Inspector Finley about them. Had the coroner made any connection between those old injuries and the most recent one, which caused Michael's death? I had so many questions and so few answers.

Chapter Eighteen

My morning bike ride was uneventful. I avoided the path where I'd found Michael's body but there were a couple of other muddy dirt roads and I had great fun testing the traction of the Donard bicycle on them. It wasn't until I got back to the hotel that I realized that I had mud splatters on my jeans all the way up to the knee.

I found a laundry bag in the closet, put my dirty things inside, and filled out the attached card, indicating that I would like everything washed, dried, and folded except for my jeans, which I preferred to have washed and hung on a hanger to dry.

I called the desk to arrange for a pickup and the young man said someone would be along to collect the laundry bag shortly. Within five minutes there was a knock on the door, and without thinking, I pulled it open to come face-to-face with Dermot Kerrigan. My first thought was *Inspector Finley is not going to be happy about this.*

This time Kerrigan stood in the hallway and took a deferential tack. "Pardon me, Mrs. Fletcher. I believe we got off to a bad start and I'd like to make it up to you. Perhaps you'd care to join me for elevenses in the dining room."

"Certainly, Mr. Kerrigan. Just let me get my purse."

I closed the door and sent a text telling Maggie where I'd be and with whom. Then I picked up my purse and followed Kerrigan down the stairs. This was too good an opportunity to miss. I had questions and hoped Dermot Kerrigan would be caught by surprise and answer them.

For the second time in as many days, Dougal Nolan called from the reception desk, "Is everything all right there, Mrs. Fletcher?"

Kerrigan answered, "Nothing to worry about here, Dougal. We're only after some elevenses in your dining room."

"See that you don't leave the building." Dougal sounded slightly menacing.

"Ah, he's determined to take care of you. That's a fine landlord," Kerrigan said.

We settled at a table in the nearly empty dining room and Breeda came to take our order. She offered us square cardboard menus but Kerrigan waved them away.

"Mrs. Fletcher is a guest in our country, so let's have the basic elevenses so she sees how it is done." He looked at me. "Would you rather tea or coffee? I know you Americans do like your coffee."

"Yes, we do, and that sounds delicious to me," I said.

"That's it, then. We'll have elevenses with coffee. Thank you, miss."

Breeda returned in a New York minute. She poured a cup of

coffee for each of us and left a carafe midtable. She went to the kitchen and came back with a plate of what I think of as oatmeal cookies, although in Ireland cookies are usually known as biscuits. Along with the cookies were some apple wedges, grapes, and a few slices of bread and jam.

"This looks lovely," I said, hoping to sound like a grateful tourist being let in on a local treat.

"Elevenses is my favorite meal. I would eat it five times a day if the wife would allow. Sadly, she is one for the green veggies and lots of protein, so I need to grab my biscuits where I can get them." He reached for an oatmeal cookie.

I sipped my coffee, opted for a few grapes, and waited to see what Kerrigan had in mind. At long last he spoke.

"I may have been too brusque when we first met. Michael O'Bannon's death itself was a shock, increased by the fact that now we are being told that he was murdered." He looked to me for agreement and perhaps some understanding.

In the hope that he would begin to be less guarded, I decided to give him what he was seeking, so I said, "It was a great trauma for us all."

"And I was foolish enough to value money over manners. For that, I deeply apologize."

He studied me as he waited for my response. Clearly, we were having a game of cat and mouse.

I held on to my goal while I waited to get a clear picture of his. "You were in shock looking at how the death might affect you personally. Your first instinct was not to think of the family, the business, and all the other people who were distressed by Michael's death. Me for example."

"Ah, yes. There's the thing. I was in shock and never thought of you suffering from the impact of finding a murdered body, especially of someone you know. The sight must have sent earthquakelike tremors right through you."

I took a sip of coffee, nodded my head, and stared at the tabletop for effect. I was beginning to wonder if he was actually sorry or just softening me for his own purposes. In the next few minutes, I got my answer.

"So, now that you have my sincere apology, I hope we can be friends." Kerrigan smiled. "And since my relationship with the family is not in any way straightforward, I did wonder if you would mind sharing any information you may have heard as to how Michael's estate will be settled. I have made discreet inquiries and cannot seem to find a local solicitor who is handling his interests."

When I returned his smile, he leaned back in his chair and relaxed as though he were the cat and had caught the mouse. Now I was ready to switch roles. "So, what is your real interest in Michael O'Bannon's estate? Is it the money Michael owed you or is it your arrangement with him concerning Worldwide Shipping?"

Red-faced, he leaned forward, reached out to grab my arm, thought the better of it, and pulled back. "What are you talking about? What would I know about shipping?"

I stood up. "Thank you for inviting me for elevenses, Mr. Kerrigan. The food was delicious and the conversation educational. Enjoy the rest of your day."

I ignored his stammering as I walked away from the table, feeling better than I had since before I found Michael O'Bannon dead in his car. I knew from Claude that Michael was supporting Worldwide as the shipper for the enlarged company once the merger was complete, and thanks to my excursion with Maggie, I knew that Dermot Kerrigan was involved with the Worldwide site if not the company itself. And yet he denied it. I had to wonder why.

Back in my room, I was pleased to see that housekeeping had been in, tidied up, and taken my laundry bag. All in all, my day was going well.

I curled up in the window seat with Seamus Heaney's poems and was particularly enchanted with "Blackberry-Picking," which reminded me of all the fun times I'd had picking blueberries at home in Cabot Cove.

There was a knock on the door, and that time, wanting nothing further to do with Dermot Kerrigan for the moment, I was sure to ask who it was before I unlocked the door for Maggie.

She stepped inside, and I'd barely closed the door before she clapped her hands and said gleefully, "You had to hear my father praise you to the skies. 'And there she goes, cool as you please, into our dining room to share elevenses with Dermot Kerrigan. The sauce of her.'"

"I had no reason to worry. What better safe space could I have than the dining room at the River Bush Hotel? And we had Breeda as our server. I am sure at the slightest provocation she would have screamed bloody murder, but not before she bonked Mr. Kerrigan with a coffee carafe."

"Aye, that you can count on. I've watched her play handball. She's a tough girlie." Maggie giggled and then turned serious. "What was your goal in spending time with the man? And did you manage to attain it?"

"Now, I did and I didn't," I said. "Come sit down and I'll tell you."

I indicated the window seat, but Maggie sat in the club chair, so I was happy enough to sit once again in the sunshine.

"Listen to you sounding so very Irish with that 'did and didn't,'" Maggie said. "Now, tell me the 'did.'"

"I managed to casually bring up Worldwide Shipping and it was evident that he was flustered. Then he emphatically denied knowing anything about Worldwide or the shipping industry at large," I said.

"And you did not believe a word he said."

"I did not. Our seeing him at the Worldwide property doesn't mean he has anything to do with ownership or operations. For that matter anyone could have seen us walking around the site and drawn a wrong conclusion. We have nothing to do with the business," I said. "The place was wide open. But based on my experience, Kerrigan was too rattled in his denial to be telling the truth."

"If it is a connection between Kerrigan and Worldwide we are looking for, I have an idea," Maggie said. "Several of my old chums from university work in various government offices. It is possible that one of them knows something about permits and operations of import-export shipping companies."

"That could be very useful. In the meantime, I would like to speak to the Frenchmen again, specifically Julien Lavigne. Claude Blanchet told me that any change in shipping arrangements would cause great harm to Julien's family finances."

"Then it looks like we both have work to do. And speaking of work, I have to check on the food deliveries for tonight's dinner. Can't have Old Joe Fogarty and his peeler at the ready with no vegetables to clean." Maggie stood and brushed imaginary wrinkles from the front of her skirt. "Will you be dining here tonight?"

"I've been invited to tea at Jane's, and after seeing how upset Niall was last night, I have no idea how that will go. Dinner may be a late sandwich in my room or a three-course meal in the dining room. It is too soon to tell."

"Niall and Deirdre would do best to avoid the aunts, if only they could. We offered them free lodging here rather than have them at Michael's house, filled with memories, or Jane's house, filled with family pressure. But Jane won that battle, as she so often does." Maggie sighed at the thought of her future mother-in-law's strong personality.

She opened the door, and apparently there was someone on the other side, because she said, "Devlin, aren't you the speediest ever? Jessica, your laundry is here. Did you want your pants to be still damp and on a hanger?"

I shooed Maggie on her way and then I thanked young Devlin with a generous tip, hung my jeans in the shower stall, and put the rest of my clothes away. I checked the time and saw that I still had more than an hour before I had to get ready for tea. I was about to call the desk to ask them to reserve a cab when the landline telephone rang. I half hoped it would be Seth or Maeve. I was starting to miss home.

Instead, it was Jane Mullen. "Jessica, I hope it won't be too inconvenient for us to have tea now rather than at four. Owen will be happy to come pick you up. We've had the most wonderful news. The police are going to release Michael's body in the morning, so Beth Anne and I have an appointment at the Mc-Avoy Brothers Funeral Directors this afternoon at five o'clock."

"Only you and Beth Anne?" I thought that was odd.

"The children are welcome to join us but I really don't see that it will be necessary. However, Niall and Deirdre are anxious to speak with you, so I thought we'd push teatime up rather than postpone." Jane spoke as if it was all settled, and I supposed it was.

I was not looking forward to visiting the family, as Jane had made it clear earlier that the conversation would center around my discovering Michael dead in his car, but it seemed easiest for me to agree to meet Owen in the lobby and get the ordeal done and gone. I still had the delivery of Maeve's paintings in front of me, so it would be difficult to avoid any of the O'Bannons.

I changed into a brown skirt and a tan blouse, fluffed my hair, and spritzed on a bit of cologne. I checked my cell phone. My only text was from my publicist, who asked me to call her when I returned home and, as she put it, was "back on East Coast time." If her latest publicity idea included travel, I knew that in my current mood, my answer would be a resounding no.

I took the stairs to the lobby as Dougal was coming in from the parking lot.

"Aye, there she is, the fearless one."

He walked directly to me and lowered his voice. "You really do like to live dangerously. Might I ask what this attraction is between you and Dermot Kerrigan?"

I arched an eyebrow at his phrasing. "There is no 'attraction,' as you call it. He had a sort of business relationship with Michael O'Bannon that interests me. I have a . . . well, a different kind of relationship with the O'Bannons. Mr. Kerrigan is interested in Michael's assets and he believes I can help him in that."

"I can well believe his motive for seeking information from you. Kerrigan is about nothing if not the money. Many a man has the bruises to prove it. That I can tell you," Dougal said.

Anxious to learn if the bruises he'd heard about matched what Tim Redding had described as Michael O'Bannon's old contusions, I was about to press Dougal for a description of the beatings he implied Kerrigan had ordered, but I heard someone call my name.

Owen Mullen was smiling as he said, "Jessica, is this man bothering you? I know the hotel owner, so I'm sure I can have this rascal removed from the premises."

I laughed and I'm sure I would have said something witty, but I was thrown off-balance when I saw Niall O'Bannon walking behind Owen, and he looked every bit as morose as he had last night in the pub.

Chapter Nineteen

Niall nodded a greeting to Dougal but walked directly to me and wasted no time explaining why. "Mrs. Fletcher, I feel I should apologize for my behavior last evening during the trad session at the Dart and the Pint. I had no business barging into what was supposed to be a social event and spouting off about James Collins, especially in front of you. I shouldn't wonder that my father's death has caused you more than enough grief."

I placed my hand gently on his forearm. "Niall, I appreciate your concern for my feelings. Right now the burden of your father's death may not allow you to think clearly. I am aware that you and your family have been through a terrible tragedy and I am afraid the ordeal may become more complex before you find peace. Thank you for your apology, but as of now, I say we forget about last night."

His relief was evident. He shook my hand and whispered, "You are a kind woman. I won't forget this moment."

As we walked out to the parking lot, Owen and I had a suitably inane conversation about the weather. One thing I was quickly learning was that the weather was always a suitable topic of Irish conversation.

"We are expecting a soft rain toward dinnertime but you can never tell when the wind will pick up and spin it all around," Owen said as we got into the car. "I've a couple of umbrellas on the floor in the back there under Niall's feet, should we need them later on."

I acknowledged that was a good idea and we continued chatting to give Niall a chance to sort out his own thoughts. He couldn't be looking forward to the afternoon his aunt Jane had planned.

A few minutes later, as if he had been reading my mind, Niall said, "I have not so much of a glimmer of an idea as to what Aunt Jane thinks she is doing by hosting a tea to talk about my da. I know she does love her fancy dos and this is a fine excuse to use the good dishes but I think it is a bit too soon."

I certainly agreed but decided it was wisest to say nothing.

Owen said, "Niall, you have to realize Mam and Aunt Beth Anne are all torn up. Your da wasn't just a business partner. They grew up together like he was their brother, not their cousin."

"Like us, you mean," Niall interrupted.

"Exactly," Owen continued. "You had to see them when first we learned. . . . Neither could complete a thought, much less a sentence. Sisters they may be but they hide their hurt in very different ways. Aunt Beth Anne is all about protecting the business relationships while Mam is all about preserving the social."

As Owen spoke, I remembered Maggie describing the two sisters having a row over notifications and which group should be called first—business associates versus social acquaintances. My assessment of the sisters was reinforced. Both were strong-willed but they used that strength for different purposes.

Niall chuckled. "You're right, cuz. Ever since we were children, that's been the way of it. When we visited Aunt Jane she would caution us to mind our manners because she had guests, while at Aunt Beth Anne's house she generally would warn us to be quiet. She was on a conference call with Dublin."

Owen laughed as well. "Now you've got it, boyo. Mam and Auntie are who they are."

"Well, then, there is nothing to be done today but grin and bear it, as they say, but I do have one request of Mrs. Fletcher."

I turned in my seat to show he had my full attention.

Niall went on. "Each of my aunts wants to hear what you have to say about my father's death, or, using its rightful name, his murder. Finding him was unquestionably a horrible experience for you. And I know my aunts will want you to relive every detail and share it with us. I wouldn't blame you if you refused to do so, but if you agree, please don't upset my sister, Deirdre, by describing how violent the scene might have been or how damaged Da looked at the end."

Owen had pulled into the driveway, so I had only a minute to answer. Fortunately, the issue of how to describe the scene had been the uppermost thing on my mind ever since I'd received Jane's invitation.

"Niall, I can tell you truthfully that your father appeared to be taken by surprise and I don't believe he suffered at all. I hope that brings some comfort to you and your sister," I said.

The family was gathered once again in the yellow parlor. Jane greeted me with outstretched arms and thanked me for coming.

Beth Anne followed her and introduced me to the slim young woman wearing outsized oval eyeglasses who was at her side. "This is my daughter Sheila. She teaches linguistics at the London School of Economics and Political Science."

We exchanged hellos and I said I was sorry to meet her under such tragic circumstances. Sheila said something similar.

Niall had walked past us to the far end of the room and interrupted his cousin Caro, who was talking to a raven-haired girl with bright blue eyes who was dressed in a charcoal gray suit and a white blouse with a frilly collar trimmed in black.

He gave her a gentle kiss on the cheek and said something to which she replied with a nod. I assumed the girl was his sister and Niall had asked if she was all right.

I broke away from Jane and Beth Anne and was heading toward Niall when Liam Mullen intercepted me.

"Thank you for coming today, Jessica. I know it means the world to Jane and Beth Anne to have you speak with Michael's children." He handed me a small glass half filled with a deep golden red liqueur. "Have a taste of Irish Mist. It is bound to get you through these touchy few hours."

I nodded and smiled my thank-you, took the glass but didn't stop to talk. I was anxious to meet Niall's sister, Deirdre. Liam was refilling his own glass as I stepped away.

Niall took his sister by the elbow and met me near the spinet piano. We moved to the bay window and Niall introduced us.

Deirdre's voice was soft and warm as she said, "I am very pleased to meet you, Mrs. Fletcher. I expect it isn't easy for you to be surrounded by O'Bannons at a time like this."

"Deirdre, I am so sorry about the loss of your father, but Maeve O'Bannon has been my friend and neighbor for decades, so if she cannot be here, I am honored to take her place."

Nora stood in the doorway and nodded her head ever so slightly toward Jane, who immediately said, "Come along, everyone. Tea is served in the dining room."

When I noticed that some of the others picked up their glasses and started to walk to the dining room, I took my first sip of Irish Mist. To my surprise, it was both sweet and mellow. I had been expecting whiskey with a stronger taste, so this was a pleasant surprise.

There were place cards around the dining room table. I found myself sitting between Beth Anne and Owen. I was sure that was a concession Jane made to her sister after some bickering. I was also sure I would need all of my fingers and toes to count up the things that caused the sisters to bicker on a daily basis.

Nora set beautiful three-tiered serving plates filled with finger sandwiches, scones, and pastries at intervals along the center of the table. Then she came around with teapots, asking if we preferred Irish breakfast tea or Darjeeling. Both Caro and Beth Anne asked for coffee, which Nora had at the ready on a sideboard.

As we ate, the conversation was light. And when someone asked Sheila about her flight from London, I interjected that the flight I'd taken seemed a hop, skip, and jump after my long flight from Boston to London.

Owen said, "I didn't realize that was how you came into Belfast. How do you plan on returning?"

When I explained that my travel agent was holding an open-ended return trip for me, Owen said, "Let's turn the agent on her ear. You'll drive to Dublin with Maggie and me. Then you can catch a direct flight back to the States. More convenient for you and we have been planning to take the trip for a while now. We've a few things we want to look into down around Dublin way. That's settled, then."

I was astonished. Susan Shevlin and I had talked about a direct flight from Boston to Dublin, but booking either the train or the bus from Dublin to Belfast meant relying on the flight's being on time. We decided that changing planes in London seemed more secure. But this was an offer too good to pass up.

"That is very kind of you, Owen, but I don't know yet when I am leaving—"

"Not to worry. You and Maggie can work out the details. My job is merely to drive the car."

Owen laughed and his cousins chuckled along. I noticed his mother did not join in the merriment.

Liam, who had seen the frown on Jane's face, attempted to change the subject. "Jessica, we are all familiar with your books but you did mention you came to Ireland at the last minute to replace a writer who'd broken her leg. I would like to look into her books as well. I'm not sure you mentioned her name."

I was quite sure I had but I knew Liam was trying to prevent a scene and I was glad to help. "Her name is Lorna Winters, and if you enjoy reading political suspense, particularly spy novels, then I think you will enjoy Lorna's books."

However, nothing was going to stop Jane from having her say, least of all a conversation about books written by an author who was unlikely ever to sit at Jane's dining table.

"Owen, whatever are you talking about? How can you possibly plan to travel to Dublin or anywhere else in the foreseeable future? Beth Anne and I are going to need your help. We are going to need this entire family to pitch in and make sure that Marine Magic stays on top of the skin care market. You can't go wandering off. . . ."

No one said a word. I looked around the table. Because they were recent arrivals, Sheila, Niall, and Deirdre seemed confused, not sure what had just happened. Everyone else seemed to understand why Jane was upset and was waiting for the finale. Everyone, that is, except Beth Anne. I caught a glimpse of her Cheshire cat grin a few seconds before she took a sip of tea and then began to study the scones on the serving tray in front of us.

I watched as Owen also looked around the table and realized this was neither the time nor the place. He said quietly but emphatically, "We'll discuss it later. As a family we have a lot going on."

"My point exactly," Jane replied.

And again, I caught just a peek of Beth Anne's grin. She took a small sip of tea and then said, "Frankly, Jane, I am glad to hear that you finally realize that Michael's death is a great loss to the company. I tried to explain that to you several times but you seemed not to be listening. I am glad that something I said finally sank in."

Beth Anne picked up her napkin and daintily patted her lips, keeping one eye on her sister for any reaction, so she was not the least bit surprised when Jane shot back, "You wouldn't know a lipid from a polymer. My knowing those things is what keeps our product line fresh and exciting. All you know how to do is count the money."

I heard several gasps around the table, and then, as if we all hadn't observed his wife's complete meltdown, Liam stood, lifted his glass, and said, "Let us all take a moment to remember why we are here today. Please lift your glasses to Michael."

When I reached for my glass of Irish Mist I was certain I would be the only one to follow Liam's direction, but everyone lifted a glass or teacup. Liam said a short prayer and then we all said, "To Michael!" and took a sip.

When Liam sat down, it seemed the war clouds had passed at least for the time being. Everyone took turns telling stories about Michael. Beth Anne brought up the story Owen had mentioned to Maggie and me about Michael falling from a tree in their grandfather's yard.

All these years later Deirdre, Caro, and Sheila became quite giggly when they talked about Michael taking them to London to see their latest heartthrob in person when he performed onstage at the Theatre Royal, Drury Lane.

"Of course," Caro said, "it was just a matter of time before another singer replaced him as a heartthrob, but nothing could ever replace the thrill for three young teens to be in the ancient and historic Drury Lane."

"And we could never forget how ancient it truly was. Da kept reminding us, didn't he?" Deirdre said.

"Did he ever! 'Now, you young ladies, remember that you are in a place where there has been live theater since the 1660s.' I can still hear him saying it." Sheila laughed. "And for many years, he did like to remind us that the heartthrob is now a has-been."

Liam followed that story with one about a particular time he and Michael were fishing on the River Bush and Michael got a phone call. "His cell started ringing just as a salmon started yanking on his line. I was telling him to let the call go to voice mail but he thought it might be a work thing, so he tried to answer the phone just as the fish gave a ferocious yank, and into the River Bush went both Michael and his cell phone. The fish got away and Michael never did learn who'd called."

The glum mood that had filled the air, surrounding us all when I first arrived, had dissipated bit by bit and now we were celebrating Michael in story after story, most funny, but there were a few that revealed his decency, such as the one Niall told about Michael hearing that the parents of one of Niall's university friends had been killed in a car accident. Michael inquired about the family finances and quietly picked up the young man's living expenses so that he could graduate with his class.

When Niall finished, I noticed Beth Anne wiping a tear from her eye. She raised her teacup and said, "To Michael." Once again, we all joined in the salute to his memory.

Then Jane said, "Our cousin Michael was a wonderful man whose life was far too short. We are blessed that today Jessica has agreed to tell us what she can about Michael's sad ending."

Everyone at the table looked at me. In some of their eyes, I saw tears, and in some, I saw dread. The only person who looked peaceful, as though she was expecting another lighthearted anecdote, was Jane.

Chapter Twenty

I began slowly. "As you have heard countless times by now, I had gone for a morning bike ride so I could explore the village and the countryside when I happened to come across a dirt road that I have since learned is an old cow path familiar to most members of this family. It was muddied from the previous night's rainfall, but I was sure the tires of Dougal Nolan's spiffy red Donard bicycle would sail through the mud without difficulty.

"There was a fair number of bends and turns in the path, and as I rounded one particularly sharp curve, I saw someone had parked a late-model blue car off to one side. It seemed as though the driver had pulled the front end into an opening of some sort between a hedgerow and a clump of trees."

The writer in me was keenly aware that my audience might need a moment to visualize the scene, so I deliberately stopped and took a slow sip from my teacup.

After a moment or two, I began to speak again. "At first, I didn't see anything troublesome, but when I looked more closely, I realized that there was a man in the front seat of the car. He appeared to be alone and definitely was not moving. I called out rather loudly, offering my assistance, should he need it. When he didn't respond, I inched nearer. Once I had a good view, I recognized Michael instantly."

I stopped at that point and looked around the table. "I warn you, this next part may be difficult to hear. Are you sure you want me to continue?"

Beth Anne immediately answered, "Please go on," as if she were speaking for the group.

But I looked to Niall for guidance. When he nodded his assent, I began again.

"Michael had a gash on the side of his head. It was the only sign of viciousness that was evident. Other than that wound, he appeared peaceful. It seemed clear to me that in the moments before he was struck, he was unaware of what was to come."

I heard a muffled sob and saw Sheila raise a napkin to her eye. Her sister, Caro, reached over and gave her a hug.

Deirdre was crying softly on her brother's shoulder, but her medical training showed through when she said, "I am, on the one hand, glad that my father didn't see his death coming but it is troubling to realize that his killer must have been someone he trusted. Or else Da would have been on his guard and moved in some way to protect himself. That would have been reflected in the positioning of the body."

I didn't reply even though Deirdre expressed what had been my thought from the first moment I saw Michael's injury—the killer was someone he trusted. I decided to continue with my description of the scene rather than comment about the circumstances. I would leave that to Inspector Finley.

"I can tell you that Michael was sitting behind the steering wheel, and when I came upon him, the driver's-side window was wide open. I tried to rouse him by reaching in to shake him gently. I was able to feel that both the shoulder and the sleeve of his jacket were wet, which led me to believe that he had been there for at least part of the time that it had been raining overnight. I was unable to see any other signs of violence, although there was a small scrape that appeared to be quite recent on the window frame of the car. I can't answer as to when that might have happened."

I folded my hands and rested them on the edge of the dining table as a sign I had finished. For the next little while, everyone sat wrapped in their own thoughts.

Jane moved into hostess mode and thanked me profusely for joining in this tribute to Michael. Then she looked at her watch and said, "Oh, dear, it is getting late. Beth Anne and I have an appointment at McAvoy Brothers Funeral Directors. I hope you all will excuse us."

Deirdre nudged her brother with her elbow and Niall took the hint. "Aunt Jane, Deirdre and I have talked about this. We'll be happy to go with you. We think it is only right that we both be part of any discussion planning our father's funeral service and burial."

Jane was halfway out of her chair but she sat down again and looked directly at Niall with the exact same look I'd seen Cabot Cove mayor Jim Shevlin give to an errant town council member who brought up something Jim considered irrelevant to the agenda as he was adjourning a meeting.

"Listen to me carefully. Beth Anne and I have been down this road before when other family members have passed away. When your sainted mother left us, your father was so broken, so heartsick, that Beth Anne and I had to step in and handle everything. Believe me, it will be better for you in the long run to let us handle this. Your memories will revolve around the actual service and burial rather than the discussions that brought them about." Jane sounded quite convincing.

I think the entire room went into shock when Deirdre stood and said, "Niall and I are our father's next of kin. We appreciate your interest and will allow you to accompany us to McAvoys'. Would anyone else like to join us? No? That's it, then. We'll be taking Niall's car and we will meet you there." And she swept out of the room. Niall waved a general good-bye to the room at large and followed behind her.

Jane and Beth Anne exchanged a look, decided their course of action, and stood. Jane looked at her husband and said, "Liam, would you mind . . . ?"

She got no further because he responded that he would be delighted to drive them.

And just like that, the room was empty save Owen, Sheila, Caro, and me. I'd never felt more like an outsider. I hoped that Owen was ready to drive me home but I hesitated to ask. Caro walked over to look out the window and said, "Coast is clear. Niall's car is gone and Uncle Liam is herding our mams into his car."

Sheila was in awe. "Wow! Deirdre said she wasn't going to have it and she was serious. And did you see our mam staying away from the argument until there was a clear winner? Here's to the next generation!"

Fascinated, I watched the sisters clink their glasses. Then they turned and held their glasses high to Owen, who returned their salute.

Owen leaned closer to me and said, his voice filled with humor, "I suppose we can safely leave now. The gathering seems to be over."

On the ride back to the hotel, Owen was unusually quiet, so after a while, I said, "Might I ask if that was a spontaneous rebellion, or was your entire generation party to the plan?"

Owen laughed. "As soon as she arrived home, Deirdre made it clear that she was going to play a decisive role in everything from the time schedule of the wake and the funeral to the musical selections played. As usual my mother and my aunt had a different idea of how things should be run. The only thing everyone agreed about was that Michael would be buried in the old graveyard next to his wife, Fionnuala, who was Deirdre and Niall's mother."

"But apparently Jane and Beth Anne did not understand. . . ."

Ordinarily I didn't like to meddle in family affairs, but since Jane had persisted in including me in the afternoon's events, I decided I could be as nosy as I pleased.

Owen sighed. "My mother and my aunt have been in charge of all the personal family matters for decades and they each have their own special domain in the business. As a result, they are used to making decisions, and if there is any disagreement about something, it is a disagreement between the two of them and not with anyone else. Somehow, along the way they have neglected to recognize that my cousins and I are no longer primary school students who need permission to go to a movie on Saturday afternoon. We are adults with lives and plans of our own."

"And I take it the five of you have had this conversation among yourselves more than a time or two?" I assumed that as spontaneous as Deirdre's speech sounded, she'd definitely consulted with her brother and probably with her cousins.

"Dozens of times. You've no idea how Sheila had to fight to work in London. Here she was offered a position in one of the premier schools in all of Europe. By plane it is barely more than an hour away and Aunt Beth Anne decreed that Sheila would be too far from home. She wasn't able to fathom that Sheila had already determined to make London *her* home," Owen said.

"It is often hard for parents to let go of their adult children," I observed.

"Don't I know it!" Owen said as he drove into the hotel car park and pulled into a parking spot. "I'll be leaving the nest soon and my mother just keeps pretending it isn't going to happen. Let's go see what Maggie has been up to while you were gone."

Claude Blanchet was sitting in a comfortable parlor chair near the lobby door. When we came in he stood up and set down the newspaper he was reading. "*Bonsoir*, Jessica. Have you enjoyed a pleasant afternoon?"

"Well, Claude, I don't know that I would call it pleasant as much as I would call it interesting. Surely you remember Owen Mullen, Jane Mullen's son?"

Claude reached to shake Owen's hand. "Of course, I remember, and if I am not mistaken, you are much smitten with Mademoiselle Maggie Nolan. Am I correct?"

Owen blushed. "You are so very correct that I have asked Maggie to marry me and I am proud to say she has accepted."

Claude offered well-wishes, and I said, "Speaking of Maggie,

Owen, why don't you go find her? I will be perfectly fine here with Claude. And thank you so much for driving me today."

Owen did not need to be convinced. He disappeared down the long hallway, where I knew he would find Maggie's office. Claude invited me to sit with him, which suited me perfectly. He indicated a small glass on the coffee table in front of our chairs.

"I am having a small sherry. Perhaps I shall order you a glass?"

"Thank you, but no. I was fortunate enough to have some Irish Mist a while ago, so I believe I have reached my quota of alcohol for the day," I said, "but please continue to enjoy your sherry."

He raised his glass to me before taking a gentle sip.

"And where is Julien?" I asked. "Out taking pictures? He seems to relish his time behind the lens."

"*Non.* I wish he was playing the world-famous *photographe.* Instead he is in his room. He claimed he needed a bit of rest, but I am quite sure that he is worrying far more than is necessary at this point in negotiations." Claude lowered his voice. "I trust your discretion, Jessica."

"Of course, Claude, anything you say . . ."

"That is *très bien* because I have already said it." Claude seemed relieved. "Do you remember my telling you that our shipping company is run by Julien's brother-in-law?"

I nodded. "Yes, I do and you also said that Belle Visage is that shipping firm's largest client."

"What I did not realize is that the entire family has drawn income from Cadieux Transport for many years. Julien is in fear that if the business relationship between Belle Visage and Cadieux is altered or perhaps disappears entirely, there will be a great deal of poverty in the future for many of his relations."

I chose my words carefully. "So when you told him about the conversation you overheard between Beth Anne and Michael, naturally he would have found that to be quite upsetting."

"*Oui*, certainly he did, but let me stop you right there. If you think Julien would harm anyone even to prevent such a catastrophe, I can assure you that is not within his range of capabilities."

Claude sounded quite confident but I was not nearly so sure.

"I agree that he is a gentleman, but in the heat of a given moment, I believe we all have a breaking point. Please do not be offended on his behalf if I ask whether you and Julien share a room here at the hotel."

In reality, I was asking Claude to provide an alibi for both of them and I was sure he knew it.

"*Non*. Friends though we may be, there is still a need for privacy. But if you are asking me if I think that Julien is capable of sneaking out in the middle of the night and murdering a man, that is simply not possible." Claude's last sentence sounded so adamant that, for him, it was bordering on rude.

I thanked him for his honesty and he graciously accepted my thanks, although I was sure he was aware that I still had some reservations. Who wouldn't?

Claude asked me if I had plans to return to America anytime soon and he did not seem surprised when I said, "Since my friend asked me to deliver some family mementos to the O'Bannon family and they are under such stress right now, my plans are of the 'wait and see' kind."

He grimaced. "I understand completely. Julien and I were most anxious to leave for Paris as soon as . . . well, as soon as the unfortunate incident occurred. However, we have received strict instructions from our board of directors that we are to remain until they order us home or the Marine Magic people dismiss us."

Owen came back down the hall with Maggie in tow. She appeared even bouncier than usual. They were polite enough to chat with Claude for a few moments. Then Owen said he was going to the shops and would be back shortly, while Maggie invited me to her office.

As we walked down the hallway, she linked arms with me and said, "This is so exciting. I can't wait for you to see what I found."

Chapter Twenty-One

As soon as we walked into Maggie's office, she shut the door and offered me a seat.

"Jessica, I am so excited. I feel as though I could be a character in one of your books. Detective Maggie at your service."

She gave me a snappy salute before picking up some papers from her desk. From a notepad she handed me a page that had a tiny piece of paper taped to its center. The small paper was exactly like something we had seen quite recently.

RT☼

I was stunned. "Maggie, you didn't go back to the Worldwide site and search on your own, did you? That certainly wouldn't be the smartest or the safest thing to do."

"I'm far more canny than that. Do you remember I told you that I have lots of old school chums in government offices?"

When I nodded, Maggie went on. "Well, first, I sent out the word that I was looking for anyone who knew about the rules and permits for international shipping. That got me a few gag text messages, including one with a picture of me from my uni days. I was constantly being teased for stuffing my backpack beyond normal capacity. Now when I look at a picture of young Maggie hunched over, struggling to carry every book, notebook, and goodness knows what else in her trusty blue rucksack, I understand the teasing, although back then I had not a clue."

"Speaking of clues . . ." I said, hoping to bring her back to the present.

"I'm almost there. Violet Dunphy called me a while ago. As luck would have it, she works in the permit office in Belfast and offered to send me whatever papers I needed for my business.

"I didn't correct her assumption that I was setting up a business and that is when I got really creative. I told Violet that I was planning on shipping some of my goods to Canada and another merchant had given me a trifold about an import-export company he highly recommends. Unfortunately, I lost the paperwork and do not remember the company's name. Then I giggled and said I was too embarrassed to tell the merchant that I had lost the trifold. He'd probably think I was too careless to run a business and I might lose my fledgling relationship with him."

Maggie looked at me as if expecting applause but I was waiting for the finale.

"Clearly 'relationship' was the wrong word to use, because then Violet veered off into my romantic life, asking if Owen and I are still together." Maggie held her hands in front of her. "Now comes the good part. Violet asked if I remembered anything significant about the company's paperwork. If not the name, perhaps the logo. I said it had a circle with spokes. She texted me a picture of a flyer from Wagon Wheel Movers. When I said the center was bigger and the spokes were smaller, she said she had something and sent me this."

Maggie picked up another paper from her desk and it was an enlarged photocopy of an application for permits from a firm whose name and logo were:

☼SUNSHINE IMPORT AND EXPORT☼

That was all it took to get my attention.

Maggie picked up an enlargement of a different part of the photocopy. "Look at the name of the applicant."

And there it was: Rosaleen Kerrigan.

"Dermot's wife," Maggie said, "and I'd bet you a salmon dinner that Rosaleen has not a bit of an idea that her name is on this document. She is a librarian over in Portrush and I can't imagine the likes of her having anything to do with Dermot's calamitous businesses. I have always been amazed that she remains his wife."

There was a polite rap on the door, and when Maggie opened it, there was Owen. He gave us a grin and said, "Ah, and would you mind telling me what nefarious deed you two are up to behind closed doors?"

I would have been more cautious, but Maggie was brimming with excitement over her discoveries and practically shouted, "Dermot Kerrigan! We are finding information about Dermot Kerrigan."

I said, "That's not exactly true. We were trying to find out information about shipping businesses and his name, or, more accurately, his wife's name, came up."

"Either way"—Maggie shrugged—"for some reason Dermot is obviously very, very interested in shipping."

"It's the merger, isn't it, Jessica?" Owen looked at me for confirmation.

"I do understand that Michael and your aunt Beth Anne were in a disagreement about shipping," I said carefully. "Marine Magic has its own shipping company."

"Absolutely. Conor Sweeney was Michael's buddy boy since primary school and his father and uncles started the company decades before Marine Magic was founded. It was a natural fit from the very start," Owen said.

"And I understand that Belle Visage has an associated shipping company as well. So why would anyone believe there was need for a new shipping company? I mean, moving a package is sort of like this." Maggie picked up her laptop from the desk and put it on the sideboard, then brought it back to the desk. "It can't be that difficult."

Owen said, "Shipping is a complicated and profitable business. And I can tell you that the entire point of the merger is to ensure that the newly combined company has enough product to expand outside of Europe. First, to the United States, Canada, and Australia. The follow-up plan is to develop specific cosmetic lines for Asia, followed by South and Central America along with the Caribbean. Basically, Aunt Beth Anne wants to take over the world!"

Maggie looked aghast, which was exactly how I felt. She stared at Owen with owlish wide eyes. "How could you possibly know all this?"

"Oh, please, Mags. You know as well as I do that conversation about the daily workings of Marine Magic is dinner table talk at my house anytime that Aunt Beth Anne joins us, and lately she and even Michael have been invited to dinner too many evenings to count."

"Owen, I want to be sure that I understand completely. Are you saying that the dinner table business conversation between the three principals of Marine Magic has increased dramatically in recent times?" I assumed the pending merger required lots of discussions both formal and informal.

"Definitely over the past couple of months. The talks were increasingly frequent and intense until they became nonstop when they scheduled the representatives of Belle Visage to come here to begin the actual negotiations. Why, Jessica? Is that important?" Owen asked.

"It might well be. Do you recall that shipping was a constant bone of contention among them?" I asked.

"To be honest, I try to tune them out, especially when they get quarrelsome, which is most of the time."

Owen looked chagrined and, having witnessed a few minor skirmishes, I could well understand.

"So, here is what we know," I said, and began counting on my fingers. "First, two European companies with global-expansion ambitions decide they can meet their goals faster and more efficiently by joining forces. Second, each company has a prior relationship with a local shipping company, and in early negotiations, the companies agree to keep both shippers. But"—I tapped my ring finger—"Michael comes up with a plan to bring in an entirely new and untried import-export company to replace both shippers and he puts up a strong fight with his cousins to make that happen."

"That sounds about right but I honestly don't get it," Owen

said. "Michael never paid serious attention to how Beth Anne runs the company. He was never interested when my mam developed a new product. His side of the business was strictly promotional."

"Owen." Maggie put her arm around him and said gently, "Michael had a lot of . . . I guess you could call them outside interests, and through them, he was often entangled with Dermot Kerrigan."

"You're talking about the gambling. No sense in hiding it. Several times the family had to cover his debts." Owen hesitated. "Are you saying that Michael was so indebted to Dermot that he was willing to put the merger and even Marine Magic itself on the line?"

I made a decision I hoped I wouldn't regret. "Owen, I am not sure if Inspector Finley shared this information with the family. I heard it from . . . another source and I believe it to be valid. It seems that when the coroner examined Michael, he found signs of a severe beating that he estimated Michael had received a week or so prior to his death."

Owen blanched and Maggie tightened her grip on him.

I waited to allow Owen and Maggie to sift through their thoughts; then I continued. "It is possible that the beating was totally unrelated to the company, but it is also possible that it was a warning that Michael had better do whatever was required of him for his own safety."

We were all startled by a knock on the door. Maggie opened it a few inches and Breeda, looking extremely anxious, said, "Your da needs you in the dining room and he asks that you hurry."

Maggie rushed down the hallway behind Breeda. Owen and I

immediately followed along. In the otherwise empty dining room, we saw Hugh Tierney, Dougal Nolan, and Claude Blanchet all crowded around Julien Lavigne, who was sitting in a chair just inside the doorway.

Dougal said to Maggie, "We've called for an ambulance."

Maggie knelt by Julien's side and immediately held his hand. I noticed that while doing so she shifted her fingers to look for his pulse.

Julien gave her a tiny smile and said, "*Je vais bien.* I am fine. Really, I am *très bien.*"

"I am sure you are, but we need to be certain." Maggie took a glass of water from Breeda's hand. "Now, take a sip, and in a few minutes—" She turned toward the sound of a commotion in the lobby. "Here they are. No waiting at all. Our medics will take a few minutes to be positive that you are *très bien.*"

Maggie stood and ordered the rest of us into the lobby, and then closed the dining room doors behind us. I was somewhat surprised that even her father obeyed her without question.

Dougal invited us all to take a seat. I chose to sit next to Claude, as I was sure he'd been quite shaken by whatever had happened to Julien.

He kept murmuring, "*Je ne comprends pas.* I do not understand. Why was he not in his room? He told me he was resting."

Breeda appeared, almost magically, with a tray that held a bottle of sherry, a bottle of whiskey, and some glasses.

Dougal poured a sherry and immediately handed it to Claude before serving the rest of us. Then he turned to Hugh Tierney and asked exactly what happened.

Hugh blinked his green eyes several times. "Boyo, I have seen strange and I have seen worrisome, and today this poor lad combined the two. It started when you called me to drive Julien from the hotel to the Giant's Causeway for more picture taking. On the brief ride over, Julien mentioned that when he died, he wanted his oldest son to inherit his cameras, because the boy loved to take pictures.

"I took it as chatter. You know, the kind of talk when you don't have much to say to each other but there you are together. It goes on in my car all the time."

Dougal nodded. "We have that same kind of talk here at the reception desk, so I know what you mean."

Then Hugh told us that when Julien got out of the cab in the causeway parking lot and Hugh asked what time he wanted to be picked up, Julien said, "Do not worry. You will get a call."

"That sounded a wee bit strange, but he is a foreigner, so I thought he got his words mixed up. No offense to the foreigners present." Hugh blushed slightly, and Claude and I both assured him there was no offense taken.

"I had driven half the way home when I was forced to stop because some of Tilly Doyle's sheep had wandered into the road—not the first time, I might add. That's when I noticed that Julien had left his cameras and kit on the rear seat. From the first I'd given him the nickname Picture Man in my head, so I knew there was something gone wrong if he'd left his cameras behind."

Hugh stopped and took a sip from the glass he was holding.

"Well, as soon as the sheep allowed, I turned the car around and went back to the causeway. It took a bit of searching, but I found Julien sitting alone on top of one of the high cliffs. His desperate sobbing was enough to break any man's heart. I feared he'd gotten some bad news from home."

"I sat down beside him and said not a word. To be honest, I

couldn't find one to say. It took a bit of time but finally Julien said, 'I confess I am a coward. And now I lack the courage to jump.' That shook me. I put my hand on his shoulder, and after a while, he was ready to leave. I walked him down the cliff and drove him here."

Dougal clapped Hugh on the back. "You've saved a man's life today and prevented a family living through years of grief. Fair play to you."

The doors to the dining room opened and one of the medical technicians, a tall, sandy-haired woman, came out. She closed the door and asked, "Is there a family member present?"

We all looked at Claude, who stood immediately. "How is he?"

She led Claude a few feet away from us and they had a hushed conversation, but not so hushed that I couldn't determine that the medics believed Julien was suffering from anxiety and could do with a proper night's rest in the hospital.

Claude readily agreed, but as we soon found out, Julien was loath to go to the hospital. Claude and the medical technicians persisted in encouraging him but he would not be persuaded. Compromise was reached when Claude offered to share Julien's room for the night.

While the medical personnel were packing up their equipment, Maggie and Claude walked with Julien to the tiny elevator, which I had barely noticed and never used.

As they walked by us, Hugh said, "Dougal, that is a fine lass you have there. She seems capable of anything."

Dougal nodded in agreement. "Aye, she is and I would sorely miss her if ever she moved far away."

I looked at Owen but he didn't comment at all.

Hugh Tierney left us, as he said, "to see what the wife has on the stove."

When Dougal moved over to the registration desk, I asked Owen who would be most likely to know any gossip about Dermot's plans.

Owen didn't hesitate. "James Collins might have overheard a thing or two. Dermot is often seen with his knee up and his elbow down at the bar in the Dart and the Pint."

Chapter Twenty-Two

Owen began fidgeting and kept looking toward the staircase. I urged him to sit down and calm down.

"Maggie may be quite a while. I am happy to wait here with you, or we could go for a walk or even take a short bicycle ride around the village," I suggested. I thought any activity would be healthier for him than his endless fidgeting.

"I would suggest we go to the Dart and have a talk with James but Maggie would be furious if we did that without her," Owen said.

"She certainly would. And who could blame her? I have an idea. I haven't seen the distillery as yet. Perhaps we could—"

A voice behind me said, "Hold that thought for another time, Mrs. Fletcher. Right now I have a question or two." Inspector Finley was walking across the lobby with Constable Breen in his wake.

They stopped in front of me and Finley said, "I understand there was a bit of a medical emergency here today, and why was

I not surprised to see your name on the witness list? Trouble does seem to follow you."

"I am not sure what you mean," I said. "I didn't witness anything."

"Breen, read the witness list to Mrs. Fletcher."

The constable opened a notebook and said, "Medical emergency report regarding Julien Lavigne at the River Bush Hotel." Then he read off a list of names. Mine was right there between Hugh Tierney and Claude Blanchet.

"Inspector, I was present here in the lobby, as were Owen and the others, but we arrived after the medical team had been called. In fact, the medics arrived a few moments after we did. The person you want to speak to is Hugh Tierney. He was with Julien even before they got to the hotel."

"All in good time. But let me ask Dougal for a quiet place where you and I can have a bit of a chat."

He walked over to reception and I saw Dougal point down the hallway. I hoped he wasn't offering Maggie's office to the inspector. I had no idea what papers we'd left in open view when we rushed out to the lobby.

The inspector asked Owen to wait his turn and then ordered Breen to locate everyone on the witness list, although what he thought we might have witnessed, I had no idea. Then he guided me down the hallway and opened a door with the words READING LOUNGE in black letters on a gold plate nailed to it. Inside, there was a wall of shelves filled with books, and five oversized, overstuffed leather chairs were scattered around the room. Each chair had an end table and lamp next to it.

"Dougal told me how to make this reading lounge private for as long as I need it. Let me see. Here we go, just as Dougal promised." Finley walked to the nearest end table, picked up a wooden sign that read DO NOT DISTURB, and hung it over the room designation. "Good man, Dougal Nolan, prepared for any eventuality. Let's take a seat."

I couldn't help but grin. The privacy of the reading room reminded me of the snug James Collins had described to me the day I stopped at the pub after shopping at Aunt Aggie's. I'd have to remember to ask him if I could go inside the snug just to get the feel of it before I left for home. I decided that a snug in a homey Irish pub would make a perfect murder site for one of my future novels.

The inspector looked at me. "And what is it you find so funny, Mrs. Fletcher?"

"Nothing at all. A work thing just flashed through my mind. Books, you know."

I waved vaguely at the shelves. I thought it wisest not to mention that I'd gotten a small thrill at discovering such a perfect site for murder.

He looked the shelves up and down as if he were examining the books. "I wonder if this room is stocked with any books written by the famous mystery writer J. B. Fletcher?"

I couldn't tell if Finley was serious or teasing, so I told him the truth. "I have no idea. Until you opened the door, I didn't know this room existed."

"Well, we can take a look later, but for now, tell me what you know about the incident with the Frenchman." He sat back, waiting for my reply.

But my mind had wandered once again. *Incident with the Frenchman.* Now, wouldn't that make a terrific title for a book?

I came to the relevant question. "Anything I can tell you is

secondhand information. By the time I arrived in the lobby–
dining room area, a small crowd had gathered and medical personnel had already been summoned. After they arrived, I did hear
one of the medical responders say that Julien was suffering from
anxiety. That's all I know. I'm sure you could get more direct information if you talk to them."

"Actually, Mrs. Fletcher, it was the medics that brought Monsieur Lavigne to our attention. I am surprised you didn't realize
that, given what Lavigne was heard to say." He waited for a response but I gave none.

After a moment Finley continued. "As I am sure you are aware,
he was in a distressed condition when he arrived at the hotel. He
was dehydrated, semicoherent, and barely able to walk. By the
time the ambulance arrived, he was seated and someone had
given him water to drink, but he still was blathering, sometimes
in English but mostly in French. As he came around, he began to
speak only English. He asked for Hugh Tierney. He asked for his
cameras. He said he wanted to rest. Is none of this familiar?"

I shook my head. "Not one word. I've already told you I was
not in the lobby when Hugh and Julien arrived. And when the
medical personnel were examining and treating Julien in the
dining room, I was in the lobby and the connecting door was
closed."

"Well, then, my final question is, have you yourself ever
thought of Julien Lavigne even as a possible suspect in Michael
O'Bannon's murder?" Finley leaned back and propped his arm
on one of the chair's wide armrests. He looked as though we were
in for a long discussion.

"Now, that is a difficult question to answer. As you know well,
Michael O'Bannon and his family were in complicated business

negotiations with the company represented by Messieurs Blanchet and Lavigne. And we were all together the evening that Michael was murdered. Considering this, of course Julien could be a suspect, and the same is true for all of the rest of us who were at Jane's dinner party, but if you are asking if there is anything that points to him specifically—"

"That is exactly what I am asking." The inspector was getting impatient, but I was careful to sort my words before I responded.

"You did interview Beth Anne about her argument with Michael in the library the night he died. And what did she tell you?" I'd been curious about how Beth Anne would answer the question and now I had a hope of finding out.

"She said it was a routine business disagreement brought on by the coming merger. Why? Do you think there is more to it?" he asked.

"You also interviewed Claude Blanchet. I am sure he admitted overhearing the argument. Did he give you any idea of what might have caused it?"

"I concede that his version had a slightly different take to it. He said Michael had suddenly brought up some new ideas regarding how the products would be shipped postmerger. Blanchet and Lavigne had been quite convinced during earlier negotiations that shipping would remain as it was both from here and from France. How many more questions will I have to answer before you answer mine?"

"I am sorry. I didn't mean to delay answering. I am just trying to determine what caused you to suddenly look at Julien with such laser focus."

"Well, I am happy to tell you that due to his fine Irish education, Robbie MacDonagh, one of our young medics, was able to understand much of Monsieur Lavigne's French-language rambling. As far as young MacDonagh could translate, the Frenchman said, 'Michael is dead,' a number of times and then he began shaking his head while repeating something along the lines of 'I don't know if the trouble is gone' or 'I hope the trouble is gone.'

"Given Michael O'Bannon's recent and unsolved murder, as soon as his supervisor saw Robbie's written incident report, she notified us immediately." He stretched out his legs as if we'd been sitting far too long.

I understood that he was sending me a signal that I'd better answer his original question, which was, basically, had Julien Lavigne had a compelling motive to kill Michael O'Bannon?

"I can tell you this, Inspector: Julien Lavigne has relatives who are financially dependent on the current shipping process for Belle Visage."

Finley drew his legs back, sat up straight, and began to rub his hands together. "Now we are getting somewhere. He had motive."

"Not exactly," I replied. "Remember that Beth Anne is the head of Marine Magic, and from what I could tell from the conversation she had with Michael in the library, she appears to be solidly against changing shipping practices. If she is, Julien had every reason to be optimistic."

"I see your point. But then how do you explain his histrionics? He actually got to the point of considering suicide, if Robbie Mac-Donagh's report is to be believed."

Now Finley leaned forward and rested his elbows on his knees. He seemed truly anxious for an explanation.

"Well, it was common knowledge that Michael, with his medical degree and personable nature, was nothing more than the spokesperson for Marine Magic. He pushed the product line to the public in exactly the way he was now trying to push a new shipping company to his cousins."

Finley was following my every word, which was a delightful change, so I plunged in and told him what I surmised.

"Unlike Michael, Julien is a top-notch businessman. According to Claude, he and Julien have worked together harmoniously for decades. So, if Julien took the time to analyze this sudden idea of a new shipping arrangement, he might suspect that Michael was filling his usual role as front man for whoever was the power broker who wanted the shipping rights for the newly merged company. Think back to Julien's words. According to your young medical friend, Julien was worried. As a businessman of so much experience, he would automatically want to know if Michael had initiated the idea for reasons of his own or if Michael was acting in his role as speaker for a third party. Thus, knowing Michael was dead, he still wondered if the trouble is gone or if the person who wants the contract is still out there, ready to persist."

"That is an interesting and, I admit, plausible concern for Lavigne to have. My only question, Mrs. Fletcher, is this: Do you have any inkling who the man behind the curtain might be?"

"Oh, yes. I believe it to be Dermot Kerrigan."

Chapter Twenty-Three

There was a timid knock on the door and we heard Constable Breen say, "Inspector, begging your pardon, sir, but you are wanted."

A look of annoyance flashed across Finley's face. "Excuse me, Mrs. Fletcher. I will be right back."

He opened the door and stepped into the hallway, pulling the door not quite shut behind him. As soon as he was out of sight, I crept over to a spot between the hinge frame of the door and the first row of bookshelves so I could eavesdrop.

Breen said, "Maggie Nolan said, since Mr. Lavigne is not to be left alone, medically speaking, she is willing to remain with Mr. Lavigne while you talk to Mr. Blanchet now. Then she would switch places with Mr. Blanchet and be your next conversation. Afterward, she can get back to work while you talk to her father and Owen. Hugh Tierney is out on a job, but he will come in as soon as he is able."

I could hear the aggravation in Finley's voice. "Maggie Nolan is now organizing my work for me, is she?"

Breen said, "Yes, sir. I mean, no, sir. At least, I was the one who called Hugh Tierney. Maggie is just suggesting the rest. Except for her-herself and M-Mr. Blanchet, of course."

Breen was beginning to stammer. I could imagine he didn't like the position he found himself in. I wouldn't have liked it either.

The inspector heaved one of those sighs I was getting used to hearing from everyone here. Then he said, "All right, Breen, you can bring Blanchet down and tell Maggie Nolan to be ready to switch places with him accordingly. Hurry along, now. I want to get these interviews done and gone."

When he came back into the reading lounge, I had my back to the door and was scanning the bookshelves intently. I said, "Sad to say, I don't see any books by J. B. Fletcher. I will have to remedy that."

"Mrs. Fletcher, we will have to continue our conversation later in the day. It seems Maggie Nolan requires my immediate attention for both Claude Blanchet and herself," Finley said, then added sarcastically, "Obviously she is a very busy young woman with a lot on her mind."

I didn't doubt that for a second. I picked up my purse and headed for the door, but before I left, he said, "I was quite intrigued when you mentioned Dermot Kerrigan. We will have to continue that conversation. Please, if you leave the hotel, make sure someone at the reception desk knows where I can find you."

I joined Owen, sitting in the lobby. When he asked about my interview, I shrugged. "It's hard to judge what Finley is thinking.

Initially he seemed focused on Julien as Michael's killer but I was able to at least drop a hint that someone else might be involved."

Owen laughed. "And based on our conversation in Maggie's office, I don't need a weather vane to tell me in which direction you pointed."

I held my finger to my lips in the universal sign for silence and pointed. Constable Breen was coming down the stairs and Claude Blanchet was walking behind him, looking for all the world as though he were being led to the gallows. They stepped into the reading lounge, and within a few seconds, Breen walked out alone and came to us.

"Owen, I am sorry you've had to wait so long, but it is likely the inspector will be ready to speak with you soon. If you leave the lobby, please let us know where we can find you. Thank you kindly."

Before Owen could respond, Breen went into the dining room, picked up a straight-backed chair, brought it to the hallway, and sat outside the reading lounge.

Owen leaned closer and said in a low voice, "I wonder if this is all really necessary. It would be different if Julien had actually . . . Well, I don't want to say it, but there seems to be a lot of fuss about something that didn't happen."

"As I said, Finley needs to be convinced that Julien's emotional breakdown had nothing to do with Michael's murder, and to be honest, I don't think he is anywhere near convinced. Perhaps if we hadn't been interrupted . . ."

Owen nodded. "I do have to wonder if Maggie is getting a little too involved in this. She's acting like solving Michael's murder is a treasure hunt and she wants to win the prize."

Answering him required some tact on my part. "Owen, think

about the many things that delight you about Maggie. Now, as someone who had a long and happy marriage with my late husband, Frank, I can tell you that the very traits you love about a person are the same ones that can sometimes drive you mad. Some of the things I see in Maggie are that she is intelligent, inquisitive, and energetic."

"Not to mention, she is kind and always tries to be helpful. Oh, I get it," Owen said. "My father always says that someone's personality is like two sides of a coin, usually when he is talking about my mother."

"I can see why he would," I said. "But going back to your relationship with Maggie, it's the very traits we mentioned that would drive her to use her energy, inquisitiveness, and intelligence to help find answers to something that has affected your family as deeply as Michael's murder has. And in turn her interest and actions would make you very nervous about her safety."

Owen leaned in and gave me a kiss on the cheek. "Your late husband was a very lucky man."

Finley released Claude a few minutes later, and when Breen came down the stairs with Maggie, she stopped to tell us that if we wanted anything to eat or drink, we should go to the kitchen and find Breeda.

"Then, when we are all done taking Inspector Finley's pop quiz, we can go to the Dart and the Pint for some relaxation."

She gave us a broad wink and was off to the reading lounge just as Dougal walked through the dining room and came into the lobby.

I was starting to feel as though I were in the audience of a first-rate production at the Cabot Cove Playhouse, watching the various characters enter and exit stage right or stage left.

"Was that my Maggie I saw go down the hall with Constable Breen?" Dougal asked us. "And why is Breen sitting outside the reading lounge? Don't tell me Clive Finley has my daughter in there."

"I suspect he is only doing what he considers to be a thorough follow-up," I said as diplomatically as I could.

"Well, I've a hotel to run, and that very sight"—he pointed to Breen—"makes it look as though someone, or everyone, is under house arrest. This has been a troublesome time, I can tell you. And why are you two sitting here, may I ask, when we've far more sunshine than is usual? Shouldn't you be out and about doing tourist things, Mrs. Fletcher? And you, Owen—shouldn't you be her guide?"

I left it to Owen to explain that he had not yet been interviewed and was waiting his turn. When he mentioned that Dougal himself was on the witness list, I was amazed at how heated the landlord got.

"Witness list! What is this, some sort of television mystery show? If I had known Finley was planning on spending the entire day yammering and hammering at people, I would never have allowed it in my hotel. When he asked for a private room, I'd no idea . . . no idea at all."

While Dougal was speaking, Hugh Tierney walked through the front door. He headed directly to Dougal, punched him lightly in the arm, and said, "What are you going on about? Has someone ruined your day by putting sour milk in your morning tea?"

"Clive Finley has only gone and taken over my premises when he has a perfectly good police station down the road," Dougal said.

Hugh looked around, saw Breen, and touched his fingers to his cap in a salute, which Breen returned. Then Hugh started to laugh.

"That's it? Eddie Breen sitting in your hallway is what's got you all rancored up? Do you think either Clive or Eddie would put you under arrest if you closed the hallway door?"

Dougal opened his mouth, then closed it. He turned on his heel, walked to the hallway, said a few words to Breen, and closed the door. Dougal returned to us a changed man.

"What say tea all around?"

When no one declined, as of course we wouldn't, he went through to the kitchen.

Hugh Tierney sat in the chair next to Owen and asked, "So, what have I missed?"

By the time we got him all caught up, Dougal was on his way back carrying a tray of teapots and cups, while Breeda was behind him with plates of biscuits and scones along with pots of jam and clotted cream.

Dougal apologized for his outburst, and as we four began chatting and enjoying our tea and nibbles, he smiled. "Now, this is how the lobby of the River Bush Hotel should look and feel."

The hall door opened and Breen held it as Maggie came through. Apparently unfazed by her interview, she said, "Oh, and wasn't I yearning for a cuppa?"

Before she sat down, she turned to Breen and said, "Go on, then. Bring in the inspector's next victim. I'll bring you tea and biscuits in two shakes."

Breen managed to look grateful and worried at the same time, which I thought was a marvelous skill.

Maggie got the message. "I'll fix a plate for the inspector as well so you can enjoy yours without bother."

With that arranged, Breen visibly relaxed. Then he said to Dougal, "I know that you and Owen have been waiting for a long while but the inspector is most anxious to speak with Hugh."

Dougal replied, "I've a hotel to run, so I won't be hard to find whenever you need, but mind you, keep the hall door closed as long as you are assigned to sit there."

Breen nodded and took a teacup and a plate of biscuits from Maggie, who quickly prepared a matching set and said, "I'll just walk these in to Finley. Da, why don't you ask Breeda to replenish the pots?"

"That's my girl, always giving orders. You'd best be ready for a life of that, Owen." Dougal laughed as he picked up the two teapots and headed to the kitchen.

Maggie was back in a minute and stood in front of Owen and me while she whispered, "Inspector Finley is on the wrong track, looking as he is at the Frenchmen. We, on the other hand, will soon have the goods."

"Maggie, it's best you know, with the way our conversation went, I felt compelled to mention you-know-who to the inspector," I said, and I did feel bad as her face fell, but I needn't have worried. Her smile was back in a jiffy.

"No bother there, Jessica. Finley tends to have a one-track mind, so while he's on his track, we can move along on ours." She took a bite of a biscuit. "Oh, these chocolate are always my favorite."

The day dragged on but at long last Inspector Finley finished interviewing everyone on his so-called witness list. I had assumed that he would call me in for further conversation about Dermot

Kerrigan but that did not appear to be uppermost in his mind at the moment.

He stood in front of us and thanked Dougal for his hospitality and for the use of the reading lounge. I could not help but notice Maggie's grin when Finley asked Dougal to notify him "at once" if Messieurs Lavigne and Blanchet expressed the least bit of interest in checking out of the hotel.

Grateful to be able to get back to work, Hugh Tierney said his good-byes and was checking his cell phone as he followed the policemen out the door. Dougal went behind the reception desk, where he always seemed most comfortable. When Breeda came out of the kitchen to see if we needed anything more, Maggie advised that she could clear the tea away.

With a glint in her eye, Maggie said, "I think it is time I tell my father that we are going for a good stretch of the legs after the day we've had. And then . . . we'll see what we can learn from James Collins about the notorious Dermot Kerrigan."

Chapter Twenty-Four

Even the short walk to the Dart and the Pint was welcome exercise. I had begun to feel as stiff as I often do during the final days of writing a book, when the words are all in my head and the only way to get them on paper is to sit in the chair and pound the keys nonstop. The sun was still high in the sky and there was a brisk breeze, which Owen told me was coming down from the ocean.

A few tables were occupied but the bar was empty when we arrived. Maggie's plan, as she told us on our short walk, was to sit at the bar and eventually engage James Collins in a chat about Dermot Kerrigan.

When I said that I thought that might be somewhat foolhardy in such a public place, Maggie scoffed. "And sure, what are we supposed to do, corral him in the snug? Not to worry, Jessica. If a person wants to socialize in the pub, they make it well known, but if they want to be on their own, they block out the talk around them."

While Owen nodded in agreement, I was not so sure. Still, I realized that a public conversation was better than no conversation at all.

We took our places at the bar, with me in the middle and Maggie and Owen on either side. I'd drunk so much tea that I might have surprised James when I followed Maggie and ordered a half-pint of Guinness, while Owen opted for a pint.

When James set down our glasses, he said, "Nice to see you again, Mrs. Fletcher. You are becoming a regular, and every publican appreciates his regular customers. They're the ones who keep the door open."

"Aye," Maggie said, "'tis the same in the hotel business. Where would we be without the salmon fishermen who show up so faithfully year after year?"

Maggie was so excited to be on the trail, as it were, that I was afraid she would jump in to ask James about Kerrigan too quickly, so I started on a completely neutral topic. "I have to say, I felt fortunate indeed to be here for your trad music session. And the dancers, well, they were nothing short of magnificent."

"Aileen and Orla Byrne have danced and won awards at *feiseanna*, as we call our cultural festivals, all over the island of Ireland. They've even participated in a *feis* or two in America. I have heard that they are considering an invitation to Australia."

"No surprise there. Those young ladies are so talented. Their coordination has to be seen to be believed. Truly amazing. All in all, it was a perfect evening," I said.

James pulled a cloth from under the bar and began rubbing

the wooden top. "Well, now, it was and it wasn't. I am beginning to get a wee bit irritated by the slovenly behavior of one of my 'regulars.' No need for names. We all know who I mean."

Maggie and Owen nodded their heads and I followed suit. It wasn't necessary for anyone to mention Conor Sweeney.

James began to rub the bar top more vigorously, which indicated to me that the incident had agitated him a great deal. "He has always liked his whiskey. Born and raised as he was up the road a ways from the distillery . . . Well, it's to be expected, is it not?"

James seemed to expect answers, so I said, "Of course," while Owen said, "And isn't it true of us all?" and Maggie said, "For generations."

James looked over our heads at the tables. Satisfied that no one was in need of his service, he continued. "The one good thing is that he knows he's often too bousy to get behind the wheel of a car, so he traded that fancy Mercedes for a bicycle that cost near as much. He gave the entire village less to worry about, I can tell you. But the issue does become when a man can't control himself in his local pub . . . I mean, what is there to be done? Can he be trusted to control himself anywhere?"

Owen muttered, "Not likely."

James was clearly on a roll. "Why, on the very evening before Michael died, I came close to asking him to leave. He was in here all well and good and then suddenly he began asking me about Audra's death. Do I still blame Michael? That sort of thing. I know I bring it up often enough, as many have witnessed, but shouldn't that be my choice, not the choice of a man not sober enough to realize when he has gone too far?"

Then, as if he'd been under hypnosis all the while and someone had snapped their fingers in front of his face, he dropped the cloth under the countertop and said, "More than enough talk about that. I've something better for ye. Here's one I heard just the other evening." And he told us a joke about an old man, his wife, and a fish dinner.

While we were laughing, a voice behind us said loudly, "James, we're off. If health allows, we'll meet again right soon."

James came around to our side of the bar to give the man and his two friends a hearty handshake; then he set about cleaning their table.

Maggie looked at the clock and said, "More folks will be wandering in shortly and needing James's attention. The next time we have him standing in front of us, I will ask about Dermot Kerrigan. What do you think, Jessica?"

I said, "I think there is no time like the present."

But in reality, I wasn't sure that we could learn anything more than we already knew. I went over the facts in my head. Michael O'Bannon had been indebted to Dermot Kerrigan off and on for years. After plans for the merger were set, Michael suddenly started to argue with his cousins because he wanted to contract a new and, to them, completely unknown shipping company. And Maggie had discovered that recently Dermot Kerrigan's wife had become the permit holder for Sunshine Import and Export. Given those facts and the bruises on Michael's body, I doubted there was much James could tell us that we didn't already know, but I guessed it was worth a try.

When James went back behind the bar, Maggie said, "When you have a free minute, I have a quick question."

Holding a glass in one hand, James put his other hand on a

tap. "I need to serve two drinks, but then I'll be right back to you with an answer. But knowing me as you do, you know nothing I ever say is short, so there will be no chance of you getting a quick answer."

We all laughed and he went off to do table service. Maggie asked me if I thought she should fish around for a while or go straight to Dermot's connection to the shipping company.

"You know James far better than I do. Trust your instinct and use whatever approach you believe is most likely to work," I said.

Maggie's smile assured me that I'd said exactly what she wanted to hear.

James came back, opened a bag of Tayto brand crisps, and put them on the bar in front of us. "Now, Miss Maggie Nolan, pop your question, and even with Owen Mullen sitting right here with us, as a gentleman, I am honor bound to say yes."

We all laughed at his implication.

I took a crisp and passed the bag to Owen while we waited to see if we'd learn anything.

Maggie took a sip of her Guinness and then said, "Would you be knowing anything at all about Dermot Kerrigan and his latest venture into the shipping industry?"

Whatever James was expecting Maggie to ask, that definitely wasn't it. He looked off into the distance as if deciding how to answer while we sat quietly waiting for his answer.

"Well, now, I do and I don't, as they say. It's a smart publican who minds his own business in all matters concerning his regulars' lives, personal or commercial, as it were."

James was stalling. I could almost see answers filtering through his mind as he rejected first one, then the next. I suspected that on the one hand, he wanted to answer Maggie truthfully, but on the other hand, it might not be wise to discuss Dermot Kerrigan's financial interests, be they business or personal.

"James, I am hardly printing a newspaper, now, am I?" Maggie teased, which lightened James's attitude.

"And you're up to promising there'll be no social media reports of our conversation?" James needed a final reassurance.

Maggie crossed her heart like a teenager vowing to keep a secret.

James took a deep breath. "Then, aye, there's been more than a whisper or two. Dermot has his hands in many tills. Not yours nor mine, the Lord be praised, but he has been known to bring in American cigarettes and Canadian whiskey in ways that are not in accord with regulations."

He stepped over to the taps and poured a few ounces of Guinness into a glass, and took a robust drink. "Ahhh, sometimes a man's throat goes dry if he talks too much."

And he smiled at us as if the topic of Dermot Kerrigan were behind him. I was sure Maggie didn't feel that it was.

She proved me correct within seconds. "Dermot's illicit activities are far from secret, but I have been hearing round about that he is considering a legitimate transport business. I wonder if you have heard the same."

James got a guarded expression on his face and then issued a long and loud sigh. "Is it important, Maggie? Is there a serious reason that you are asking, not just idle chatter?"

Maggie reached across the bar and covered his hand with hers. "James, I would never put you in a position of struggling with someone else's confidences unless the matter was truly life or death."

He nodded and became clear-eyed. His decision had been made. "I suppose this is all concerning Michael, with what's happened and all."

Maggie nodded.

James said, "You and all the village know that I make my snug available to those who wish a bit of privacy. They've only to ask me to leave the door unlocked. Well, some time ago there was an evening that Dermot asked me to leave the snug door unlocked. So of course, I did.

"As is my custom, once I heard movement and the hum of voices in the snug, I kept one eye and one ear on the window." He pointed to the stained glass panel in the corner. "Sure enough, it opened a few inches and himself ordered four glasses of Black Bush. I put the glasses on the window ledge and tapped on the window. It was opened by Callen O'Shea, one of Dermot's thugs, so I had a quick idea of the kind of goings-on that could happen that evening.

"Now and again voices were raised, and I stuck close here behind the bar, worried that I might have to intercede if things got too rowdy and I heard some punches being thrown. During one of the moments that the window was open for glasses to be passed, I heard a voice. Now, I couldn't swear it was Michael but it sounded quite similar." James stopped for another sip from his glass.

"Do you remember what the voice said?" Maggie prompted.

"Aye. Close to exact as I can come, it was, 'I keep telling you, I'm not in charge.' Then Callen took the glasses from the ledge and closed the window." James shrugged. "I cannot swear it was Michael."

Owen and I exchanged a glance. Those words sounded exactly like what Michael likely would have said if he was being pressured into hiring a new shipping company, which was clearly outside his purview.

Maggie was effusive with her thanks and was sincerely promising that none but we three would ever know of this conversation when James interrupted.

"I've one thing still to mention. It was nearly closing time when Dermot tapped to tell me they were leaving the snug. And he said the room was a bit more manky than usual, so I should add an extra twenty on his account to pay for the cleanup. The only thing I found was a couple of bloody bar towels dropped on the floor, looked like someone had had a bloody nose." Then James folded his arms across his chest and smiled, relieved that his ordeal was over.

Or got punched in the nose, I thought.

We stayed long enough not to look as though we were the "take the information and run" gang, but Maggie was so antsy that we were barely on the sidewalk when she threw her hands in the air and yelled, "Talk about your fine *craic.*" Then she flung her arms around Owen and gave him a smacking kiss.

Next she put her arm around my shoulder and planted a kiss on my cheek. "Couldn't have done it without you, Jessica."

I hated to burst her enthusiasm but I was compelled to ask, "Couldn't have done what, exactly?"

Maggie grinned. "We solved Michael's murder. I cannot wait to see Inspector Finley's face when we tell him. Oh, but first we have to tell Da. And, Owen, how do you want to tell the family? We can't have Finley stealing our thunder."

Owen looked at me over Maggie's head and shrugged help-lessly.

I stopped walking, which forced Maggie to stop as well. Then I said, "Calm down, Maggie. We haven't solved a thing. All we have done is gather some relevant information. Our next job is to find out if it is useful or not."

Chapter Twenty-Five

Maggie was dejected but only for the moment. By the time we'd walked the few short blocks to the hotel, she was back to her usual bouncy self.

As we walked in the front door, she asked me what I thought our next step should be. Then she stopped and pointed. Inspector Finley was sitting in the lobby with a cup of tea at his elbow.

"Does the man ever take a minute off from work?" Maggie was annoyed. "I'd rather not see him again until I have something concrete to tell him."

"I have a feeling he's here to see me, not you," I said mildly.

"Why would that be?" Maggie asked. "Aren't we a team?"

"Because it was my interview that Finley abruptly ended earlier today to allow you and Claude to skip the line. At your request, I might add," I said.

For the first time Maggie looked repentant. "I only wanted to be done with him because I wanted to continue sharing the information I received with you."

"I know, but for now it is best that we not go barging in to Finley with accusations we can't back up."

"I'm sure we can." Maggie saw the look on my face and stopped. "Can't we?"

"No, we cannot. Without James's testimony all we can say is that we heard from *someone* who said he heard Dermot demanding that Michael do *something* concerning Marine Magic that would benefit Dermot financially. And if James is willing to speak to the good inspector, all he can say is that he heard a voice that sounded like Michael's. He never saw Dermot and Michael together. He saw only Dermot and Mr. O'Shea. Who is to say anyone else was with them?"

We spent so much time talking that Finley eventually saw us, stood up, and started our way.

"Owen," I said, "why don't you and Maggie go to her office? I will speak with the inspector."

The last thing I wanted was to have Maggie flashing an imaginary "amateur detective" badge and running her suppositions by Inspector Finley. I greeted the inspector as I walked directly toward him while the young couple slipped away.

"Mrs. Fletcher, I understand you and your friends went for a walk. Beautiful evening for it."

"Yes, it is." I smiled pleasantly.

"I hope you are not too tired to finish our conversation. Let's go see if the reading lounge is available?"

Which, of course, it was, since Constable Breen was sitting in the chair nearest the door, thumbing through a salmon fishing guide. The moment we entered, Breen jumped up from the chair and dropped the book on the table.

He said, "I'll see you are not disturbed, sir," and went into the hall, closing the door behind him.

Finley and I sat in the same chairs we'd occupied earlier. He crossed one knee over the other and said, "When last we spoke, you told me that you believe Dermot Kerrigan, a man I know well, was behind Michael O'Bannon's request to give the shipping contract of the newly merged company to an import-export company that Kerrigan now controls. Have I got that right?"

"Yes, that is completely correct," I said.

"And where did you get such an idea?" he asked.

I couldn't help but smile while I said, "Why, I got it from you."

His head snapped up and his eyes bulged but he didn't say a word.

I went on. "Don't you remember, Inspector? You told me that you suspected Kerrigan of smuggling and that he had an interest in a property on Bayhead Road."

"I'm not likely to forget such things. Our sources who keep track of people like Kerrigan have been seeing signs of packages moving in and out of a house he owns that happens to be nicely set back behind the hedgerows that grow along Bayhead. How would that have anything to do with Michael O'Bannon? You don't think that Kerrigan would dare to try smuggling huge quantities of ladies' face cream out of Ireland?" He leaned back in his chair, chuckling as he did so.

"No, I don't."

As I said it, Finley nodded as though I had at last come to my senses.

"What I do think is that Dermot Kerrigan is a smart man who

saw an irresistible opportunity. Easy as it might be to get a limited number of products into or out of the country while avoiding taxes and fees, an ambitious man might want to move large amounts. What would make that easier?"

I smiled mischievously again. I leaned back in my chair and waited for him to think it through.

"Well, I suppose the contraband could be stashed away here and there among legitimate import-export products. Besides running afoul of the law, there would be the danger that Kerrigan's products would be discovered by the legitimate shipper." Finley's head began to bob slightly as if he was deep in thought.

"Unless . . ." I said, and waited for the light to dawn.

"Unless . . ." Finley pursed his lips and squinted his eyes. I could see he was almost there. Then he boomed, "Unless he owned a company designed for international trading like the one Michael O'Bannon was proposing. That is where you were going all along, isn't it, Mrs. Fletcher?"

"I was only going where you led me, Inspector. You brought up Kerrigan's interest in smuggling and one thing led to another," I said as if it was the simplest thing in the world.

"Why do I get the feeling there is more that I should know?" Finley's voice was sterner than it had been all evening.

"Well, you might want to search the government records for newly issued or newly transferred import-export licenses or permits or whatever paperwork is required in this country."

He merely raised an eyebrow and waited for me to say more.

"Remember, the paperwork needn't be in Dermot's name. It could be issued in the name of any relative. Or even a friend, but I would look for a relative first. In fact, I shouldn't wonder if setting up the business could be done in such a way that the person who is named has no inkling they are now the proud owner of a shipping company."

"Mrs. Fletcher, you sound quite positive that such paperwork will be easy to find. I have to wonder if you are something other than a mystery writer. Have you access to Interpol, or perhaps your CIA or some other stealth organization?"

"I have to admit that I do have friends in various law informant circles, and I do hope that one day I will count you among them, but for the purposes of this conversation, I am speaking entirely of my own suppositions," I said. "Now, is there anything else you require of me this evening?"

He looked to the ceiling as though searching for whatever questions might still be left to ask. Then he found one. "I was wondering if you'd made any plans to leave Bushmills and travel home."

"I plan to remain until Michael O'Bannon is properly buried. Then I will share Maeve's paintings with the family and be on my way," I said, and when he didn't so much as nod his head in reply, I asked if he had any objection to my leaving.

"Not at all, not at all. The thought crossed my mind that when you go home, you'd like to be able to tell the American cousin that Michael's killer has been brought to justice."

He looked directly in my eyes as if daring me to deny it, which, we both knew, I could not.

I nodded, and I tossed the ball back to him. "That's true and I hope you can make it happen swiftly. In the meantime, if there is nothing else, it has been a very long day."

When I picked up my purse, Finley stood, which I took as a signal that we were done for the time being.

"One more thing, Mrs. Fletcher. Should you decide to leave

for home, I hope you will do me the courtesy of giving me ample notice."

"Of course, Inspector. Have a nice evening."

I walked down to Maggie's office, and when I saw the door closed, I made sure to cough loudly and clap my hand against my purse before I knocked, just in case the couple had decided to take the opportunity to steal a kiss or two.

I needn't have been concerned. Owen opened the door immediately and Maggie was sitting at her desk, digging through a pile of papers.

"Jessica, how did it go? Please sit down. Can I get you something? Owen can bring tea from the kitchen."

"My conversation with the inspector went rather well. I do believe he will spend the next little while searching for a shipping license that is connected to Dermot Kerrigan," I said.

Maggie clapped her hands gleefully. "You only hinted? You didn't tell him outright?"

"The information wasn't mine to tell. All I saw, for a fleeting few seconds, was a piece of paper purporting to be a permit that you told me was sent to you by a friend who worked in a government office. We would have to verify the permit, get your friend's permission to give the inspector her name, and then tie it all together and present it to him.

"As to the tea, I'd dearly love to have supper sent to my room. Sandwiches with a side of vegetables and a nice pot of tea. Breeda will know. She brought me room service the other night and it was heavenly. Delicious and tranquil."

Maggie picked up the desk phone and relayed my request. When she hung up, she said, "Jessica, it is no wonder you write such excellent mystery books. You have such a wondrous understanding of the difference between gossip and fact. Gossip is guessing. Fact is supported by solid evidence."

"That's kind of you to say. And you have done a bang-up job collecting evidence. I must say you dove into investigating with boundless enthusiasm."

Maggie blushed and giggled at the praise.

Owen said, "I don't know if Finley mentioned to you that Michael's body has been released and he is being moved to McAvoy Brothers Funeral Directors. Right now everything is on track for a wake tomorrow evening followed by a church service and burial the next morning. My mother and my aunt are furious. They wanted a long, drawn-out circus of a wake but Deirdre and Niall stood firm."

"That is good news," I said. "And I hope taking those traditional and time-honored steps will help everyone adjust to the loss, especially Michael's children."

I was also aware that once the burial was over, I needed to find a time and a place to fulfill my obligation to Maeve.

The thought of Maeve reminded me of something. "Maggie, I had great luck at Aunt Aggie's Attic as far as gifts to bring home go, except I didn't find anything for Maeve O'Bannon. She is a difficult person to buy so much as a birthday card for, much less what I believe should be a special gift from her ancestors' village. Can you recommend anywhere else I could look?"

She popped right out of her chair. "Can I ever! Come with me."

Dougal was behind the reception desk, and when we approached, he boomed, "Aye, there you be. I was beginning to think Clive Finley had arrested the lot of you."

Maggie rushed around the counter to give him a kiss on the cheek. "Don't be daft. We are the most innocent sort you'll ever meet. Here is what we are after." She opened a drawer and took out what I thought was a pamphlet but turned out to be a folding map.

She spread the map on the counter, picked up a pen, drew a circle, and said, "Now, here is Danaher's. It is a stationery store that stocks far more than pens and paper. There are all sorts of games and knickknacks. You might find something there."

She went on to draw more circles and tell me about each of the shops she'd marked. Maggie was so thorough in recommending several different types of stores that I was confident I would find the perfect gift for Maeve.

I went off to my room, map in hand for tomorrow. I planned to have a quiet evening reading Seamus Heaney's book of poems and perhaps watching some local television. The evening was relaxing, right up until the moment my phone rang.

Chapter Twenty-Six

The tray Breeda brought to my room had a delicious array of food. Along with a ham and cheese sandwich made with fresh-baked brown bread, there were fresh broccoli and sliced tomatoes and an iced raisin scone.

"We've a special treat tonight," Breeda said. "One of the local farmers is testing out his recipe for yellowman and Mr. Nolan was inclined to buy some for the kitchen."

"Yellowman?"

Breeda pointed to something bright yellow that looked like a honeycomb. "It's a toffee candy of sorts and a tradition at the Auld Lammas Fair held in Ballycastle each year. Most of the stalls will cheerfully sell you a piece or two. Mind your teeth when you try it."

"I will be careful, I promise." I smiled and Breeda bounced out the door.

I finished the main portion of my meal and set the scone and the yellowman aside for a later treat. After scrolling through some television shows and finding that none caught my attention, I picked up the poetry book and was feeling more relaxed than I had in days when the room phone rang.

"Sorry to disturb, Mrs. Fletcher, but you have a visitor. It's best you come down. I've put him in the reading lounge."

I'm afraid I was a bit snappish. "Honestly, if Inspector Finley thinks I am going to jump each time he says come, he had better think again."

"It's not the inspector, but just the same, I suggest you come downstairs," Dougal said, and there was something in his voice that prevented me from arguing any further.

When I got to the lobby, Dougal barely acknowledged me other than with a slight nod, and then he slewed his eyes toward the hallway. When I got to the reading lounge door, I was not surprised to see the 'do not disturb' sign was already in place. I was surprised, however, when I opened the door and James Collins was standing inside, twisting and twirling a flat cap in his hands.

"Thank you for coming, Mrs. Fletcher. By way of explaining, I need to tell you I have two daughters, one safely married and one away at university. You know their mam is gone, so I have to do the watching over them on my own."

Normally I would have stopped him there to ask what any of this had to do with me, but he was so agitated that I decided to stay quiet for the moment.

"I'm sure you remember our earlier conversation about the snug. Well, not an hour ago, Dermot Kerrigan himself comes in and sits at the bar. After I served his pint, he asked me, casual-like, if anyone had been around the pub inquiring about him. He specifically mentioned young Tim Redding, who comes in for a pint now and again. Kerrigan supposed he might be coming to the Dart for his pint as a spy for Finley."

I was beginning to see where this was going. I nodded to encourage him to continue.

"It would be worth my life to tell Kerrigan that I spoke to you and the young ones. Might be worth your lives as well. So tell me true. Have you told Finley anything about . . . about the snug?" James asked.

"James, you've nothing to worry about on that account. As I explained to Maggie and Owen, since you never saw Michael and cannot be sure the voice you heard was his, all we have is supposition, and your guesses won't help Finley find a killer. Now, if you were to go to the inspector yourself . . ."

"And who would watch over my daughters if I did and Kerrigan found out and he arranged for me to go off the cliff top at Fair Head? No, Mrs. Fletcher, Clive Finley will have to discover Dermot Kerrigan's wrongdoings strictly on his own." He put his flat cap firmly on his head. "I bid you a good evening."

And he was gone. I took the 'do not disturb' sign off the door and turned out the light. When I stepped into the lobby, neither Dougal nor James was anywhere to be seen.

I asked the young man at the reception desk if Maggie was available and he said she'd gone out for the evening.

There was nothing I could do for James Collins until I was able to speak with Maggie and Owen and encourage them to keep our conversation with him completely private. I decided to go to my room and call Maeve so I could fill her in on the details of the planned wake and funeral. With any luck the sound of her voice would inspire me to find the perfect gift for her when I went shopping in the morning.

I woke up energized and ready to face a busy day. I'd showered, dressed, and was putting the finishing touches on my hair when there was a light tap at the door. It was Maggie.

"There was a note on my desk this morning to let me know you were looking for me last night. Owen and I spent the evening with the cousins. It is so rare that Deirdre and Niall come home. . . ."

"No need to explain. You didn't happen to mention what James Collins told us about Kerrigan and the snug?"

"Not at all. It was purposely a fun evening with lots of talk and laughter about our adventures when we were children and all that's been since. Why do you ask? Is there news about what happened to Michael?" Maggie looked fretful.

"No. Not that. It's just . . ."

I told her about my conversation with James and his concerns about loose tongues causing him difficulties.

Maggie was truly horrified. "Jessica, when you explained to us the difference between gossip-based and fact-based information, I understood what you were saying but I never gave a thought to the potential costs for anyone involved. Thank you for trusting me enough to share James's concerns. I promise there will be no need for James or you to worry. The snug is forgotten. And I will be sure Owen tells James so at the first opportunity."

"Well, that is a relief. Now I can focus on my next problem: finding the perfect gift for Maeve O'Bannon. I am going to take a bike ride around to the shops and see what wonders they hold."

"Good on you." Maggie pointed out the window. "That sky is promising a good soft rain before too long. I'd recommend a waterproof jacket and hat. If you are in need of either, we've plenty in the hall closet off the lobby."

"That is thoughtful, but this isn't my first trip to Ireland, so I have come prepared." I opened the closet door and pulled out my tan rain jacket complete with a hood.

"Ah, then, I'll not be worrying about you." Maggie's face turned serious. "And I promise you'll have no cause to worry about me flapping my jaw."

I went to the shed and was happy to see the red Donard, and I put a folding umbrella and my purse in the basket. I took a final look at Maggie's map and began pedaling toward Main Street.

After more than an hour of shopping, I found a toy car that represented the Police Service of Northern Ireland. I was sure Mort would love it. I bought myself a T-shirt that proclaimed *THE RIVER BUSH best fishing in the world.* I couldn't wait until I wore it on my next fishing trip with my Cabot Cove friends. It was sure to cause a stir.

I patiently let an older gentleman in one shop try to talk me into buying a shamrock bracelet for Maeve, but in all the years I'd known her I'd never seen her wear jewelry of any sort, so that was an automatic no.

In a more touristy shop, I found a set of tea mugs with a picture of the Giant's Causeway on each. It might have made the perfect gift except that Maeve had lived in her house forever, and that meant, at least to me, that she had enough mugs and cups to serve tea to dozens of people at the same time.

I was disheartened when I left the shop and more disheartened still when I saw that my front tire was nearly flat. I'd pulled out Maggie's map to see how far I was from the hotel when I heard a voice say, "Now, this is my lucky day. A damsel in distress. And I believe I can be of some assistance."

Conor Sweeney was behind me on a sharply designed black bicycle. He saw me looking over the bike and said, "I know Dougal Nolan brags about his Donards, but believe me, there is nothing finer than a Krencker—made in Denmark, excellent craftsmanship. I actually order my tires directly from the manufacturer. I keep them in my garage. I've never had a flat." He looked soulfully at my tire. "I ride everywhere, so I change both tires on a regular schedule."

I complimented his taste in bicycles even as I was wondering how he would propose to help me.

Conor got off his bike, dropped the kickstand, and said, "Although I have never had a flat tire, I am a firm believer in there being a first time for everything, and so, Mrs. Fletcher, I am here to save your day."

He reached down and unzipped a long black bag that was attached to his seat tube and took out a tire pump. He knelt on one knee, opened the valve on my tire, and attached the pump. Then he stood and put a foot on the pump to hold it steady while he wrapped his fists around the handle. He was stronger than he looked, and in fewer than a half dozen strokes, my tire was nice and taut.

Conor put his hand on the tire and pressed hard. "There you go. I don't hear any air hissing out, so it must have been a slow leak. Come on, give the tire a squeeze."

As I leaned over to do so, I noticed a dent in the side of the tire pump. "Oh, my, what happened there?" I pointed to the spot that was misshapen and discolored.

Conor looked surprised. "I have no idea. I guess that happened the last time I was being a Good Samaritan. I'll have my mechanic take a gander. This Krencker ensemble cost far too much money for any part of it to appear beat-up or worn-out."

He slid the pump back into its case and zipped it shut. "Now I'll ride along with you to the hotel."

On the way we chatted lightly, and when we stopped in the hotel driveway, Conor said, "I hope that being able to wake and bury Michael will give the family a sense of healing and closure. He will be missed by us all, and, at least for the young ones, the funeral will be like a marked end of one part of their lives and the beginning of the next."

"And what about Beth Anne and Jane? How do you think they will reorganize Marine Magic to replace Michael?" I asked.

"I think we'll be just fine. I will see you at McAvoys', then, will I? I would offer you a ride but I don't think sitting on my handlebars would be overly comfortable." Conor laughed and pedaled away.

I put my bicycle in the shed, and when I entered the lobby, I was glad to see that Dougal was behind the reception desk and no one was waiting to see me. I told him what had happened with the Donard's front tire and he said he would have it looked at.

"Next time you go out, take the blue one as a precaution. Although I don't see you'll have much time for bike rides in the near term, what with the wake and the funeral. And now Maggie tells me we are all invited to the big house for a reception after the burial. I'll have to rearrange the staff schedule, with the both of us gone for the better part of this evening and tomorrow."

While Dougal mentioned his schedule, I realized that mine could soon change. Once the burial was over and before the younger generation scattered back to their homes, I would have to take care of Maeve's presentation, which meant I should call Susan Shevlin so she could arrange my trip home. I couldn't help wishing that Michael's killer would be discovered before I left.

Chapter Twenty-Seven

I was still sorting through my packages when there was a knock on my door. On the off chance it was Inspector Finley testing me again I asked who it was and was surprised when Claude Blanchet answered.

I opened the door and invited him to come inside but his demeanor indicated that the very idea of being in a lady's bedroom made him uncomfortable, so we stood in the doorway.

"Julien and I have hired Monsieur Tierney to drive us to and from Michael O'Bannon's wake this evening. We would be honored if you would join us."

"Thank you both for thinking of me. I would be most appreciative. It is awkward being a relative stranger at such an intimate event."

"*Oui, exactement.* And I have an ulterior motive. Julien likes and trusts you. If he should become somewhat filled with the anxiety as before, well, I am confident that you and I can keep him calm and remove him from the venue before there are any consequences."

I nodded. "I see. That makes sense."

"We shall await you in the lobby at seven o'clock. Is that convenient?"

"It is absolutely perfect."

With one scheduling issue settled, I decided to move on to another. Susan Shevlin answered her phone on the second ring.

"Jessica, it is so good to hear from you. Are you ready to come home?"

"I am more than ready, and circumstances being as they are, we are getting closer to actually booking tickets," I said.

"I am glad to hear that. What did you have in mind?"

I could mentally see Susan opening her computer to my file and placing her fingers on the keyboard, ready to take notes.

"Well, we can't book quite yet, but Maeve's cousin Michael is being interred tomorrow, so I expect that I should be able to present her family gifts within two or three days, and then there will be no reason for me to stay," I said.

"Oh," Susan asked, "did the police arrest the murderer?"

I knew she was hinting that it would be difficult for me to leave the scene of an unsolved murder and she was absolutely right, but I was here only as a favor to Maeve, and once that favor was completed, I intended to leave.

"Not to my knowledge." I tried to sound offhand. "Before we book anything, I'd like to talk about coming home another way."

"You mean, by ship?" Susan knew that I had enjoyed a number of transatlantic cruises that she had booked for me in years gone by.

"No, what I meant was, I'd like to avoid that lengthy stopover in London and just fly directly from Ireland to Logan Airport, or if not Boston, I would be happy to fly into New York and visit Grady for a few days. I was fortunate to receive an offer of a ride from here to Dublin Airport."

"Bushmills to Dublin is a long ride. It's nearly three hours by car. Dublin to Logan is generally quite manageable. If you are sure you want to sit in a car that long, I am sure booking your plane tickets won't be a problem," Susan said.

"Well, in any event, it's too soon to make definite plans. I will call you back as soon as I have a date certain. Now, what Cabot Cove news am I missing?"

Promptly at seven o'clock, I walked down the stairs to the lobby. Claude was hovering over Julien, who was seated in a chair. As I walked closer, Julien appeared to shake off Claude's attention and he stood to greet me.

"Madame Fletcher, I must apologize for my recent erratic behavior," he said.

"There is no need to apologize. I am glad to see that you are feeling well. It is quite kind of you to attend Michael's wake," I said.

"I am much cheered by the fact that we will be going home," Julien replied. "I miss my family."

Claude explained, "Beth Anne called me and said that it is best for all concerned that we wait a few weeks to begin negotiations in earnest. She will need some time to focus on family matters. Julien and I will attend the funeral and then prepare to go home."

"Understandable on all counts. Oh, here is our ride," I said as Hugh Tierney came through the front door.

"And don't I appreciate passengers who are on time? I do indeed. Good evening to you all." He walked directly to Julien and clapped him on the back. "And how are you feeling tonight, me boyo?"

I think Julien surprised us all when he clasped Hugh in a warm embrace and kissed him on both cheeks. "Monsieur, you are the reason I will see my family again. I cannot express my thanks."

Hugh turned a delicious shade of red and mumbled something that sounded like "Aye, you would have done the same for me." Then, as if to change the subject, he waved to Dougal, who was at the reception desk, and said, "See ya there, yeah?"

Dougal waved back. "Right behind you, laddie."

The ride to McAvoy Brothers was a short one, and Hugh offered a bit of advice. "Never wise to be the first ones to get to a wake. The family needs time to settle in, don't they? So I will drive past McAvoys' car park, and if there are more than four or five cars, well, then, I will circle back and in we go. Fewer cars and we'll take a spin around the village. Agreed?"

Whether or not we agreed with his logic, I can't say, but none of us disagreed with his statement, so he looked at the parking lot, declared it empty, and drove us to the center of the village, then up past the distillery, and finally back to McAvoys', where there were now enough cars in the lot to satisfy him.

Owen and his cousin Sheila were greeting guests at the door, and when we arrived, Owen escorted us to the casket, where Michael lay in repose. After a few moments with our own thoughts, we expressed our condolences to the family and then were on our own.

Claude and Julien chose to sit in armchairs near the back of the room. I decided to stand near them with one eye on the door.

I watched dozens of people enter. Hugh Tierney finally entered. I supposed he wasn't kidding when he said he preferred a larger crowd in the funeral parlor.

Maggie and Dougal Nolan came in a few minutes later. After they met their obligations to the family, I saw Dougal pair off with Hugh Tierney, and Maggie was at my side.

"Any news?" she asked, and when I didn't respond immediately, she whispered, "You know, about the murder."

"Maggie, this is probably not the best time or place. I think we should hold off investigating until Michael is buried and the family is back on an even keel," I said.

She looked dejected, so I suggested we go join her father and Hugh Tierney, who were standing on the far side of the room. "Those two are always good for a joke or a funny story."

"That they are," Maggie agreed, and she linked her arm through mine and we walked across the room.

Dougal was saying, "You don't see many Aston Martins in Bushmills."

They both laughed. Then Hugh said, "Truer words, as they say. And that color—midnight blue, is it? So close to black, but ah, the shine."

"Car talk, is it?" Maggie mocked. "Have you two no respect for the deceased?"

"Sure, and isn't it Michael's car we're talking about?" Dougal said. "The most gorgeous piece of machinery."

Maggie laughed and turned to me. "When Mam was alive, she used to say that she never feared Da would leave her for another woman, but fancy cars always made her a wee bit nervous."

All three of them laughed, but I was a second late in joining them. My mind had stayed on the midnight blue of Michael's Aston Martin and my eye was on the door. Dermot Kerrigan had just come in.

I excused myself from the group. They were enjoying their conversation so much that I was sure I would never be missed. I waited until Kerrigan paid his respects and then managed to nonchalantly put myself in his path.

"Mrs. Fletcher, how are you?"

"I am fine, Mr. Kerrigan. I was about to say I am surprised to see you here, but then, I suppose I'm not."

"No reason why you should be. Michael O'Bannon died before he could pay me what I am due. My presence is a reminder. It won't be long before I am standing in front of the family demanding what I am owed." His smile was so insincere, it made my skin crawl.

"And what if the family refuses?" I asked.

"I am sure that long before now Michael taught them that stiffing me financially, or in any other way, for that matter, is never a wise course of action. Now, if you'll excuse me, I see an associate." He gave me a brief nod and walked away.

Maggie was by my side in a heartbeat. "What did he want?"

"I believe he would like me to be a messenger to the family. 'Give him what he wants or you could end up like Michael.' He's far too careful to have said it directly but"—and I looked at Claude and Julien chatting with Jane—"he may not have given up on his shipping plans, which will cause the Frenchmen a lot of grief."

"Not to mention Conor Sweeney. And the aunts will be infuriated. They are happiest when squabbling between themselves about who is in charge. I cannot imagine how they would react to being forced into an alliance with the likes of Dermot Kerrigan," Maggie said.

"Maggie, you are one smart woman. You will do quite well when you marry into that family. Now, have you seen James Collins here this evening?"

"He was out on the porch with the pipe-smoking auld ones a few minutes ago," she said.

"Thank you. You have been very helpful."

And I hurried outside, where James was in a cloud of smoke and surrounded by three ancient men with pipes. When he saw me signal with a brief finger wave, he came right over.

"Always glad to see you, Mrs. Fletcher, even under such sad circumstances." He shook my hand.

"I need a favor, Mr. Collins, and I don't want to answer a lot of questions about why I need it."

"You've only to ask." His smile was far more sincere than Kerrigan's.

"I would like you to leave the snug door unlocked after the funeral tomorrow, during the time that the reception at Jane's house is in full swing."

"Ah, found yourself a handsome young Irish lad, have you?" James's laugh faded away when he saw I remained somber. "You are not in any trouble, are you? You are not going to do something foolish?"

"Not in the slightest. You have nothing to worry about. I will be cozy in your snug and your snug will be in good hands with me. And since you still look skeptical, I promise to explain everything to you after the fact," I said.

"I agree on one condition. I will skip the reception and man the bar myself. Should you be in need of assistance, you've only to holler." He sounded quite adamant.

"Agreed. I am sure I'll be safe, but I appreciate your concern. And I thank you for offering to be the barman. Now go back to your friends and swap outrageous stories," I said, which made him laugh.

"Ah, you've been here but a short time yet you have gotten to know our ways."

He was still laughing when I went back inside. I had a plan in motion but I needed to pull my ideas together. There was a staircase to the upper floor, and as I walked past it, I saw some chairs and a few end tables farther down the hall. I suspected it was an overflow space, and for the moment, there was no one there. I knew what I wanted to do and where I wanted to do it. Afterward I could go home happily. But for now I needed a few minutes to organize my brain.

I sat alone while the hum of voices from the next room provided background noise to my ever-evolving thoughts. It didn't take long for me to become certain that my plan would succeed. My step was peppy and I had a big smile on my face as I went back into the main room.

Jane Mullen was acting as the hostess, walking around the room and being sure everyone was thanked for coming to honor Michael. She came up to me and gave me a warm hug.

"It has been such a blessing having you here during this terrible time. But you must come back to see us in happier times, and we'd love for Maeve to come with you."

"I appreciate how kind everyone has been when I know you are all under such stress."

Jane smiled her pleasure. "And you know we would like you

to come to my house for a small reception after tomorrow's services. The family would be so disappointed if you weren't with us."

I assured her I would be delighted to attend the reception. After all, being there was crucial to my plan. All that was left for me to do was call Inspector Finley.

Chapter Twenty-Eight

After a heartwarming church service, I accompanied the O'Bannon family and friends to the cemetery where Maeve's cousin Michael would rest for eternity.

And then, as I'd promised, I attended the reception at Jane's house. People stopped by to express their sorrow, and in some instances their shock at the circumstances of Michael's death. And then there were those who were merely curious.

An elderly woman, her body completely covered in a long black woolen coat, was wearing an ancient black pillbox hat with a veil covering the top half of her face. She began her conversation with me by saying, "Bad luck to ye, finding young Michael like that. Did ye know it was murder right off or was it the constables who figured it out?"

I gave the constables full credit and excused myself as quickly as I could and moved into the yellow parlor.

I scanned the crowd and was pleased to see Dougal Nolan

walking toward me. "I may not have mentioned but when your neighbor Maeve O'Bannon was a wee girl and would come to visit her grandparents, she and my oldest sister, Doreen, became great friends. Those two used to get up to all sorts of mischief but my mam would have none of it when Doreen blamed Maeve as the instigator." He laughed at the memory.

"I'd love to meet her. Perhaps take a picture. I am sure Maeve would enjoy reliving the memory," I said.

"Ah, but she's long gone." When Dougal saw the look on my face, he laughed again. "Not *that kind* of gone, such as we celebrated for Michael today. Our Doreen married a Canadian fella and moved to a small town, Sainte-Anne-de-Beaupré, just outside Quebec City. Jean André is French-Canadian. His accent sounds a lot like those two." Dougal pointed to Messieurs Lavigne and Blanchet.

"If Dora is short for Doreen, I suspect Dora Fournier is your sister. I have met Dora and her husband a number of times when they've visited Maeve. And I've kept an eye on Maeve's house when she's gone north to visit Dora. I never made the connection between Dora and Bushmills."

"Well, now you have it. You've had a friend in the Nolan family for donkey's years, as it were." Dougal was gleeful. "Now the next time I pop over to see Doreen, we'll have to make it a get-together."

Then a shadow flitted across his eyes. He looked around the room, and when he saw who was and wasn't in hearing distance, he said, "You know, it is one thing to cross an ocean to visit a sister, but I would be an unhappy da and granda if I had to cross the Atlantic every time I wanted to see my daughter and play with whatever *weans* may come her way."

"Do you mean Maggie?" I asked. "I had no idea she was thinking of emigrating."

"It's that Owen Mullen. Oh, he is a fine lad and I have long forgiven him the earlier sins of the family, but he is an ambitious one and his ambition has nothing to do with growing the family business."

Dougal was getting worked up; his voice began to squeak as if he were trying to sing a note several octaves above his range.

I wasn't sure why Dougal was upset, so I said, "I understand that Owen studied architecture. I suppose he could pursue a career anywhere."

"And there you see the problem. Maggie has been dropping sly hints, talking about a honeymoon tour of the United States. All the big cities, New York, Chicago, San Francisco. Suppose it's more than a honeymoon? Suppose it is a job and a house hunt? I can't stop her, now, can I? Maggie is a grown woman who knows her own mind but . . ." Dougal trailed off.

"Yes, I see that you're worried, but are you sure you should have a concern? Has Maggie said anything at all about leaving Ireland permanently?" I asked.

"Not a word, but—"

"And what are you two gossiping about like two old hens?" Maggie came up and linked her arm cozily through her father's.

Dougal turned red and clearly couldn't think of a quick reply, so I said, "Well, I will be planning my trip home quite shortly but I have my original chore to complete. I was just asking your father if there was a meeting room at the hotel that I could use to serve an afternoon tea to the O'Bannon family while I show them the paintings Maeve entrusted me to deliver and read the note she sent."

Maggie clapped her hands. "How exciting. I think the bridge room would do nicely. It is a small, warm, and friendly room perfect for a family-sized group. What do you say, Da?"

"Exactly what I would have picked, had my darlin' daughter not said it first." Dougal smiled and gave me a nod in thanks, I was sure, for the rescue.

I was looking at my watch more often than I should have because I was not one hundred percent sure that Inspector Finley would keep his part of the bargain. When we first spoke last night, he flatly refused to listen, much less consider my plan. It took some persuading but I was ninety percent certain that we were set.

Hugh Tierney came over to talk to us and soon enough he and Dougal were telling funeral jokes, jousting about, and enjoying each other's company. Twice I had to move out of their way. I excused myself when, through the window, I saw Dermot Kerrigan come toward the front door. I quickly entered the hallway and managed to bump into him.

"Mrs. Fletcher, unhappy circumstances these are, but still nice to see you. And wasn't the funeral lovely?" he asked.

I was having none of it. "What I noticed was that the burial was especially hard on Deirdre and Niall, losing their father so unexpectedly. That is going to take some getting used to, I would imagine."

Apparently Dermot didn't want to dwell on the sadness, because he suddenly saw a friend he needed to talk to immediately and he hustled away.

I wandered into the library, where about a dozen people were gathered, sitting on chairs and sofas. Then I saw Conor Sweeney standing alone, leaning against the mantel of the fireplace with a glass in his hand.

As I approached, he gave me a wan smile and said, "I came in here to hide from Michael's family and closest friends, who seem to all be in the yellow parlor. I just can't pretend to be cheerful. Michael and I were friends all our lives."

He drained his glass and placed it on an end table.

"I expect this is harder for you than anyone realizes," I said.

He looked at the floor for a moment and then raised his eyes. "Well, I am glad you are here. It's time I shake off my misery. As a writer you must enjoy seeing such a fine home library. Shall we scour the shelves?"

"I'd enjoy that very much."

We took a leisurely stroll, looking at books on the south wall of the library. I stopped and said, "Oh, my, what a wonderful collection of Seamus Heaney poems. Maggie left *Opened Ground* in my room and I have been reading a few poems each day. Jane has quite a collection."

"Not Jane. It's Liam who is the poetry bug in this house. That, I can tell you. Why don't you decide on a volume? I'm sure Liam would be happy to lend it to you."

"Really? Do you think so?"

"I'm certain of it. Now, you take your time and then we'll go find Liam and let him know where old Seamus is going to be for a day or so." Conor seemed his cheerful self once more.

I closely examined the titles of each book and then said, "*Wintering Out* is an intriguing title for a book of poems written by a man with such a wonderfully descriptive way of writing about nature."

I made a halfhearted attempt to take it from the shelf but it was just out of reach.

"Please let me," Conor said, as I had hoped he would.

He reached over my shoulder, I ducked my head, and in a few

seconds, he placed *Wintering Out* in my hand. I riffled through the pages and said, "Oh, this is fabulous. Will you come with me to find Liam?"

Conor laughed. "I can tell you where we'll find him. He is in the dining room standing next to the open bar. To tell you the truth, I wouldn't mind visiting the bar myself." He offered me his arm. "Shall we go?"

Liam was talking to the bartender, who seemed to have a lull in customers at the moment. When he saw us come into the room, Liam said a little louder than I thought necessary, "Well, Billy boy, here's some business for you."

I was shocked when he came over, put his arms around me, and planted a sloppy kiss on my cheek. He reeked of alcohol. I hoped it was due to the stress of the day and wasn't a regular occurrence.

Conor was busy placing his order for a double Black Bush with the barman, so he was no help. I managed to shift away from Liam and showed him the book I was carrying.

"Seamus Heaney. Now, there's a lad. And if you want to treat yourself to another fine poet, look for the works of Patrick Kavanagh." Liam seemed to be losing his balance and leaned over to prop himself up against the bar. "Take good care of my friends. I'll be right back." And he wandered away.

Conor said, "Well, it seems like you've earned yourself complete access to the Mullen family library, or at least to the poetry section. Shall we walk through the rooms and see who we find?"

"Actually, I did want to speak to Claude and Julien. I suspect they will be leaving for France soon and I want to be sure to have a chance to say good-bye," I said.

We entered the hallway and made our way through the visitors who were either coming or going. Conor stopped and greeted several people. At one point he introduced me to a married couple, telling me he and the husband had been friends since primary school days. When their conversation became quite lengthy, I slipped into the yellow parlor, where Claude and Julien were sitting on a small love seat by the rear window. As soon as I approached, each stood up and offered me his seat. I patted Claude on the arm and thanked him; then I sat next to Julien.

"You have both been such delightful company. I wanted to be sure we had some time to exchange phone numbers and addresses so that we can stay in touch after we all go home."

I took my cell phone out of my purse and dropped it between the cushions. Julien fished it out and handed it to me. They each recited their information and took mine in exchange. We were in the middle of saying that out of all the chaos of the past few days the one bright spot was that we had met and spent some time together when a newcomer caught my eye.

I hardly recognized Constable Tim Redding, dressed as he was in a navy blue suit, a white dress shirt, and a blue-and-green-striped tie. He stood casually in the doorway until he was sure I'd seen him and then he stepped into the hallway. I said my good-byes to the Frenchmen and walked out to the foyer. One of the huge doors was propped open and I saw Tim pacing at the bottom of the staircase.

I hurried to meet him.

"You look rather handsome in your suit and tie," I said.

"Inspector Finley ordered it. He said I would fit in better with this mob. He didn't want me to stand out in the crowd. I also brought my own car. We are just two ordinary mourners leaving the reception."

I nodded. "That is exactly how we look."

We were in Tim's car and heading back to the village when Tim asked, "So, did you manage to do whatever it was you set out to do?"

"Oh, yes. Now, would you mind telling me exactly what directives the inspector gave you?"

"He said I was to show up in mufti, pick you up, drop you off, and go on my way. He also ordered me not to ask any questions of you but to call him as soon as I'd accomplished my mission." Tim laughed. "He actually called it a mission."

Then he turned serious. "When I leave you, can I be sure you will be safe?"

"Where would I be safer than in the snug at the Dart and the Pint?"

Chapter Twenty-Nine

Tim stopped his car at the end of the pub's back ally.

"I have to tell you, Mrs. Fletcher, I do not like this one bit. I am not sure who is more daft, you or the inspector."

"Inspector Finley would tell you that it is definitely me." I laughed and opened my door. "Please wait here until you see me enter the snug, and then go a few blocks away and call the inspector. You can tell him you delivered the goods."

"I think you are enjoying yourself far too much, Mrs. Fletcher. This is serious business."

"Never fear, Tim. I am very aware of that and I will be cautious," I said before I closed the car door.

I walked up to the snug door, and as James had promised, it was unlocked. I waved to Tim, and when I heard him put the car in gear, I went inside.

The snug was a small, charming room with two high-backed wooden benches on either side of a table. There were soft candelabra-type electric lights on the walls and a sweet glow came through the stained glass window that was behind the bar in the pub. I tapped lightly on it.

James raised the window a few inches and peeked through. "Ah, glad to see you there. Once the snug door is unlocked, I never know for sure who's going to bang on the window looking for service. Can I get you something?"

"No, it wouldn't be wise to let my visitor know you realize the snug is occupied," I said.

"I understand. Remember, all you have to do is yell, throw something at the wall, make any noise at all, and I will be there in a flash."

"You are a good friend, James, and I appreciate your trust in me."

"And I yours in me," he said before he closed the window.

I sat down and took out my cell phone and played with it while I was waiting. I looked at my watch. Enough time had passed that the person I was expecting should have found the note I had placed in his jacket pocket.

Just as I was getting really bored, I heard a noise outside the snug door. I slipped my phone in my coat pocket and stood, ready to greet Conor Sweeney as he walked into the room.

His face was a mask of surprise when he saw me. "Oh, I am sorry. Am I intruding? Are you waiting for someone, Mrs. Fletcher?"

"I see you got my message, Mr. Sweeney," I said emphatically.

"You? You are the one who slipped this into my pocket?" He looked incredulous as he took the piece of paper out of his pocket and threw it on the table. I didn't have to look at it to know what it said.

*I KNOW WHAT YOU DID. I AM WAITING FOR
YOU IN THE SNUG AT THE DART AND THE PINT.
MICHAEL MUST BE AVENGED.*

When I had typed it I thought it was rather dramatic, but I wanted to be sure to get his attention.

Conor walked to the table and sat down as though his knees had suddenly gone weak. "And here I thought in a drunken moment I had said something to alert one of my pub mates. On my way here, I never thought of you as a possibility. Tell me how—?"

"I presume you rode your Krencker here."

He nodded. "It is how I travel everywhere."

"I have to say that kindness was your downfall. When you came across me with my flat tire, you used your almost new, rarely used tire pump. I noticed it had a dent and a discoloration on one side. When I mentioned it you explained it away as something that must have happened when you helped another bicyclist, and I never gave it another thought until Hugh Tierney reminded me of the wonderful midnight blue color of Michael's car. And I realized that discoloration on your black pump was a very dark blue.

"Then I remembered that when I discovered Michael's body, I noticed a ding where the color had scraped off the window frame on the side where his assailant must have stood during the attack. You were the assailant and the tire pump was your weapon."

Conor put his elbows on the table and rested his head in his hands. "I knew that Michael would take the cow path home once he dropped Beth Anne at her house. I parked my bike in the lane and took out my pump. When Michael came along, he stopped as soon as he saw me. I pretended that I had finished pumping my tire as he pulled up. He offered me a ride home but I said I needed more than a ride. I needed an assurance that he wasn't going to put me out of business.

"That's when he told me about Dermot Kerrigan wanting the very business I had always had. The business that fed and clothed my family. I was enraged. I understood Kerrigan—he was always a crook—but I didn't understand Michael betraying me. He was my lifelong friend. I lashed out. I am not even sure I knew I had the pump in my hand. But there it was. Next thing you know, Michael was dead and I was sorry that I hadn't killed Kerrigan instead."

We sat in silence for a few moments. Then Conor said, "I suppose there is no way you could keep this to yourself?"

I pulled my cell phone out of my pocket as I walked to the door and opened it. Inspector Finley and Tim Redding were standing there. I held up my phone. "Did you hear all that, Inspector?

"Aye, I did, Mrs. Fletcher." He held his phone to meet mine. "I suppose we can disconnect now."

Two days later I walked into the bridge room of the River Bush Hotel and was happy to see it was arranged exactly as Dougal and Maggie had promised. The display table in the center of the room was covered with a white tablecloth and had four easels awaiting the pictures that I had unrolled and flattened as best I could by putting them on the dressing table in my room and setting my suitcase on top of them. Dougal had provided cardboard and a box cutter so I could make a backrest for each of the paintings.

I arranged the four landscapes on their easels and set them in a straight line, but that didn't look quite right. I moved the Giant's Causeway and the fishing spot on the River Bush forward and put the paintings of the clocktower and the Old Bushmills Distillery between and behind them. I'd stepped back and taken a final look and was feeling quite satisfied with the display when a voice behind me said, "At long last we get to see the O'Bannon family treasures."

Jane Mullen continued. "Liam is parking the car and Owen went off to find Maggie, but I rushed right in here. Aren't these adorable? Granda wasn't an artist, but he did try. They'll fit perfectly with the antiques display I showed you, don't you think? Of course, I will probably frame them and hang them on the wall with a note saying they were painted by Finbar O'Bannon. Do we know what years he painted them? I'll have to ask Maeve. If she doesn't know, I suppose I can put his birth and death years, as if he was Picasso or someone else important."

She stopped to inhale briefly and went on. "Perhaps I'll move the blue quilt. That wall would be perfect. What do you think, Jessica?"

I didn't want to burst her bubble, so all I said was, "I suppose it would be best to wait for the others to arrive and then we can read what Maeve has to say."

At that moment Deirdre O'Bannon and her brother, Niall, came into the room and walked directly to the table.

Deirdre said, "I remember these paintings. When we visited America, we always stayed with Maeve for a while, and these pictures hung in her upstairs hall. Niall, did she ever tell us that our great-grandfather painted them? I was so little, I don't remember."

Niall said, "Oh, yes, I knew who painted them although I am not sure who told us. Mrs. Fletcher, it is very gracious of you to host our family today in honor of Cousin Maeve and these paintings."

Before I could answer him, Beth Anne swept into the room with her daughters, Caro and Sheila, in her wake. She looked around as if to say, *I'm here. Now we can begin.*

As much as her "I am the most important person in the room" attitude got on my nerves, I greeted her politely.

Maggie came in carrying a tray of teapots and was followed by two waitresses bearing scones and sandwiches. They quickly arranged tea stations on several tables around the room.

Once Owen and Liam joined us, I was ready to fulfill my duties. I opened my purse and took out the letter Maeve had written. I got everyone's attention and began to read. "'My dear cousins, many years ago our beloved grandfather Finbar O'Bannon gave these four of what he called 'paintings from home' to my parents as a wedding gift. As I am getting on in age and have no O'Bannon relatives here in America, I thought it time that the paintings be returned to the town Finbar called home. I wanted Jessica to show the paintings to all of you together so you could decide the best place for them to reside.'"

I looked at the gathered family members and saw Jane preening. I supposed she was still imagining the pictures on her wall. I continued reading. "'I send you all my love and hope we meet once again, either here or in heaven. Your cousin, Maeve O'Bannon.'"

Deirdre was the first to speak. "We've certainly had sadness in this family of late, but we all can look forward to the joy of a wedding when Owen and his Maggie become man and wife in a few months' time. I suggest, since Owen is the first of our generation to be brave enough to wed—"

"And smart enough to woo one of the finest girls in the county," her brother Niall injected.

"I say," Deirdre continued, "that our great-grandfather's paintings should go to Owen and Maggie to hang on the walls of their new home, wherever that may be."

Jane huffed and started to object but Caro overrode her with a loud "Deirdre, well done, you. That is a grand idea."

The four young cousins stood and clapped while Owen blushed, slipped his arm around Maggie, and gave her a light squeeze. Then he saw the look on his mother's face. He might have declined but his father saved the day.

Liam stood, teacup in hand, and said, "All raise your cup to Owen and Maggie, the new owners of four true O'Bannon family heirlooms. *Sláinte.*"

Knowing she was hopelessly outnumbered, Jane stood and joined the well-wishers, raising her cup to Owen and Maggie.

Chapter Thirty

The next twenty-four hours were a blur. So many people dropped in to see me at the hotel to say good-bye, and I was touched by how many asked me to please come back soon for a longer visit: Inspector Finley, Constables Breen and Redding, Agatha Mason from Aunt Aggie's Attic, even Breeda from the kitchen, who told me that Old Joe Fogarty wished me safe travels. I had an especially warm talk with James Collins.

"Missus, the man I refused to trust was murdered by a man I held close as a friend from boyhood. I'll not let emotion get the best of my judgment again. Count on that. I'm ever grateful to ye."

At last my final morning in Bushmills arrived.

Maggie and I stood in the parking lot, watching Dougal and Owen fill the car with our luggage. Then Maggie handed me a tote. "Here is your perfect gift for Cousin Maeve. I guarantee it is the perfect gift for any O'Bannon."

When I looked inside, I knew she was right. We put it carefully in my suitcase.

Dougal surprised me with a kiss on the cheek and told me in no uncertain terms that the best room in the River Bush Hotel would be mine forevermore. "You've only to show up at the front door."

Then he turned to Owen and said in a voice filled with emotion, "See that you bring my girl home again."

Owen responded, "You can count on it. Always. I promise."

And they began jabbing at each other in that way men sometimes do that often ends in a bear hug, just as theirs did.

Then the three of us were off in the car to Dublin, where Maggie and Owen would be staying for a few days after I got on a plane to fly home at last. The Irish countryside was as lovely and welcoming as it had been since I arrived in Belfast, and Maggie pointed out places I should put on the list to visit on my next trip.

"Speaking of travel," I said, "Maggie, do you realize that your father is quite worried that you and Owen will move far away from Bushmills, perhaps as far as America or Canada? Although your plans for a family may be years away, he is worried about being able to spend quality time with his grandchildren."

I couldn't believe it when Maggie began laughing and Owen said, "You are a wicked girl, Maggie Nolan, a wicked girl indeed. Poor Dougal."

When Maggie tried to control her laughter, she began to hiccup, and when that finally subsided, she said, "Jessica, by now you've seen that the parents in both our families share a common trait. They think Bushmills is the center of the universe and want their children to stay there forever."

I was beginning to understand. "So it is all a trick."

"A trick of sorts, you might say. Owen has job offers under consideration in Dublin, Galway, and London. All of those would sound so far away to my father unless they were alternatives to, say, Alberta, Canada, or to California in the USA."

I couldn't help but laugh along with her. And for the rest of our ride to Dublin, we talked about Owen's job prospects and their upcoming wedding plans.

Just as Owen pulled up to the curbside at the airport, Maggie said, "You must come back for the wedding, Jessica, and you must make sure that Cousin Maeve comes with you. She hasn't come for a visit in donkey's years. I barely remember what she looks like. It's long past time."

I hugged Maggie and Owen good-bye and I promised to attend the wedding and to do my best to bring Maeve along.

Dublin Airport was a favorite of mine. The shops were all duty-free and had a wide selection of gifts. Although I was perfectly satisfied with the gifts I'd already bought, it didn't stop me from browsing.

The flight from Dublin to Boston was smooth and storm free. The plane wandered through the occasional puffy white cloud, and from my window seat, I watched the ocean below us turn various shades of blue, depending on its depth. When I arrived in Boston, I was happy to see Jed Richardson waiting for me at baggage claim. As it turned out, he was in a terrible rush.

"I know you've been traveling all day and I hate to hurry you along, Jessica, but our takeoff time has been moved up. Grab your things. I have a golf cart waiting. And no need to worry. I texted Demetri, so his taxi will be at Cabot Cove Airport when we land. I thought Doc Hazlitt might be picking you up, but when I checked in with Susan Shevlin, she said your travel plans were so uncertain, we were going with professionals all the way."

"Uncertain" is one way of putting it, I thought, but I said, "I can't tell you how happy I am to be home."

Which is exactly what I said to Demetri when we pulled up in front of my house a little more than an hour and a half later.

"And home looks so cheery. Your lights are lit and welcoming. Let's see if you have company," Demetri suggested as he removed my luggage from the trunk of his cab.

"I'm sure when Seth checked the house he just left them on to give it a lived-in look while I was gone," I said as I opened the door and found Maeve and Seth sitting in my living room.

Demetri laughed. "I told you, Jessica. A welcome-home party."

He parked my luggage in the foyer, waved good night, and was gone.

There were plenty of hugs to go around, and then Seth said, "A man could starve waiting to get an invitation to the kitchen in this house."

Well, that got me flustered. I pointed to the kitchen. "I've been gone for weeks, and traveling all day today. You'll be lucky to find anything other than tea bags but you are welcome to help yourself."

Maeve looked insulted. "You know better, Jessica. While you were gone, I took as good care of your kitchen as I did of your seedlings, which are in fine fettle, even if I do say so myself. Take a snuffle now."

I turned toward the kitchen and took a deep breath. "Brown bread. You've baked a loaf of your delicious Irish brown bread."

"And the kettle is on the boil." Maeve shooed us into the kitchen and ordered me to sit. "I will do the serving."

On the table she'd put my second-best tea set out around an array of butter, jam pots, and honey. Then she opened the oven and placed a warm loaf of brown bread on a platter midtable.

"I sliced the bread and put it back in the oven on warm. It should be perfect just about now."

As I took my first bite of bread, Seth got a mischievous twinkle in his eye. "Ayuh, I suppose you've had tastier bread in Ireland."

"Never," I said. "There is no bread anywhere like Maeve O'Bannon's brown bread."

Seth laughed. "Now, that is exactly what I thought you'd say."

"I had no doubt," Maeve said, and then she asked about the family.

I told her everything as gently as I could. Although we had talked about Michael's murder on the phone more than once, Maeve had a lot of questions. She was particularly concerned about how all her family members were coping with the loss.

"There is a major bright spot. You were right about Jane's son, Owen, and Dougal Nolan's daughter. There is to be a wedding. And I think it will be fairly soon. I am invited to return to Bushmills for the festivities on the condition that you come as well. The family would love to see you again."

Maeve hesitated, and the best answer she could come up with was "We'll see when the time comes."

We'd been friends and neighbors for so long that I was ready for her wavering. "Didn't I tell you that the cousins voted unanimously to present your grandfather's paintings to Owen and Maggie as an early wedding gift? Now, how would it look if you turned down your invitation to the wedding?"

"I'll give it a good think," Maeve said, and I took that as a giant leap on the road to a positive response.

"And what about me?" Seth asked. "Won't you ladies need an escort?"

"Oh, Seth, won't *you* need an invitation?" I teased.

"I'll go on Maeve's invite. She's family. Her invitation will undoubtedly have a plus-one. Not so sure yours will, Jess."

Touché, I thought. "You both stay right here. I forgot something."

I went to my luggage and brought back to the kitchen the package containing what I believed was the perfect present for Maeve.

When I set it in front of her, she got nervous. "Now, Jessica, I am only after sending some of my old things to Ireland, and here you are bringing something back to take up more space in my house."

"Go ahead," I ordered. "Open it."

She pulled off the wrapper and read aloud the label on the long black box. "'Bushmills Irish Whiskey Black Bush.'"

Maeve laughed. "Set out the glasses, Jessica. I can guarantee this bottle won't become one of those dusty unopened presents found in the back of a closet when I die."

I put three short Waterford Crystal tumblers on the table and Maeve poured a hearty serving of Black Bush into each, and then led us in a toast to the increasing size of the O'Bannon clan. I suspected that meant we three would be traveling to Bushmills for an Irish wedding very soon.